I0831833

The Garnet Red

A Novel By

Joseph Crisalli

ISBN 978-0-6152-0075-0

To my parents:
For sunlight on the Mississippi…

I
The Red

Rosa Frobischer

Heat always makes me irritable. Perhaps it's because I don't enjoy being wet. Something about damp clothing makes me feel less than human and I act accordingly. George always told me that irritable wasn't a "good color" on me. Oh, my dear George—he could say something like that and appear urbane. From me, such a statement simply seems senile.

"Driver," I addressed the burly black man in front of me so softly that I wasn't certain that he had heard me. How silly to be intimidated by a cab driver. But, that was before. Or was it after? I'm never sure how to describe time.

There was no time. For seven decades, time ceased. And, when it started again, the whole of the Earth jerked from the shock of it all. Do my metaphors make sense? They were never my milieu. George was the wordsmith.

I was the bookstand.

"Did you say somethin', ma'am?" The driver asked me.

"Oh, yes." I wiped my brow and tried not to breathe in. "I was wondering if there was…" I let my voice trail off. Did I need to bother that poor man?

What would George have done?

"Somethin' on yo min', ma'am?" The driver asked.

"I'm thinking about my husband." I fanned myself with my hand. The diamonds sparkled.

"Where he at?" I could see the driver's grin in the rear view mirror. "He should be here with a nice lady like you."

"Oh, thank you," I nodded timidly. You see, I was timid. That was before. Or was it after? "You're right. He should be with me. But…"

God, I was uncomfortable. The cab seemed suddenly small and close. I could feel the driver's heart beating. I could hear the movement of his rough hands on the steering wheel. I could smell his life on him. It reminded me of the bayou…of…

Of what?

Stay calm, Rosa. It's just a cab trip home. No, not home. Marionneaux.

Steady, girl. Steady.

I discreetly brushed the tip of my nose, letting the first two fingers of my left hand linger so as not to smell the driver's pungent, heat-activated cloud of cologne, sweat and stale beer. Directly under my eyes, my wedding and engagement rings sparkled in the filtered Louisiana sunlight sending flecks of color onto my flushed cheeks.

I had worn those rings for over six decades. Those diamonds had since taken on a more urgent purpose—having to take the place of George's hand in mine. Empty hands have a habit of grasping, you know.

"What was I saying?" I asked the cab driver.

His great sad horse's eyes looked up at me in the mirror, dark and wet. "Yo' husband, ma'am. You was tellin' me where he at."

"Yes, of course. He's…I…he's passed on. The son of a bitch." I laughed. One tear snuck out from the corner of my eye. I hated that tear. And, yet, I loved it, too. George would have said I was foolish to cry for him. But, George never had the challenge or the joy of being married to himself. George never had to deal with George. That's why he had me. That's what I was for. I did the crying. George did the talking.

George, of course, did a lot of talking. He once joked that for every word I ever spoke in my entire life, he must have said about one million. You see, my husband spoke to everyone in the world. But, my whole world was George. He built an empire with his words. I built a home for him with mine.

George—the sun rose and set on George. I never knew a life before I knew him. And, I wondered if I'd ever know one after.

I let my body shake for just a moment. Old bodies shake whether you let them or not, but I figured I'd give mine permission just that once—as if my consent would make the process a little easier. If anything, a spasm of grief might have served to cool me down.

"I'm sorry ta hear dat, ma'am." The driver said somberly. I think he meant it, too. How odd. I didn't distrust him. Why not?

"You sure you okay?" He asked me.

"I'm fine." I answered. "Thank you." Oh, why, for the love of Pete didn't I just tell him I was roasting like a brisket in that horrendous tin can of his? Why didn't I ask if he had a fan or if he could crack a window? Why didn't I want to bother him?

I remember one time that George and I were dancing at Ciro's. He wanted to spin me and dip me as if I were Ginger Rogers complete with feathers. I just stiffened up. I didn't like to be the center of attention. I didn't want to put anyone out. George laughed. He took my face in both of his hands and said something that I thought very strange at the time. "A jewel that doesn't know it's a treasure is just a hunk of rock."

My response was an ever so eloquent and refined, "Huh?"

He laughed. He spent a great deal of our life together laughing near and, yes, at me. I laughed too. He never did answer my "huh." That's all right. I answered it myself seventy or so years later.

Now, I think, the girls would say something like, "What had happened to devalue you, Rosa?" Well, Shelby would ask me that. She reads all those magazines. Dove wouldn't ask me that. Dove…she'd just hold my hand. But, I didn't know the girls then. I only knew George. I was small then. I was precious.

What had kept me so small for so long?

I couldn't have answered that question then. George, I think, could have. But, if he knew, he never told me. He never said to me, "Rosa, when this happened to you…this is when you lost your sense of self-worth." He wouldn't have said something like that even if he had been willing to do so. We didn't say such things, then. But, we do now. We most certainly do now.

But, then…then we had metaphors. Ah, George…why'd you have to leave me all alone?

Oh, but if he hadn't…well, I'd always have been a hunk of rock.

As it was, I was an overheated old woman. Yes, that's when it started. My renaissance began as most births do—hot, wet, smelly and with some shouting.

I couldn't help but wonder how George would have regarded me at that moment—damp, frizzed and clearly cranky. Would he have been disappointed or proud? What would he have said?

I supposed it didn't matter. George was dead.

I felt a giggle tickle my lungs from the inside. I knew what George would have thought. Yes, I did. He would have shouted at me, "Goddamn it, Rosa. I'm dead. Let me rest!"

He was a moody bastard. But, thank God…he was *my* moody bastard.

I was no longer his or anyone else's muse. I was no longer a companion. So, what was I? That's all I knew how to be: Mrs. George Frobischer.

A dead man's wife…

What was I? On that sticky day—sitting there in the stench of that cab—what was I?

I was simply an ancient crone in search of a new life by way of an uncertain past. A past that was so far removed from what I had become that I could only recall faint flickers of it—like forgotten footage cut long ago from one of George's films.

A crone in diamonds and silk…

"The costumes aren't as important as the motivation!" I heard George shout that once on some film set. I think it was 1942. Oh, yes, it was '42. I remember because Joan walked off the set and wouldn't come back. They had to recast. Yes, I was to have had lunch with her that afternoon. But, Crawford wouldn't dine with me after George bellowed at her. How small the world was then. How smoothly it spun.

The cab stopped—lurching before it shuddered to an abrupt halt. I gasped and inadvertently inhaled two lungs full of stench. Slapping the back of the driver's seat, I admonished him to be careful before I demanded to know how much longer we had before we arrived in town.

I heard George's voice, "'Atta girl, Rosie."

Again, I could see the reflection of the driver's eyes in the rearview mirror. He rolled them toward heaven before answering me. "A few more minutes ma'am. Then we be in Marionneaux." He punctuated it with a sheepish grin that quickly told me that I was
being formidable.

I giggled.

The driver chuckled, too.

At least I had gotten a quick response.

“You somethin’ else, lady.” The driver chortled.

“You think so?” I asked him with a grin. “I’ll tell you a secret. I’ve never been quite sure what I was.”

He laughed. “I could tell ya.”

“How about you just drive?”

“Yes’m.” He couldn’t help but snicker a little bit more. I brushed away another tear and did the same. Damn tears.

“And hurry up,” I sighed…simultaneously embarrassed and proud to be speaking so forcefully to someone. I was shocked that he didn’t turn around and smack me.

“Like I say, ma’am. Just a few more minutes.”

I grinned.

Perhaps irritable was a better color on me than George had thought. I sat back in the seat and my hand returned to its perch beneath my nostrils. What were “a few more minutes” in the context of a lifetime?

Nearly seventy years earlier, George had taken me from rural Louisiana and sculpted me into an angel—wings feathered in prose, punctuated by a halo of post-deco grace. For a while it positively oozed Pygmalion, but soon, I was the perfect mate to a man of his stature. I draped myself in gowns and jewels, smiled and posed…an animated mannequin with the disposition of a saint and the manner of an oil painting. I smiled my way through opening nights and movie premiers, through cocktail and wrap parties. I laughed and nodded on film sets and in restaurants. And, I liked it. I was the perfect accessory—a flower in his buttonhole. With a chuckle, he had always called me, "Rosa, my thornless rose."

I thought of that as I placed a red rose on his casket before the remaining mourners filed from the cemetery. That rose had thorns. I had nothing.

The day of his funeral, I had not only buried him, but also in large part, interred myself. Even George's obituary in the Los Angeles Tribune concluded with the words, "he is survived by his wife of sixty eight years." No name. Just a simple, "his wife." I read it aloud and laughed. He was survived by no one.

Damn tears.

In the weeks following, I had a strange sense of detachment as I made phone calls for various necessities. It occurred to me that I couldn't remember the last time I had said my own name. What was it again? I spoke it as if I were referring to someone else—some Rosa Frobischer that I had never met—a stranger. Some mysterious…

…Veils…women don't wear enough veils any more. I think I should very much have liked wearing a veil over a large, wide-brimmed hat. I'd have worn it always. Yes, perhaps with Groucho glasses underneath. No one would know. I'd be "Rosa the Hat Lady." That would be something. Wouldn't it?

Wouldn't it?

Oh well. I had never had to refer to myself. George had handled everything. George had always introduced me. George had created me.

I vowed I would meet this "Rosa Frobischer" one day. And so, I set about making plans for her. I sold the house in Beverly Hills and almost everything in it. When all that was left were a few boxes and my two suitcases, I boarded a plane to Louisiana.

As the cab chugged forward, I was jolted back into the moment and my attention was grabbed by the Spanish moss flowing from the trees like torn and tattered shrouds—an image that seemed somehow appropriate. How George would have gone on and on about it…imagery. He loved his imagery.

I loved him.

He was my home when I knew no other.

I just realized…tears are wet.

It was to be a wet year.

In the following days, I settled well enough into my new cottage and my new role. I planted bougainvillea. I walked up La Colline Cramoisie. I wept on D'Arbonne Street.

I found a bookstore.

Maybe I did wear a veil after all. Who can remember? That was before. Yes. Yes, it was before. I know that now. I wonder if anyone else noticed. People were certainly watching me.

The residents of Marionneaux quickly flocked to the widow of screenwriter George Frobischer—formerly one of their own. I was quite the nonesuch, in fact—a living museum of film history. But, I felt lost in their expectant stares, trapped within their hollow looks of sympathy which were laced with a distinct tabloid curiosity.

Where was my veil?

Being a slave to another's expectations had never been a goal of mine. With George, I was a willing accomplice, but I felt no affection for these people and instead of a desire to mollify them, I felt a need to which I was unaccustomed—a need to master them.

At 86 years of age, I wasn't about to become an exhibition. Not quite Norma Desmond, not quite Baby Jane Hudson. So, as much as I missed George and as much as my heart was broken, I knew that the only way I could mend my soul was to live for myself. For my…

For myself? Yes. I would live for myself. In Marionneaux? Yes.

George would probably agree with that and might even secretly applaud my newfound assertiveness. "'Atta Girl, Rosie!"

I would have to pave my own way. And, no, not only for me…thank God.

For, of course, there are the girls. Always Dove and Shelby…

Is it okay?

Oh, I shouldn't waste time when there are so many things to be done. I'm wanton and slothful. Selfish, like papa said.

But, is it okay?

I can't not think. I can think and work.

Is it okay to be sad when someone else is happy?

I am what papa said. I am.

I was sad that day. I shouldn't have been. It was wrong to be sad. See, Mr. Allemand was happy. He was going to sell the bookstore. He said he was glad to do it. He wanted to retire, to live in Shreveport near his sister.

I didn't want him to. What would happen to the bookstore? What would happen to me?

I'd miss that store. It was my only escape. And, I'd miss Mr. Allemand.

Selfish Dove…only thinking of herself and what she can get to put in her mouth or what she can find to make her waste more time. That's what papa said.

But, it was true. I was going to miss Mr. Allemand. He was my only friend. Is that weird? I didn't have much choice. I found friends where I could. After all, no one wants to be friends with the fat girl.

Mama would have said not to. She'd have said I was too old. "Girls of fifteen don't do that!"

But, I did. I cried.

I made sure to dry my eyes before I went home.

"Mama!" I told her. "Mr. Allemand is going away!"

"Quiet, girl!"

Papa was angry. "Noodles…cut the noodles."

Cut the noodles. Sure, I'd cut the noodles. I'd like to make a noose out of noodles.

That's a terrible thought. I was ungrateful. I cut the noodles.

"Hurry up, girl!"

They shrugged their shoulders at me. They were busy. But, I felt like someone died. I guess. I didn't know death right then. But, I mourned. Who? Maybe me. Or maybe, deep down, I already knew.

"But, Mama." I tried again. "I'm all alone now."

No one said anything. They cut the noodles. And, yawned.

They were tired.

"Help us!"

"Yes, Mama."

I wonder if they listened to Jade when she talked. I wonder if they played with her. I think they must have. But, I guess after Jade grew up, Mama and Papa had no energy left for me.

My mother must have always been old.

Even when she gave birth to me, she was old. She always seemed so much grayer, so much more wrinkled than the other mothers. Could she have been so much older? We never talked about it. Who had time?

They were old. That was it, I guess. They were old and I was in their way. If I wasn't helping, I was in the way. That's why I first went to the bookstore. Where would I go?

That was a bad day—the day Mr. Allemand said he was going to sell the store. I remember I drew. I drew pictures that weren't like my usual ones. Different colors. They were red pictures. Swirls of red.

They made me feel better. Drawing them made me feel better, I mean. Looking at them didn't. But, isn't that how art is? Books, too.

Papa called them wastes of time. "Chickens don't feed on paper! Can't cut noodles with a paint brush!"

I read *The Raven* until Mama called my name out angry and loud. Nevermore. She wanted me to go to the restaurant. It wasn't far. It was right behind our little house.

I brought my drawings with me. I thought I would show her. I kept trying. Why is that?
There was this book that I read once. It was about a dog whose master was really mean to it, but the dog loved the master anyway. The dog would come up to the master and wag his tail, but the man kicked the dog.

"Look Mama." I showed her my pictures.

"No time! No time, girl!"

The dog in that story got kicked each time. Then one day, people came and took the dog away. They brought him to a nice home where he could wag his tail and get hugged instead of kicked.

I showed Papa my drawings, too. Or I tried to anyway. Papa nodded. "Feed the chickens, girl!"

Girl. Why'd they always call me girl? Didn't I know I was a girl? Did they think I might decide I was...I don't know...a chicken? Maybe they'd pay more attention to me if I was.

I looked at the coop. Would it be so bad to be a chicken? At least then I'd be useful to someone. And, maybe the coop was nicer than our house. It was cleaner anyway. I kept it really clean. Clean for those chickens. Lucky chickens.

I looked for Jade. There she was. She had her vine basket. It was all brown and twisted and curvy.

"Dove." She whispered and waved me over. "Hurry up."

"What?"

“I want to show you.”

“Show me what?”

“You.” She said softly. She took my hand and led me behind the coop. She pointed to a tree branch. “Look.” I looked. “It’s a nest.” Her mouth grinned. Her eyes didn’t. Her eyes were far away.

“My nest?”

“Dove nest…look, with eggs. Dove eggs.”

“Wow.” We looked at the nest.

“We gotta hurry,” She said finally. “Get the chickens done.” She looked at the papers I clutched in my hand. “Watchoo got there, Dove?”

I wasn’t a chicken—not to Jade. I was Dove. I offered the papers to her.

She looked at my pictures.

She always did. Jade made the time even when there wasn’t any. Jade was my friend. No…not really. She was my sister. She lived with us then. I wish she had stayed.

She knew how to be lonely. I know she did. She never said it, but I know.

I’d draw her. I’d draw her mouth and eyes.

Once I read about a girl that was caught in a trap. It dug into her leg and if she tried to get free, it made her bleed. In my head, when I read the book, I pictured Jade as that girl. I drew a picture of Jade in the teeth of that trap. I never showed the drawing to her.

Jade wouldn't have liked that picture. She liked to act like she was happy. It wasn't a happy picture. But, I didn't use red in it. I wonder why.

I used to wonder if I'd be like Jade when I was older. Jade was a lot older than me— eighteen years. But, she played with me when I was a little, little girl. We'd sing together. We'd even play hide and seek at the bayou. Those were the very best times! We'd even stop to look for frogs in the dark water. Her eyes sparkled. But, I knew she was sad.

I guess it is okay to be sad when other people are happy.

We were saddest when it was time to go home. But, we both smiled anyway.

Other times I couldn't make myself smile.

When Jade turned thirty-three, she moved out. She went to work as a maid at the gray mansion on La Colline Cramoisie. She was to work for Miss Rittenhouse. I always heard about Miss Rittenhouse.

Was living with her better than staying with us?

I knew Jade was unhappy living in our little house— sleeping in the same bed she had slept in when she was a child. She wanted more out of life than chickens and mein. I was proud of her. She was a grown up lady. But,

I cried when she left. Without her in the house, I was totally alone.

That was another reason to be at the bookstore. I wasn't so alone at the bookstore. But, I thought that would have to stop, too. Everything stops, I guess. Well, no, not everything. I didn't think Mama and Papa would ever stop. Jade did, though.

She came to visit on Saturdays…for a while.

It didn't matter, I guess. When Jade did visit, I was allowed only a few minutes with her. It was short, but nice—sisterly chat. But, then Mama would call to her. Or Papa. But, when Papa called, it was different.

I sometimes felt that Jade liked the work. She worked like she had a fever like if she worked hard and fast, she'd never know she was working. Or maybe she'd never have to think about other things as long as she had something to do. I don't think she liked having nothing to do. That was when she would glance at her watch and stare off far away.

I drew a picture of her watch. I didn't show it to her. She wouldn't have liked it. The watch was red. That was right after she moved. Right before Mr. Allemand found someone to buy the store. Right before my sister visited for the last time.

That last time, she seemed like she was dreaming. I asked her why. She told me that she prayed that one day I would feel the way she did.

"How can I, if I don't know what you're feeling?" I had asked.

But Mama and Papa had called her away before she could answer. I sat alone in the restaurant's storeroom and tried to dream, too. But, my dreams weren't like Jade's. Mama scolded me back into washing the dishes. She told me I was fat because I was idle.

I let the sound of the running water fill my head. Maybe, if I tried, I could be far away, too. Maybe I could get away in my own head like Jade did. I tried to trick myself with the little poem. A long time ago, someone had made it into a song. I had learned it from Jade when I was very small. I think Mama had taught it to her, but by the time I came along, there was little time to waste on silly tunes.

I sang-talked the poem to the rhythm of the water sloshing over the dishes. The splash and clatter was a little like music.

The shadowed river listens,

Waiting for the rain,

Lies lost in such sharp silence

Her beauty will wane:

She wears her hope like diamonds

All colors save but one

Diana's orb will free us

Reflected in the sun.

Was that shouting in the dining room?

I liked that part about Diana. She was a goddess. When I was really little, I thought that the poem meant Princess Diana from England. To think of her made me feel sad because she died. She died running away from people that stared at her. But, the poet was writing about the Goddess Diana. I didn't feel sad for her. She was a goddess. Goddesses don't have to run away. A goddess doesn't hide.

Chickens hide.

Yes, I think that was shouting.

I could barely tell over the water. It was not unusual for Papa to lose his temper with Jade. Surely, it was nothing new. I turned the knob to make the water run harder. The words of the poem played across my lips as the little tune welled up in me like the water around the dirty dishes. Maybe I was dreaming. Were they the same dreams as Jade's? I hoped so.

I pictured the words in my head—all color, all alive.

Down deep below the surface
Weary roots do drink
The water rich with Heaven:
Closer than we think.
In darkness it is stagnant
In light only will grow
Proud branches strong and sturdy
Where darkness once did flow.

Soon, the sound of the water overtook me. I imagined that I was aboard the proud ship sailing with Captain Ahab and Ishmael in search of the Great White. Always searching.

More talking. Loud talking. It was so loud that it broke my dream. It shattered like a mirror.

My dreams were different than Jade's.

That's because I was fat. And selfish.

My father was shouting at Jade in Chinese while my mother wailed. They always used Chinese when they didn't want me to know what they were saying. Jade had learned the language from them as a girl. But, no one had taken the time to teach it to me. I could only guess what they were saying, but from their volume, I could tell that they were clearly upset about something again. Poor Jade…she never visited again after that.

I wished I could go to the river.

Even more, I wished I could go back to the bookstore.

Both wishes came true. But, not all at once.

Several weeks later, I met Mr. Allemand on D'Arbonne Street. I knew he would be there. I wanted to say goodbye to him. He told me that he had found a buyer for the store. It was being taken over by "the Hollywood Widow." I thought that all hope was lost. It made me think of Dante. Dante, at least, had Beatrice. I had no one.

But, when I met Mrs. Frobischer, everything changed. Everything. She was my Beatrice. I would draw her.

I was shy with her at first. I had heard all the things that the people around town were saying about her. When you call someone "The Hollywood Widow," you expect her to be like the ladies you see on TV. You expect them to be like the lady in that movie I saw. The one with the dead monkey…what was her name?

Norma.

When I heard them say, “The Hollywood Widow,” I pictured Norma in my head. She was in her big house with her dark glasses and she was giving angry speeches about microphones and being a star.

But, Mrs. Frobischer wasn’t like Norma. She wasn’t like any of the black and white ladies.

She was…what was she? It was hard to tell at first because she didn’t seem to know either. In a way, she was kind of like Jade. But, she was funny, too. And, she was so nice.

After a little while, I knew what she was. But, I didn’t dare say it out loud. See, she was the kind of lady that likes to take care of people. She was like…well…she was the way I wished Mama would be.

She was so nice that I had to talk to her. And, talking is hard. Talking to new people is especially hard. But, she made it easy. After a week, I felt as though I had known her all my life.

I drew a picture. It was a picture all in blue. It was ocean blue and I showed it to Mrs. Frobischer. You know what she did? She hung it on the bulletin board!

She was pretty, too. She was old…older than Mama even. But, she was so much prettier.

And what was most surprising was that she thought I was pretty, too. She told me things…nice things. She always spoke to me as if I was her equal. One day, she even asked if I would like to make some extra money by helping her in the store. I was so happy!

So, that's what happy felt like.

Is it okay to be happy when someone else is sad?

But, I had to be happy. I wasn't just a bookish fat girl any more.

I was needed.

I was a person.

I…I was…

Someone thought I was pretty.

Shelby Halifax

Good Lord! If anyone had ever told me that I'd be hanging out with that Dove girl, I would have told them they were crazy. She certainly didn't look at all like the sort of person I'd want anything to do with.

At first I was ashamed to be seen with her. Who could blame me? Really! Everything was against her—her looks, her clothes, her weight, her family.

I mean…God! Their house always smelled of garlic. I suppose that's to be expected. They lived behind their restaurant, after all.

But, suddenly, there was this chubby girl. And, she was always around. It's totally understandable. I mean, I understand why she would want to be my friend. Look at how we lived compared to her family! My family's big yellow house midway up La Colline Cramoisie is a world away from the dirty shack behind their wonton hut. They have chickens for God's sake!

I was talking to Therese, our cleaning woman, just the other day. Mommy says it's nice to engage the servants in chit chat now and again. It makes them feel important.

Anyway, Therese had the nerve to tell me that I've been a much better behaved girl lately. The fool! How dare she? I've always been extra kind to her. As angry as I was, I just smiled and nodded. I didn't want her to think I was irritated. You must never show your subordinates any weakness. Besides, she'd only go right to Mommy and tell her I was being petulant—the snitch.

She should be more careful. It's easy to replace a cleaning woman.

But, get this! Then, Therese suggested that my change of attitude was due to Dove's influence. Jesus! I haven't changed. And, if I have, well, it's due to Mrs. Frobischer more than anyone else.

I remember that first day when I saw Mrs. Frobischer behind the counter, she looked so severe—all in black. Really, for a woman of her coloring, she should have been wearing something a little brighter. But, of course, she was in mourning. I wondered how long she had to dress like that. How awful it must be to have your wardrobe limited. I felt very bad for her.

She did have a rather impressive diamond on her left hand—almost as big as Mommy's. I wondered if it was real. I'd have to get a better look. But, still, the stone wasn't enough to brighten her up and her appearance was unsettling.

Maybe she just needed some moisturizer. I know that always helps Mommy—especially after she's been…never mind that. Grandmother says family business must be kept in the family. Where was I? Oh, Mrs. Frobischer….

I remember. What upset me most was the suspicious way that she looked at me when I walked in and went to my usual place at the little table by the magazine racks. Did she think I wasn't going to pay?

I always buy the magazines that I thumb through—well, most of them. I just like to have a few moments to look at them first. God! No one likes to be rushed. I tried to ignore her stare and sat with my back to her. But, it was hardly five minutes before she came up to me.

“Can I help you?” She had asked. I wondered if she was mocking me.

“No.” I said firmly.

I began to feel a twinge of guilt as she walked away. How could I be rude to an old lady? And, it was especially awful to be so forceful with a recent widow. I knew I had to do something to be kind to her. It’s the duty of those that are more fortunate to be gentle with the grief stricken.

“Pardon me,” I said as sweetly as I could, “Is there anything I can do to help you?”

She turned back and raised an eyebrow. Again, she looked suspicious, but she forced a smile. I had to use all the strength I had not to reprimand her for looking at me that way.

“No,” She said, “I think I’m just fine.” She sounded almost amused. I couldn’t tell, though. She wouldn’t let herself look me in the eye. Was I that intimidating? Daddy says I can be a brat sometimes.

I tried to be softer with her…poor fragile thing.

“But, surely you couldn’t be ‘just fine’,” I answered. “Your husband is dead.”

She frowned, “Yes.” She opened and closed her hand a few times. Palsy—must have been a palsy.

I figured I’d talk to ease her mind.

"I read all the movie magazines. I know how you people are." I added sympathetically.

She raised that eyebrow again; "We people?" She made a little noise in her throat. It was like a giggle. "What sort of people am I? I'd like to know."

"You know, you entertainment types," I explained slowly. Her grief must have made her slightly simple. "Your husband must have left you with all sorts of debt or else you would have stayed in Beverly Hills. That's why you have to work in a bookstore."

She laughed—rather rudely, I thought. But, I let it pass. She waved her hand in front of her face—her rings glinted under the florescent lights. I would just have to get a better look at them! She focused her eyes on me. Perhaps I had misspoken, but those movie people are notorious for losing fortunes. Those rings, if they were genuine, were probably all she had left in the world.

"I own this bookstore," she answered. "I was born in Marionneaux. That's why I moved back here. I suppose, at any rate, that's why I moved back here. " She looked at her left hand and then looked around the store. "I remember that I came to this shop when I was a little girl." She chuckled. "I thought it would be fun to own it."

"Of course you did," I nodded gently—not believing her.

"What's your name?" She asked me with a hint of sharpness in her voice. I think she must have noticed her rudeness, too, because her cheeks turned pink. Poor dear, I thought. Her grief must have made her completely senseless.

I stood and gave a pretty curtsy. "Shelby Halifax."

"Shelby," She nodded. "You asked me if you could help me. Do you still want to help?"

"Oh yes, very much." I smiled, thinking she meant for me to listen to her woes of poverty and isolation.

She giggled and blushed again. "There are books to be shelved. They're in the back room. Follow me." She twisted her mouth into a triumphant smile.

I just had to gasp a little. But, I couldn't back out then. One had to consider one's pride. So I did as she said. I followed her to the back room. That's where I saw Dove—looking all squatty as she piled books onto a cart.

"I'll let Dove tell you what to do from here." Mrs. Frobischer smirked before walking away.

As she left the storeroom, I heard her mutter, "What do you know? 'Atta girl."

I sighed and looked at Dove who smiled weakly. Who would have ever thought that I would be doing this sort of labor? And, in such company. I felt rather guilty when I began to enjoy it.

Amelia Rittenhouse

Damn her! Damn her to Hell!

I could show her the way if she's forgotten. *Easy, easy now, Amelia.*

Why? For the power these hands once had…no. For the power they have…small talons to slice and cleave all that threatened me. *Such talk from such a small, hollow…* Small, yes, but I have a big voice. Though withered I am not spent. Not yet! *You fool. The difference in your ages is slight and yet look at her. She's your superior.*

The sheer enormity of my spirit can crush anyone. Even her. Even Rosa.

Rosa! Our paths had never actually crossed when she was a girl in Marionneaux. She, the daughter of bakers, came from D'Arbonne Street on la Rue de Marchands and I was a débutante on La Colline Cramoisie. *You wore white?* I was the daughter of Dorset Rittenhouse and she was the "Meat Pie Man's" girl.

I couldn't recall a time that I had ever calculatedly been near her—at the very least, not in Louisiana. If I had, I was sure to have dismissed her as if stepping over a dead rat! *Such talk.* No matter what we had in common, she wasn't worthy of my time. She was beneath me! Still, I, naturally, knew who she was. She was considered the town's great beauty—a reputation that father's money could not buy for me.

What could it buy for me?

I'll tell you. Permanence!

You confuse opulence with permanence.

My contribution is permanent! Damn it all, but I conquered beauty! I've filled this house with beauty that will last longer than Rosa Frobischer's. My art. That will live forever. There you were wrong, Father! Some things are forever! Some things can be kept and protected. I've clawed and fought to guard them—clawed and bled and ripped myself to shreds! And, I'll be damned if…

No! She'll be damned! Damn you, Rosa Frobischer! You should have stayed in California.

You flatter yourself, Amelia, you shriveled sack.

That's where we really met—California. Many years after she left Marionneaux, we were finally introduced at a party in Brentwood. She didn't associate the name Rittenhouse with her past. I was more relieved than anyone could imagine. Ostensibly, she was so far removed from everything that she seemed to have no memory of Marionneaux or anything outside of her newfound station as Mrs. Frobischer. *She had a husband, old girl. Where's yours?* A husband, yes, but, she had no memories.

Or perhaps she did. Still, she'd not best me! Each time I saw her afterwards, I always felt her eyes on me when I wasn't looking. A sharp panic would flood my veins in those moments. I wondered what she had heard or seen. Or remembered. But surely, she wouldn't remember me now. *Don't worry. Feel me. Trust me.*

I hoped she wouldn't. I hadn't been to Hollywood in forty years—not since Unwin…well, not in forty years.

Where's your fight now?

I just knew she'd come back one day. I knew she'd threaten it…me…us. *She's your Trojan Horse, Amelia. Remember? From out the great belly, they came in the night. Trust in me!*

When I heard the front gate creak open, I thought it was the postman. But, when the doorbell rang, my heart froze with terror. Ninety-one years old and I am still paralyzed by the unknown.

When that dim-witted housekeeper, Jade, went to answer the door, I almost begged her not to open it. However, I decided that I couldn't be controlled by my fear. Bitch! Chinese Whore! She'd be punished, too. Cry for me more, Jade! Are you alone?

So am I. *Loneliness is for the weak, Amelia. Are you weak? Are we? Give yourself to me!*

Forty years alone is too long. *Ah, what are you complaining about, old girl?* Forty years alone in the finest house in Marionneaux isn't such a tragedy, true. *Chin up, Amelia, you're made of sterner stuff.* I know father would have been proud that I'd ruled his empire as firmly as I have. *Firm hand? Hard heart. Cold like stone.* When he built this house it was the pride of the state, the grandest mansion within a hundred miles, a testament to his wealth. Our monument! *Your reliquary.*

My father took Rowan Rittenhouse's—his father's—few paltry mines and founded one of the greatest jewel importing business in the world! This house is a symbol of my father's empire. Our empire. My empire! We were royalty! We needed a palace to match. *To hide...*

Father said it was the only house in Louisiana with "a foundation of jewels." *What else did he say?* It was his fortress. *What else? Arm yourself! To arms!*

Is that the doorbell? I'm ready! *Amelia, you're an old, damned, ugly, useless...*

I'm such a fool. This house—now, it is simply a prison. I wonder if anyone else sees it but me. *Trust in me.*

I wonder if anyone else hears the silence in our prison. It speaks to me where no one else will. *Our prison. Trust in me. It's a path to freedom.*

I have to finish what I've started. I do. I owe it to...the family. I owe it to the proud Rittenhouse name!

And, I'll be damned if Rosa Frobischer undermines all my hard work! *Our home. Trust in me! Come to me, Amelia! I'll remind you.*

Tapestries can hang like dirty convicts and marble columns can feel like iron bars. Or the ribs of a beast—yes, a great beast. I'm trapped in the belly of a whale. Alone.

Such poetry. It's a family tradition. I'll give you poetry. Let me stroke your hair when no human hand will. Let me whisper in your ear, dear one. Dear, inadequate, hateful...

I lie. I am not actually alone. I have my secrets. And my silence...

Dear, dear, Amelia…always.

Rosa Frobischer

I had often heard the townsfolk speak of Amelia Rittenhouse. She was referred to by a multitude of *Wonderful World of Disney*-ish sobriquets most of which began with some derivative of "Old Lady" and ended with Rittenhouse. That phenomenon didn't surprise me. Everyone of any importance in Marionneaux had a nickname. Mine, I learned from Dove, was "The Hollywood Widow." I never thought it fit me. But, then again, I felt the same about some of the gowns that George bought for me. So, I chose to pretend to ignore the epithet. I was good at pretending and at ignoring. Some people have golf.

Did Amelia Rittenhouse ignore the ever so lovely things that the people in town said about her? Amelia Rittenhouse. I wondered at the name. Could it have been the same woman that George and I had known all those years ago? Could it have been the spirited girl that danced until dawn? The girl whose life so sparkled in her peridot eyes that their very glint dimmed the sequins with which she dripped?

I remembered her plainly. She was not conventionally beautiful—rather pinched in fact, but she had an air of elegance which when combined with the wildness in her apple green eyes was quite breathtaking. She was always desperate to be the center of attention and yet when she was lavished with it, she retreated. A war always seemed to be playing out in her little body—two great forces tugging her to the point of ripping in half.

I understood the result if not the cause. I was at once drawn to and repelled by her.

She had fascinated me. At first, it was because there was something so familiar about her. But later, because she seemed so pathetic—a lost puppy in satin and beads. Or maybe a wolf.

Amelia Rittenhouse in Marionneaux—had she always been here? Why didn't I remember?

I decided that my curiosity about the woman in the huge house on the red hill was great enough to risk inconveniencing people with questions. It was a close call, but one day, I found the gumption to query Shelby about this Amelia Rittenhouse. When she told me that Amelia was something of a hermit (and, as typically is the case, rumored to be a witch), I couldn't imagine that she could possibly be the same vibrant, confused, butterfly George and I had known.

Dove confirmed what Shelby had said, albeit in a more rational way. Dove's sister works as a maid at the Rittenhouse Mansion, and while there had never been a mention within the Ji family of witchcraft, Dove did suggest that I keep a thick skin if I were to visit the sprawling manse. Miss Rittenhouse was known for her sharp tongue.

"But, you know something? I feel sorry for her, Mrs. Frobischer." Dove sighed.

"Why is that, Dove, dear?" I asked her.

"Because…" She cocked her head to one side, "I don't know. It's hard to say. Maybe because she's all by herself."

"She's not. Your sister is there. Right?" Shelby smirked. "And there's gotta be more staff in that huge place. Honestly! I'll bet she's not at all alone. If 'The Hag of La Colline Cramoisie' couldn't find other people to work there, I'm sure she'd just stitch some up in her basement lab."

"Shelby." I scolded her.

"Sorry," She rolled her eyes. "Dove, it's just if you want to feel sorry for someone, feel sorry for me. We have to live a few houses down from Old Lady Rittenhouse. I'm always afraid that some of her spells will backfire and she'll turn our maid into a toad or something. You know, a toad can't wash a sweater."

"No, but a toad can wear one. I saw it several times in Los Angeles." I teased Shelby. She always tried to be so serious and sophisticated. But, I knew she had a silly side. I was so glad when I could get her to laugh a little. I thought laughter might do her some good.

She chortled and looked a little embarrassed about it afterwards.

Dove ignored us. As usual, she was lost in her worries. "Sure, Jade's there. But, Jade's all by herself, too. It's like no matter how many people are in that big house, they're all still alone."

"And being alone is bad?" I asked, clasping my hands together.

"Oh, yes." Dove nodded with tremendous seriousness.

I swallowed. "I agree."

"I think that's why Miss Rittenhouse is so…mean." Dove continued.

"Loneliness makes you mean," I nodded. "Sometimes. Other times it just makes you scared."

Shelby looked at me. "This boy I know at school, Averill, says that if you don't talk for at least four hours a day, your vocal cords will dry up."

"You'll have no problem, then." I chuckled.

"I wonder if Miss Rittenhouse has dried up vocal cords," Dove tried to hoist herself up on the counter to sit next to Shelby who was perched near the cash register. "That would be terrible—not to ever talk again."

I nonchalantly rolled my task chair over to her so that she could use it to climb up on the counter. She smiled and climbed upon it before settling in next to her friend.

"Would serve her right," Shelby laughed, "The witch."

"Why?" I asked the girl. "Does she deserve to be lonely?"

Shelby's cheeks flushed.

"Do you think she chose to…" I felt wetness in my eyes and under my arms. "People sometimes leave…"

Dove pushed herself off the counter and quickly embraced me.

“I’m sorry, Mrs. Frobischer.” Shelby said quickly and sincerely. “I didn’t mean to upset you.”

“I know.”

“I wasn’t thinking about you at all.”

“How strange that I was.” I laughed.

“You’re not anything at all like Miss Rittenhouse.”

“I’m not?”

Dove still held me.

Shelby answered me. “No, she’s a dried up old hag. And you…you’re not that at all—especially if you keep using the moisturizer I recommended for you.”

I nodded.

“See, you’re not anything like that old witch at all.”

I knew I had to see for myself.

After I took the girls to the marketplace for beignets and chocolate, I went home and paced the blue carpets in my living room. Did I dare? I found my answer on my left hand. George’s rings sang to me in a shower of light. They told me that I should.

That’s what I get for listening to my jewelry.

•••

Who was that brave woman that dolled herself up that late afternoon so that she could intrude upon an ancient, reclusive heiress that she may or may not have met a few times in Brentwood? Was this Rosa Frobischer? Maybe I'd find out as she and I walked that afternoon.

As, I strolled down D'Arbonne Street on my way to La Colline Cramoisie, I could smell the tangy scent of still water wafting up from the Bayou Vin Atténué. It made me want to sneeze or blow my nose.

Good Lord! The day was hot. Or was it me? I wasn't given to adventure seeking. Quests weren't my forte. If you needed an impromptu post-theatre soirée organized, I was your woman. But, I wasn't used to storming citadels.

"Should I turn back?" I asked myself after sneezing again. "Ugh! The swamp stinks today. It's a sign. A sign that I should go home and wait for a less humid day."

No, it wasn't a sign. It was just standing water. George wouldn't have turned back. Did he retreat when Irving Thalberg showed his fangs? No. Did George hesitate before he threw a director's chair at Miriam Hopkins? No. If George could take on Miriam Hopkins, I could certainly handle Amelia Rittenhouse. Right?

I told myself that it was too late to turn back anyway. If only the air wasn't so thick and moist…and pungent.

I tried not to think about that odor of dirt and swamp and attempted to change my focus by taking myself back to those Hollywood parties.

I took a deep breath. It was quite a hike for a woman my age. But, easier than driving. I let my scratchy memories distract me from the labor of the journey.

The image of Amelia Rittenhouse with champagne flute aloft came rushing back. Her yellow-green eyes were like an animal's—expressive and never still. Her gaze would dart from person to person as if she were looking for their souls through their skin. She would drink herself into a frenzy before invariably diving into the omnipresent swimming pool—clothes and all. I half expected her to howl at the moon as she came up for air—or sob. I was never sure which.

I shut my eyes as I remembered those endless parties. They always seemed to end up centered on some body of water. Why was swimming such a paramount activity for us then? I never joined them.

In fact, I remembered one evening poolside, watching George splash water on Joan Crawford (never a good idea—especially given their already rocky relationship), when Amelia Rittenhouse was staring at me for an unusually long time. I swore she never blinked once. I thought by speaking to her, I could break whatever trance she was in. I mentioned something about how everyone was having a good time in the pool, but that I didn't care for swimming. She said, "I know," before turning away. It was the only time we ever spoke.

I had that strange feeling that I get sometimes when I remembered the manic spasm of her eyes at that moment by the pool—the way they burned me like fire before their savage gleam was extinguished by some hidden fear. While, I dreaded the trap of her eyes, I was called to answer my questions and so, I began my quest—my sweaty, peculiar, unexpected quest. And, there it was…that dreary stronghold. Why give up then? I had, after all, walked all the way from my cottage.

How funny that I preferred thinking my bravery was purely circumstantial. I was still just a rock—as much of a rock as the wedges of stone that made up those massive gray walls that swelled before me.

The Rittenhouse Mansion stands atop La Colline Cramoisie with its deep red soil—the color of dried blood—unusual for this area. The Renaissance Revival villa peers down upon the bulk of Marionneaux. And, while it is truly an architectural masterpiece, there's something not quite right about it. The windows seem dim and vacant and the overall appearance of the gray marble of its walls makes it seem cold and pallid, almost cadaverous—almost like a hollow, weather-dulled skull.

Surely, it couldn't be the same Amelia Rittenhouse.

Nevertheless, I pushed past the wrought iron gate and made my way up to the massive front door. Just as I was about to convince myself that it wasn't too late to turn back, I caught sight of a mature woman—plump and impish with raven hair streaked with silver.

She was strolling one of the side gardens, stopping to touch the white blooms on the azaleas. She kicked at the skirt of her olive green dress as she walked. She half-muttered, half-sang as she walked. I could barely hear the words, but they struck me as some local verse, which made me feel foreign and familiar all at once.

The shadowed river listens,
Waiting for the rain,
Lies lost in such sharp silence
Her beauty will wane:
She wears her hope like diamonds
All colors save but one
Diana's orb will free us
Reflected in the sun.

I paused a moment to listen to her—being careful not to disturb her. She seemed very intent on something almost as if she was forcing a thought up through her skull. After a moment, she wandered out of my sight toward the back of the house beyond the loggia. I took a deep breath.

It wasn't without hesitation that I rang the bell. But, I did it. I felt somehow compelled to do so after I heard that round woman's song. However, I wasn't sure if I was yet ready to face Amelia Rittenhouse—whoever she may have been.

Frankly, I was relieved when a maid opened the door. She resembled Dove. I smiled and greeted her as an old friend, "You must be Jade. I know your sister. She's a lovely girl."

I wanted to smooth the wrinkles out of her apron.

Jade nodded skittishly and said nothing, the hot flush of her cheeks told me that she had best not be seen talking to a guest. I smiled warmly to tell her I understood before she flitted off to fetch the mistress of the house.

After a few minutes, Jade returned to the vestibule where she had left me standing. Poor thing, she had a tired, withered look about her that made her seem very much like a stray cat whose tail had been pulled too many times. The only color anywhere on her was a pair of pearl earrings backed in gold. The pearls were small and rather unimportant, but she wore them as if they were priceless.

She saw me looking at her ears and quickly clasped one earring between her fingers, letting her thumb stroke the pearl for a second before artfully unfurling a strand of jet black hair from the bun behind her head and letting it settle in front of her earlobe. With a twinkle in her eye, she quickly did the same on the other side. In that brief moment, she seemed filled with life—a vitality that quickly passed through her as she said, "Miss Rittenhouse told me that you should be asked to wait."

Jade ushered me into a grand and impressive hall and scurried off. I hadn't seen such opulence since the last time George and I went to Florence. The walls were rich red between heavy marbleized and gilt moldings. The crimson expanse was interrupted by magnificent portraits and paintings—the majority of which looked to be masterpieces of museum quality. I was amazed. What a sin to pall these works of genius.

Above me, in a row, hung three massive Maria Teresa style crystal chandeliers—their brilliance hidden as they begged to be lit and yearned to sparkle. Even in the dimness of the room, I could tell that albeit majestic, the house lacked joy. Everything in it seemed to tremble with frustration as if it struggled to be released from the bath of its own staleness.

As I surveyed the room, I could have sworn I saw a shadow pause on the landing before darting off. A lean, tall, black shadow. Shadows don't pause, nor do they appear without a body to which they can be attached. And, yet, a specter didn't seem out of place in that setting. It was all too much like visiting the set of one of George's movies. I was simultaneously amused and doubtful. But, most surprisingly, I didn't wish to flee. Shockingly, I wanted to charge forward. George would have patted me on the back and offered me a cigar. I was almost proud of myself. But, that quickly faded.

Suddenly, I had the unmistakable feeling of youthful paranoia—unbecoming in a woman of my age. I was no longer a creaky octogenarian, but a girl in her late teens. A pink self-consciousness bubbled inside of me and I put my hand to the back of my neck as if to brush away nonexistent spider webs—thin, sticky threads of memory.

I was a girl again, in a ball gown—alone, but not. And, someone was watching me hungrily. Someone familiar. I glanced back to the sweep of the stairs; a shimmer on the landing watched me—if darkness can shimmer.

My left hand automatically smoothed the errant wisp of silver hair that tickled my forehead. When had I felt this way before? Why was the room so stiflingly warm? I began to perspire and as I did I was overcome by an agitation that made me shudder.

I wanted George.

No, I wanted my daddy. Eighty-six years old and I wanted my daddy.

Dozens of eyes peered down at me from the portraits on the walls. They closed me in. I took a deep breath and challenged the soulless images to take me.

I screwed my face up into a defiant grin and had to laugh at my own foolishness. Humility had made me even braver than I thought I could ever be and, once again, I looked to the landing. Nothing. No shimmer, no shadow, no looming stalker—only a bronze bust of Dionysus on a pedestal. I chuckled again—convinced I had been overtaken by a spell of my own imagination. A bust—armless and harmless—had been my lurking observer. I started toward the stairs. I would have to have a word with that bust—finally, an argument I would win.

The creaking of a door signaled that my time to debate the bronze had drawn to a close. And, I was greeted by another specter. This one, very real. She stood, framed in the doorway of what appeared to be a maple-paneled library. She had shrunken, and grayed and yet she was still recognizable in as much as a death mask resembles its predecessor.

There she stood, still dripping in sequins which quivered in the folds of her faded scarlet finery—now a sickly mauve. She was the dusty, decayed shell of the woman I had watched drink champagne and dance on tables.

"Damn you! Why did you come?" She asked me. No, she demanded of me.

"Amelia," I responded uncertainly, "It's Rosa. Rosa Frobischer. We ran in the same circles when my husband and I lived in California."

“I have never run in any circle,” She answered with a weary contempt. She then retreated, shutting the library door behind her.

“Well,” I muttered to myself, suddenly alone in a page out of Poe. I hastily and quietly saw myself out.

Unwin Rittenhouse

Rosa Frobischer came today. I saw her. She did not see me.

Jade Ji

Oh, oh, the mistress was awful today. A real bitch. She was like an animal at the zoo. So mean. And, I don't know why. You know, I brought in her lunch, she was all shouting and all spitting like I did something. I turned around to see if I dropped something. I made no mess.

I only looked away for a second, you know, but somehow she knocked over the tray. Tomato soup flew into all the corners and all over the walls. Then, she blames me, calls me "careless." But, what did I do? I made no mess! And, she says that I'm a "heartless devil," you know, and that I was "depriving an old lady of her soup."

Somehow…I don't know how because I was picking up the spoon…she got to pick up the bowl. She threw it at me. It spun like a Frisbee. A straight, thin line of tomato went across my white apron. What a spatter! It looked like when I painted my nails on Mama's table cloth and slipped. Ugly stain. I got whooped.

Even after I cleaned up her mess and brought her a new tray, she still made moans and complained. You know, I don't think it was even about me. She kept repeating something about being "invaded by Huns" and how we must "slaughter the infidels lest we be defeated again."

I wonder what she meant.

And, she didn't even eat the soup I brought the second time! I hate to waste food. Papa would have smacked me good if I ever did that. One time when I was little, I didn't finish all my mein and Papa whooped me.

But, Papa's not here. I guess that's why I am. Which is worse Papa or Miss Rittenhouse?

But, she didn't scare me anymore—not her. I wouldn't let her. Douglas says she's a witch. He teases me. But, not as much as I tease him.

Later, I felt *it* again. That thing.

I know it's what made the last three maids go away. There's something upstairs—or someone. I know there is. I wish I couldn't feel it. But, I can. I can always feel things. Shadows and things. I always could. Mama says that's why I'm going to Hell. But, I know that's not what she meant.

You know, I'm not going to go to Hell.

Douglas says I'm like an angel. I wonder if angels clean.

And, there's so much to clean, you know. So many stains.

Why doesn't Miss Rittenhouse allow me to go down the other hallway? The one on the left. Only Agathe is allowed there. It's not fair. I should clean that instead. Why should I have to care for the rest of this big old house when Agathe only has three rooms to look after? And, I'm stuck with the mistress' room. It always smells in there. Like old lady.

Oh who cares? Why make such noise? The cleaning keeps my head quiet.

You know, when I went upstairs to tidy the mistress' bedroom I knew *it* was watching me. When I turned around there was nothing. But, I know I heard footsteps. It was the shadow. I know it was.

I thought of Douglas to make me feel better—how strong and warm his arms always feel around me. I wish I could always be with him. He would protect me.

But, it isn't our night. We always have to be so careful.

If only it was Saturday. I might have gone home to stay with Mama and Papa. I could have talked to Dove and listened to her chatter about all her books and her pictures. All those words she uses. Where did she learn those words? Same place she learned to draw like that, I guess.

Maybe I should have gone home. And, if only for a night, I could have slept in my bed without having to lock the door.

But, too much has changed to go home. Besides, too much to clean here, you know. By the time I got back in the morning, I'd already be behind.

•••

Finally, the day is over and Miss Rittenhouse went to bed. I know because I heard her nasty coughing in her sleep when I walked by her door. I stopped for a second and listened at the curving door that goes to the hall to the left. I only heard silence. Agathe must have been sleeping, too.

Should I? Should I call Douglas? Could it hurt? I ache for him. His love has made me feel more like people. I am real when I am with him. I am.

I like to touch one of the earrings that he gave me. I do it whenever I can. I even did it when that other old lady came today. I pretended that the pearl was his love.

Nice old lady that one…kind of sad. She looked scared. I know how that is.

I wish I could have worn the earrings home to show Dove. She never gets to see pretty things. But, that would have made everything worse. I just would have been more trapped.

When I think of Douglas, I am free. But, no, I don't dare call. I wish I could do something. I want to run through the halls. I want to break things and shout—spin around like a crazy woman. I am alive. I want to feel something. I want to be free—always. But, I want to be with Douglas. Free with Douglas.

Sometimes, I think I hear someone else breathing. And I turn around to look. I am alone. I guess it's my own breath I hear. Because I'm always alone—always alone without Douglas. So, why am I always afraid? How can you fear nothing?

I have decided that I will never be afraid again. I have decided that starting now, I will sleep with my door unlocked.

Distractions are a hazard. Lord knows George distracted himself into the grave. Anything was better than actually feeling his pain and he searched for new ways to avoid himself. For ninety years he toiled under his denial, letting each slight, each snub, every inconvenience and frustration take residence in his gut until the amalgam burst forth in an effluence of agony. He would then coddle this infant rage—making sure it did not starve without its placental indignation. He would spend days bouncing the hungry terror on his knee—feeding it to satiation with his self-pity. Within a week, his offspring would perish on its own; having asphyxiated in its own acrimony. This happened with a chilling regularity. The torture was his alone to suffer. My torture was watching it.

At first, I had tried to leave George alone in his bouts of melancholy and spleen. I knew that his moods were a byproduct of his artistic mind—the muck and progeny of his genius. His frustration was unrelated to me and I knew that his eruptions could have only been avoided if he would have stopped hoarding his emotions. But, as decades passed, I could not sit back and watch him rear these demons and so, I tried to help him create his diversions in the hope that an unending stimulation would keep him from ever feeling anything negative.

I often wondered if I was only making things worse by distracting him further. I should have forced confrontation. But, angels are, by nature, passive.

I suppose it was inevitable that I, too, would begin internalizing my emotions if for no other reason than to protect George. Besides, it was the house agenda. And, although I am keenly aware of it, I still have trouble stopping this behavior. Therefore, the larger the hurt, the more dyspeptic and internally uncomfortable I become. And the more distressed I feel myself becoming, the more I try to distract myself from dealing with it.

Such was the case after my aborted encounter with Amelia Rittenhouse.

The evening after I had visited the Rittenhouse Mansion, I angrily stormed back to my cottage—a cloud of negativity billowed out behind me as I walked like so much poisonous exhaust.

I was unaccustomed to being as self-indulgent as to openly feel that much irritation. It didn't suit me. George could carry it off. Not me. I wasn't big enough. But, that was before.

On the way home, I stopped at the hobby shop before they closed. I picked up some drawing pads for Dove. I didn't want to get something for one girl and not the other, so I got a pretty pen on a beaded string for Shelby. I felt better, then.

If it hadn't been for the smell of the bayou, I could have relaxed even more. But, by the time I reached my cottage, I was keyed up again.

I tried to calm (yes—distract) myself by lining the kitchen shelves with pale pink paper, but that only served to infuriate me more as the paper was uncooperative and the scissors disobedient in my tired hands.

I threw the scissors down and chuckled as the metal clattered on the worn wooden floor. One loan drop of moisture escaped my eye.

I left the project unfinished and retreated to my bed. As drowsiness crept over me, I heard in the distance of my own thoughts, the words that the stout woman had hummed in the mansion's garden:

The shadowed river listens,
Waiting for the rain,
Lies lost in such sharp silence
Her beauty will wane:
She wears her hope like diamonds
All colors save but one
Diana's orb will free us
Reflected in the sun.

I was immediately swept into a fitful sleep.

That night I dreamt I was dressed in a beautiful gown of celadon colored silk…the gentle gray-green washed over me and made me feel young.

"George," I called out. "I'll be down in a minute."

I stopped to admire myself in the glass and noticed three claret colored spots on the bodice of the gown.

"Oh no, I can't go out like this."

I scratched at the three stains with my fingernail, glancing back into the mirror to see if they were gone.

This time, I was not greeted by my own reflection, but instead, I saw nothing but dozens of lidless eyes—unblinking. They made me feel heavy and dark as if I was being soaked through.

"Blink!"

Were they leeching the light from me?

I raised my leg high and kicked the mirror. It didn't shatter, but instead disappeared into vapor. I stood alone in an emptiness which seemed to crush me. How can nothingness crush you?

Without warning, a thick warm rain fell and coated me—making me wet and furious. I cursed the rain and wondered why the water felt so heavy, until I realized that it wasn't water that fell from the blackness above, it was red…a scarlet, like blood and just as thick.

"But," my dream-self thought, "It doesn't smell like copper."

Each crimson drop landed painfully on my warm and tender skin. The pelting of each droplet became sharper and more painful and soon, welts had begun to rise on my flesh. They burned and itched and soon a swell of my own blood arose in the wounds.

"George!" I screamed for him.

"He doesn't exist yet." My own voice answered back. I heard it in the staccato sting of those red globules.

I tried brushing away the droplets as they fell only to find that they had begun to solidify before they struck me.

Their red was a deep fire of crimson beneath bright hot flashes. Hard and faceted, the droplets had become cut rubies—no, not rubies. They were darker. Garnets, yes garnets. They hit the blackness of the ground with the abbreviated sound of ice pellets, and soon they began to pile up around me—suffocating me. I was drowning in them and as I struggled to be free of the carmine, my arms and legs were sliced by their razor edges.

My green silk dress was being ripped to shreds and had become streaked by the muddy color of port, which had begun to rise in jagged stripes as my flesh was torn. My body itched from its wounds.

I awoke—sweating—and turned on the light. I threw off the bedclothes and sat up—shivering as the cool stillness of my bedroom met my skin. I looked at my arms. They were scratched—a deep pink swelled in the lines my fingernails had made on my arms and legs. I had scratched myself raw in my sleep.

I did not try to slumber again that night. I sat in my bed—propped against a pillow, my arms limp—and watched the sun paint coral over the violet sky before those gentle hues retreated behind a wall of gray.

•••

The following morning had started out pleasantly enough, I suppose. Perhaps dull is a better description than pleasant. After the mediocre sunrise, everything was as lacking in spirit and as devoid of color as my dream had been red with life. I dressed simply in my favorite dark gray blouse and black damask skirt, hoping the softness of the fabric would soothe my raw skin. I finished the outfit with a black cardigan sweater, being careful to cover my injured arms without snagging the ragged skin around the scratches.

Once outside, I found the day to be as dull in energy as it was in appearance. Was it really as lackluster as all that? Or was it my own dreariness projected onto my surroundings? Very often, dullness—numbness—is worse than actual pain.

As usual, I walked as quickly through the Marionneaux town square as I could. As I did, I glanced upward to La Colline Cramoisie to the gray monster of a mansion and I suddenly felt a tight queasiness squeeze my innards. I tried to ignore the stares of those that I passed—their too-polite bows behind narrowed eyes reminded me too much of my dream.

D'Arbonne Street seemed unusually crowded and I began to feel claustrophobic especially after passing the building that once had been my family's bakery. I paused outside of it for a moment and took a deep breath. There was no smell of fresh baking bread, no sweet white haze from people lazily eating beignets—only car exhaust and damp earth.

A corpulent, rather flamboyantly dressed woman around my age putted past me on her motorized cart—nodding her salutation with a smirk.

"Why does she hate me?" I wondered to myself.

Perhaps we had been classmates and she harbored some frayed seventy-year old soreness over losing the Christmas Essay Contest to me. Or perhaps her resentment was deeper. Maybe she hated me for having escaped the narrow streets and small minds of this town. The people of Marionneaux didn't take kindly to those who deserted them. And yet, by returning—even after decades—their collective countenance suggested a triumph at my return as if I had failed without them. Again, I felt that tightness in my stomach.

I shut my eyes and was shocked by the crimson I saw behind the lids. I cursed the dream. I cursed my lack of sleep. My wounds itched.

When I opened my eyes I saw that she had stopped her scooter a few feet from me and had paused to watch me out of the corner of her eye.

"Good morning," I said as brightly as I could—frankly, surprised at myself for challenging her.

"Good morning, Rosa," she belched in a voice rough with gravel. She smirked again before the corners of her mouth wilted into a frown—a speck of spittle shone in one of the trenches of skin on either side of her lips. "So sorry to hear of your misfortune."

I nodded, wondering if she meant the misfortune of losing George or perhaps some other perceived tragedy of which I was not yet aware.

"I can't imagine what it would be like to bury a husband," She continued, answering my question for me. "Mine is still with me, thank God." The gravel of her voice was suddenly coated in an unctuous solution of mock sympathy and bile.

"Oh how nice for you," I answered gaily.

"You may remember him. Augustin L'Ebène," She snarled sweetly.

I nodded again, "Of course."

Augustin L'Ebène. Oh yes, Augustin L'Ebène—he had courted me feverishly, but I rejected him. Although he came from a "good" family, I found him cruel and repugnant. After my rejection, a vicious-tongued tart named Marie Badeaux had quickly snatched him up. They were well suited. I laughed when their engagement was announced. How could I have taken such delight in something so trivial? For a moment, I felt lost, as if struggling against a great gust of wind or an ocean wave. Why had I laughed? I noticed Marie had begun to look at me with an odd mixture of triumph and curiosity. I drew in my breath.

Thinking of these things—remembering a time pre-George—was making me feel light-headed. My heart raced. But, to admit my discomfort would be inconvenient for Marie. Most people aren't at ease with other people's emotions—especially people like Marie L'Ebène.

Besides, I heard George's voice in my head. He was bellowing, "Don't let her get to you, Rosie." Perhaps I had some facets after all.

I smiled as big and pretty as a Louisiana sunset, "I'm glad he's well, Marie."

She raised her eyebrows, as if confused. I could tell she was at once impressed that I had remembered her and slightly defeated that she no longer had the upper hand. The spittle still sparkled on her cheek.

“We are all well,” Marie growled, “I have three beautiful daughters…all married above....” She paused, “They married well. Augustin is retired now. After over sixty years in the medical profession, he’s earned the right to relax, to work on his hobbies and enjoy his grandchildren.” Widening her eyes, she set her jaw as if about to make a proclamation, “You of course know my granddaughter, Shelby.”

So, Shelby Halifax was of the same bloodline. This explained a lot. But, Shelby was still salvageable.

Marie continued, “You seem to enjoy making her work in your little bookstore.”

“She seems to enjoy it herself,” I pulled my lips into something resembling a smile. Was that a cheer I heard from deep within myself? Nah, couldn’t have been. Could it?

Marie coughed. “I suppose there is comfort in having children around when one has no man for company. I understand why you make her stay to help you. The loneliness…” She whispered “loneliness” as if it were a curse.

—You bitch—I thought. “Well, one is only as alone as she allows herself to be.” I answered, not giving her the satisfaction of letting her see my irritation. I hoped she wouldn’t notice that I had begun to sweat. I tried to listen for that cheer again. I couldn’t hear it. My hands itched.

“True,” Marie said wryly, leaning over to flick at a fly on the handle of her scooter. As she did, the folds of her face fell forward like a cascade of salmon colored rags.

I put my hand to my still smooth face and touched my cheekbone.

"You want lessons on being alone, you go there." Marie pointed to the crest of La Colline Cramoisie. "Old Rittenhouse could teach you." She paused and whispered again, "You know what kind of people she keeps?"

I shook my head. I wanted to ask her what she knew of Amelia Rittenhouse, but I didn't want to hear her particular brand of interpretation nor to give her the satisfaction of telling me. She seemed too eager. There was that cheer again.

Suddenly, a dimness passed over Marie's eyes which indicated that she thought that she shouldn't share her gossip with the likes of me anyway. "I don't want to keep you from your work," Marie said, placing a finger on the joystick of her scooter. "I know how you must need it."

I felt my neck tighten.

She began to speak again, but held her breath as a young Asian couple passed by, holding hands. Her face grew even more sour and she looked as if she might spit. "Some people," she began after the couple had passed by, "Need to stick to their homes."

I wasn't positive if she meant the couple or me.

"I'm very sure you're glad to be back in Marionneaux." she added. "You were probably lost without your roots."

Before I could speak, she oozed, "Good day," and rolled slowly away.

I leaned on the brick wall to my left and clenched my eyes shut—again startled by the red.

I rubbed my eyes. "A rose without roots," I muttered. "No roots, no thorns." I've spent too long waiting in a vase to let that woman wilt me. I chuckled at my metaphor. George would be proud.

"What a cow!" I shook my head as I remembered Marie. I was antsy. Too antsy.

From there, I decided to take my time getting to the shop. I didn't think I could stand to be cooped up behind the counter so soon after that harrowing encounter with yet another specter from my past. Besides, the girls wouldn't be at the shop until much later in the day, so it wasn't as if they'd be disappointed if I opened up late. What to do what to do?

I glanced up La Colline Cramoisie. I was torn. I thought I'd enjoy looking at the restored Victorians and old plantation homes along the hill, but I rather dreaded going near the Rittenhouse estate.

I decided to walk up about halfway, turning back before the zenith. That way, I could clear my head and guarantee that I'd avoid further mental muddiness compliments of Amelia or any of her minions. George always called me the "Mistress of the Compromise," after all.

And, so I started up the hill—trying to preoccupy myself with admiring the architecture of the row of unexpectedly austere mansions that led up La Colline Cramoisie. Distractions.

Midway up, I was greeted by a nasal shout. It was Shelby Halifax, running from her parents' pale yellow clapboard castle. She shouted for me again—her voice sounded strained. The biting eyes of their cleaning woman regarded me with what I perceived to be a mix of curiosity and aversion as Shelby panted her way to me.

Out of breath, her face pale, Shelby took my arm.

"What's wrong, dear?" I asked uneasily—still shaken by my encounter with her grandmother. I wanted to scoop her up and protect her. I couldn't bear to see her so upset. "Whatever could have happened?"

"Dove's sister," Shelby panted. "She's dead."

II
The Silence

I am free.

Shelby Halifax

Those awful shrill sirens woke me. At first I was very angry and I threw one of my imported Dutch eyelet pillows toward the window. I just hate it when I have to get up too early. But, I suddenly became afraid as I realized that the sounds blaring up the street were coming from ambulance and police cars. It wasn't a sound I was used to. I thought maybe our house was on fire. How would we get all of our clothes out in time? But, luckily, I didn't have to worry about it. The sirens passed our house. It was someone else's problem. I smiled. It always was someone else's problem. But, whose? I simply had to find out.

I knocked on the door to Therese's room on the third floor. As usual, she didn't know what had happened. How can you expect someone like Therese to know anything about stuff that doesn't concern her directly? So, I went downstairs. I didn't walk as slowly as I usually did. Something about our beautiful staircase made me want to descend like a beauty queen or a movie star and so I always made a careful and elegant entrance—even when no one was around. But, I didn't bother that morning. I was in a hurry and, anyway, I was in my nightgown. I laughed a little bit.

I was walking around the house in my nightgown. I knew Mommy would disapprove, but I didn't care.

I found Mommy in the morning room. She was reclining on the chaise, talking on the phone. Her breakfast sat untouched on a silver tray which Therese had placed on the pouf to her right. Mommy never ate at the table. Mommy actually never really ate, now that I think of it. It was all just for show—the trays of food and such. But, she always told me that a woman of a certain class has, at all times, the right props at hand.

She looked at me crossly when I came into the room and put her hand over the receiver. "A girl of your age isn't to parade around the house in her nightclothes. You're too old for this."

I ignored her and sat down. She sighed loudly into the phone and wiggled her right foot at me.

I knew what she would say. The closer I got to my sixteenth birthday, the more Mommy would become angry with me over little things. But, I also knew I would have to risk her anger. If anyone would know what the sirens were for, it would be Mommy.

She shot me another dirty look and said in a forced voice to whomever she was speaking, "I have to call you back. Shelby is being awful again."

I blushed. I could feel my cheeks turning pink. I hated feeling like that. I picked at the weave of the dupioni silk upholstery.

She hung up the phone and propped herself up on her sharp, thin elbow, using her free hand to fluff the back of her bleached curls.

"Why must you disobey me?" She asked huskily.

I chose to ignore that question. I'd show her. I wouldn't even look at her.

"Well!" She glowered at me. Making facing like she was isn't good for your skin—it causes wrinkles. "For Christ's sake, you little shit, stop mangling my fabrics!"

I stopped picking, but I wouldn't apologize. Her shoes were far worse for the upholstery than my fingernails. No, I wouldn't apologize. "What's going on?" I asked instead. "Why the sirens?"

She narrowed her eyes and sighed.

Before she could answer, Daddy came into the room.

"Hello, my girl," Daddy said to me. He looked nervous. "You shouldn't be out without your robe," he added for Mommy's benefit.

Mommy shut her eyes and lay back on the chaise again.

"Voletta," he nodded at her.

She nodded back coldly—without opening her eyes.

Daddy's face fell and he scratched absently at the side of his thumbnail. He then looked at his hands and began to purposefully run the nail of his right index finger under the nail of his left thumb. He looked tired.

I looked first at Daddy and then at Mommy—waiting to see if they would continue talking. They did not and I wasn't surprised. They didn't seem to talk much anymore. Not to one another anyway. But, that's the way parents are.

“Mommy, what about the sirens?” I asked again, hoping my impatience wouldn’t show. It did, however and Mommy noted it.

“What about the sirens,” She mocked me in a shrill nasal voice. “Must you know everything?” She added.

“I must,” Daddy answered, winking at me.

“What makes you think I would know,” Mommy answered sharply as her lips curled back into a smile.

“Is there anything that happens in Marionneaux that you don’t know, Voletta?” Daddy asked.

I felt a shiver. I made a note to myself to ask Daddy to buy me a warmer nightgown. In pink. No, no, white. I’m too old for pink.

More silence.

“Voletta?” Daddy asked again.

Mommy continued to smile, “The Chinese girl that the old Rittenhouse woman keeps.” Mommy began. “She’s been murdered.” Her eyes sparkled as she said it.

Daddy’s face was like stone. He didn’t change expression at all. But, all the color drained out of his cheeks. He sank into one of the Chippendale chairs by the sideboard.

Mommy still smiled.

More silence. It was weird for Mommy to be quiet. I looked at her hair and reminded myself never to color my own—or at least never to bleach it. Too much work to keep the roots in check.

Daddy began digging at his nails again.

"Stop acting like a farm hand!" Mommy snapped.

She was right. It was unbecoming. I smiled at Daddy and nodded so that he would know I agreed.

He turned away from me.

"Don't you want to know how?" Mommy asked—thoroughly enjoying herself. "Isn't your curiosity at all aroused?"

"Not in front of the child." Daddy said softly.

"I'm not a child, Daddy," I whined.

Mommy rolled her eyes. "She was sliced," She said flatly even though her eyes didn't lose their steely glint.

Daddy's shoulders tightened and his head went back a bit.

"Slashed to death," Mommy continued very matter-of-factly. "Like a ham."

"NOT in front of the…Shelby!" Daddy shouted and stood up quickly. He put his hand on the wall behind him as if he were afraid he would fall.

Mommy laughed, "Why not? She'll hear all about it soon enough."

I smiled. She was right. Mommy rolled over on her side—facing us. She was beginning to look old. I promised myself I would dress better when I was Mommy's age and that I wouldn't make so many faces. No one wants wrinkles. I'd have to practice keeping my face still.

I looked at Daddy. He had nice skin for a man. But, I couldn't tell what he was feeling. He seemed disgusted, I thought—as if he was served something for breakfast that he didn't like. Like turkey sausage. Suddenly, I felt my heart contract and I wanted to cry. I had to look away from him. I never felt things like that. Averill Cage, this boy in my science class, says that a girl starts to have strange feelings around our age because of hormones or something like that.

Mommy sat up and grabbed her coffee cup from the silver tray—stirring it viciously with a spoon. The clanking was noisy and I didn't like it.

I looked at Daddy again. He had closed his eyes tightly, but other than that, his face hadn't changed expression. Again, I felt cold.

"Was she cut into pieces?" I asked.

"What?" Daddy asked raspily.

"The Chinese girl?" I continued.

"Shelby!" Daddy shouted, "Get out of here!"

"Please," Mommy began. She hated when anyone shouted, especially so early in the morning—anyone except her, of course.

"What did I do? Am I being punished?" I asked, prepared to cry—but, not real tears.

"No," Daddy said more gently. "Just go get dressed and go somewhere. Go to the bookstore or something."

Mommy scolded him, "Don't encourage her to spend time doing labor for that Frobischer woman."

"GO!" Daddy shouted again.

I quickly stood up.

"You'd better go," Mommy said softly, but her eyes were like fire.

I left as quickly as I could.

Once I got into the foyer, I paused for a moment on the stairs and listened.

"You're happy?" I heard Daddy say. "A girl is dead and you're happy?"

I heard Mommy laugh. "You really are a fool."

Then, someone shut the door.

With nothing else to listen to, I decided I would go upstairs and get dressed.

I washed up and went to my closet. I had to be careful what I chose to wear. When something as serious as a murder occurs on your street, you don't want to look too flashy. But, you also don't want to look like you're in mourning because you don't want the neighbors to think you have any real association with whatever's going on. So, whatever I wore had to be tasteful and conservative, but not too somber.

I thought about everything Mommy had said. I wondered what it would feel like to be sliced to death. She never did tell me if the girl had been cut up in pieces. Maybe she was just sliced and she bled to death. That seemed worse. I ran the handle of my brush against the flawless skin of my forearm and tried to imagine it. I shivered again. I must get Therese to turn the air conditioning down.

I chose my taupe sweater set and beige pants and lay them out on the bed while I fixed my hair. In my mirror, I could see my doll collection reflected. All of their glass eyes sparkled at me. I sighed heavily as I thought about the passing of my childhood and my budding womanhood. Soon, I'd have to put my dolls away because I'd be too old for them. What would people think if they visited me and saw I still had dolls out in my room?

But, they were all so beautiful. My favorite was the one that Grandfather L'Ebène had gotten for Grandmother long ago. It then had been Mommy's and she gave it to me. It was the figure of a Chinese girl dressed in silk. She seemed to be laughing. It was so old…probably worth a lot of money now.

My eyes burned. I studied them in the mirror—opening them wide. I shivered again. I looked back at the Chinese doll. Was she laughing? Or was she screaming?

I shook my head and got to work on my hair. Making sure each dark curl cascaded in the proper place.

Daddy was right, I decided. It was a good idea to go to the bookstore. I couldn't wait to tell Dove what I had heard. "But," I thought, "Maybe I shouldn't. It might upset her what with it being a Chinese girl."

I continued to fluff my hair.

"But," I thought again, "Maybe Dove's sister knows the girl. She works for Old Lady Rittenhouse, too."

I laughed, "Daddy always calls that Rittenhouse woman a witch."

I sprayed my hair.

"Yes, maybe Dove's sister knows the girl. Wouldn't that be something?" Another shiver.

"Oh my God!" I dropped my hairspray and ran from the room without even finishing my hair. I saw the Chinese doll out of the corner of my eye as I ran. She was definitely screaming.

Why? Why? They wasted no time in finding an entrance to my life! Didn't they? I won't let them invade my home! I won't let them destroy what I've built!

I knew what had happened even before Agathe came screaming into my bedroom. I smelled death. I knew it wouldn't be long before the maggots began to feast on us all! *It'll be all right Amelia, they won't compromise his safety.*

At first, I let it get to me. I sat paralyzed for hours as the sun came up. Dust particles sparkled in the light that slit through the heavy gray velvet drapes—making incisions of brightness on the deep red carpet. I watched the dust hang in the slash of sun.

The feeling was unmistakable. I had never forgotten it even after all these years. Death. I couldn't drink it away.

When Agathe burst through my door, sobbing, I didn't even move. The way her black and white hair flapped behind her as she flounced in made her resemble a frenzied nun who's found a man in the convent.

"We have to call someone!" She demanded.

"No," I whispered.

She ran off.

It was then that I knew I had to act quickly.

I rose as quickly as I could and I shouted out to her, "Damn you Agathe! Leave it alone! If you so much as compromise…" She was too far away. *Save your energy for the real marauders, Amelia.*

Jade lay on the floor—the claret pool of her blood lost in the crimson lake of the carpet. Her eyes were open. And, so were the curtains. The light made her pallid face seem almost like marble—or porcelain. It was a tableau out of a Caravaggio—his "Death of the Virgin," or maybe simply his "Portrait of a Courtesan."

It was beautiful—sick and awful and beautiful. *Don't let it get to you, old girl.*

Agathe had covered the girl's nakedness with a blanket. It had been, unfortunately, white. The wool blotted her life—making red veins in its weave. Seeing that stain made my skin itch.

"A white blanket? Damn it!"

I pulled back the mantle. The girl was cut—neatly. It was the same pattern I had seen before. Done with a surgeon's precision—or a sculptor's.

The red lines on her skin were the only color except for her swollen purple earlobes—bloated on either side of the short tear that had cleft each lobe from the hole of her piercing to the tip.

I covered her again. This time, making sure her face was hidden. I didn't want to see her eyes. Even in death, she reminded me. I let myself shrink if only for just that second. But, I didn't stay down for long. *You'll feed before they do.*

"Stupid girl," I hissed at the corpse. "You did this to yourself."

How I had hated her. She was so much like the other one.

Agathe came thumping into the room—covering her mouth with her shaking hand.

"I've called the police," She declared though her fingers.

"Idiot!" I screeched with a renewed passion. "You know we can't let them in here!" If only I could have, I'd have ripped her to shreds.

"I had to," Agathe whimpered. "If he did this…"

"Shut up!" I shouted. "Say that again and I'll..."

Agathe sank against the wall.

"Don't speak of him!" I continued to rail her.

"I had to call them," Agathe rambled, "It was the right thing."

"I haven't kept you here to do the 'right thing.'" I snapped. "They'll search the house."

"I don't care," Agathe began to sob.

"Listen you!" I continued. And, then I heard the sirens followed by the knock at the door. Agathe ran to answer it. *It's all over! No, no, it isn't. Don't think that!*

"Vultures!" I shouted.

I looked down at the mound under the blanket that was Jade. I wanted to kick her.

I made my way to the landing just as the police were coming up the stairs. Five officers and two ambulance men—I felt as if I was being eaten by ants.

I pointed to Jade's room without saying anything. I'd lull them into my confidence and then…

Three officers and the ambulance men went that direction. Two of the officers started down the other side of the hallway—to the left.

"What are you doing?" I demanded.

"We have to search the house," one of them answered gruffly.

"I won't allow it," I said as calmly as possible. But, it was too late. They had gone.

When they entered the door to my past, I couldn't do a thing. In my head, I pictured myself screaming, hurling myself in front of them. But, I couldn't. *Is it time to let go? No! Never give up!*

I sat on the low Empire bench on the landing as still as the bronze. I was planning.

Moments later, they came out. I heard one mutter, "Nothing in there."

My heart leapt. "Nothing," I repeated. *Be calm, Amelia. They'll know.*

I stayed on that bench—barely breathing as the men carried the girl's body out. I watched as they searched the house. I watched as they sealed Jade's room. I answered their questions mechanically. I don't even remember what I said. I was waiting—waiting for it all to be over—waiting to pounce.

They ordered us not to go into Jade's room or touch anything until they gave us permission, said that the kitchen door was unlocked, and then they left. *I'll go where I like, parasite!*

They left.

I remained on the bench. Agathe had said something to me. I don't know what. I don't even know how long any of it had taken.

They left. They found nothing.

"Amelia!" Agathe shouted at me. I looked at her. "Where is he?" She asked shrilly.

"That's your job," I answered slowly as I felt my life slowly begin to awaken. "He's your…" I chose my words carcfully, "rcsponsibility."

"I know what he is." She screeched—challenging me.

"Find him, then." I answered—disturbed by my own calm. *There it is, Amelia. There's your undoing. Again.*

She sputtered and started to plod off.

"Wait!" I said—fully alert.

She turned back.

"Did you tell them about him?" I asked.

"No," she answered boldly. "But, not for you," she added with an unusual force.

"Not for him either," I glared at her.

"No. For me. I'm going to get what's due me." She whispered and her eyes flashed.

"You are your mother's daughter," I nodded.

She smirked. "Am I? I think I'm more my father's." Her pewter eyes flashed brightly.

I knew then that I had lost. I was to be a slave to that plump devil.

"Just find him." I answered flatly.

She went off, presumably to find him.

I leaned against the wall; shaking my head and feeling my legs fall asleep from the hardness of the bench beneath them. *You lost again. Didn't you? You old, stupid bitch.*

No, I hadn't necessarily been beaten. I still had some fight left.

I watched the dust again. I smelled the death.

"This time, Unwin," I vowed, "I won't allow us to be defeated."

I am free.

I got up early. I was working on a new drawing. The first sound I heard that morning was the phone ringing. The sound startled me and I jumped. My hand darted up and left a stray line with my scarlet pencil.

Such an early call. But, I thought nothing of it. It was probably another catering order or a waitress calling-in sick. When I heard my mother's moan, I quickly put down my drawing pad and ran out of my room.

Mama was on the floor. She was curled up in a little ball. Papa also came running in, wiping his hands on his apron. He had just butchered a chicken. I watched as his hands streaked red on the white of his apron.

Mama shrieked.

"What is this?" Papa demanded, "What is this, Niu?"

"Our baby," Mama wailed.

Papa looked at me.

"Jade!" Mama shouted through her tears.

Papa wiped his hands on his apron again. It took me a minute to understand.

But soon, I knew that my sister was dead.

I felt my stomach turn over. I felt cold and hot all at once.

Papa said. "She brought shame to us."

Papa turned and went back to the kitchen.

"Hsin!" Mama shouted his name. She rose up from the floor on her hands and pulled herself to the kitchen door. "Only to you!"

Those were the last words I would ever hear my mama say.

She collapsed back onto the floor. She sobbed silently. She would never speak again.

I sat in the living room for a very long time and watched Mama cry.

Jade wasn't the only one who was dead.

I can't say exactly what happened after that. Everything happened quickly and yet in slow motion at the same time. Some people in uniforms knocked on the door. I remember opening the door. I remember nodding when told that I should look after Mama and Papa. I remember hearing how Jade died.

Mama sat until the sun went down. She was like a candle, like wax. And, then I helped her out of her chair and put her to bed. I told her that I would protect her and take care of her. She said nothing. I shut the light and told her good night. She said nothing.

I read a story once where an old man's son dies in a car accident. He never said another word. He just sat around and stared at things and never said another word to anyone. I thought about that. I decided that when I could, I'd go to the library and check that book out. I'd bring it home and rip out every page. And, I'd burn the whole thing up in the incinerator in the back yard. That's what I'd do. And, then I'd get the book about the man who beat his dog. And, I'd burn that one, too.

I went through the dark living room. My feet made no noise on the yellowed carpet. I thought about going into the kitchen to tell Papa that I was scared. I thought I'd tell him I was sad and worried about Mama. I walked by the door and saw the razor of light cutting around the door edges into the dark, dark living room. I said nothing.

That night, I sat in the dark—alone. I thought Jade was with me for a second. I thought I smelled her sweet scent. I must have fallen asleep because I never saw Papa come out of the kitchen.

The following morning, I fed the chickens. And, then I fed Mama. At least I tried to. I had propped her limp body up in her bed. She would not eat. She would not drink.

Papa told me to go through the things that Jade left behind when she moved to the Rittenhouse Mansion. He told me to pick a dress to bury her in. He said to throw the rest away.

"Why can't we give her things to the shelter?" I asked.

"They are not good enough!" That was all he answered. I didn't know if he meant Jade's things or the people at the shelter. He added in his thick accent, "Do as I ask, girl!" With that, he left.

"Do as I ask." I breathed heavily and wanted to scream at him. Why did he hate Jade? What had she done?

Instead, I said nothing. I did as he asked.

I ran to the small back bedroom that once was Jade's. It was then that I let my tears out. They fell all over my gray shirt and made little black dots.

The closet door creaked when I opened it. The faint remains of Jade's scent—her ginger shampoo and lavender water. Those made me cry all the more.

I carefully touched each dress, each sweater, each skirt. They felt cold to my touch.

I selected a dress for her to wear. It was the pale gray-green silk with flowing sleeves. It was her favorite. It was her "princess dress." That's what I called it. She had picked it out herself to match the tiny celadon-glazed vase that Mama kept on the shelf by the front door. She loved that vase. She always dusted it with such care.

I listened for a moment. Nothing.

I lay the dress out on the narrow bed. The mattress was bare—no cover, no sheets. I pulled each arm of the dress out to make a T. I lay down on the bed next to it and wrapped the right arm of the dress around me, resting the cuff on my nose. With closed eyes, I remembered Jade. In my head, I could still see the way she looked in that dress on her twenty-first birthday. I was very small, then, but I remembered it anyway. We were all happy then.

Maybe Jade wasn't happy. Maybe she wasn't. After all, it's okay to be sad when other people are happy. Poor Jade. Was she ever happy?

I got up and went down the hallway to look in on Mama. Her mouth had fallen open. It had been her only movement. I quietly shut the door and went back to Jade's room.

Alone, I opened the top drawer of my sister's bureau. In that skinny drawer, she kept her most prized possessions. It was filled with plastic and cheap trinkets, a pressed flower, a ticket stub, old letters. It was all so much junk, but she always treated these meager objects as if they were royal treasures.

Maybe Jade was a princess after all. People always stared at her. She didn't need a crown or jewels. She was pretty all on her own.

She had only the one real piece of jewelry—a small, silver pin with three red stones which Papa had given her when she turned twenty-one. He had loved her then. What had happened?

I pinned the brooch to the front of the dress. What did Papa call the stones? He had a terrible time trying to pronounce it. Rubellite. Jade had loved the way the stones sparkled and flashed with a red fire. She swore she would wear it always and she kissed Papa on the cheek that day. He asked her at that moment if he would always be her favorite man. She said he would.

I sat on the bed for a minute and decided that pinning those stones to a corpse was as good as throwing them away. That should please Papa.

I don't know how long I sat there after that. In awhile, I went back to the narrow drawer and I ran my fingers lightly over its contents.

I pretended that I was one of those people that could talk to the dead. I read an essay about it once. These people can touch stuff that belonged to someone when they were alive and then they can get messages from them even though the person is dead. I didn't get any messages. It didn't work for me.

I looked around the drawer. At the very back, there was a small black velvet box. It was the kind that jewelry comes in. I reached in and took the box out, opening it. It was empty. I felt guilty about going through Jade's things. But, they were all that we had of her.

I removed a stack of letters—each carefully folded. I opened the top one.

"My beauty," It began. My eyes welled with tears and I could not read on. I looked at the signature. "I love you...Douglas." Someone had loved her. I was glad of that. I remembered how her eyes danced the last time I saw her. Maybe that was why.

"Someone loved her!" I shouted to no one.

Very slowly and carefully, I began to take Jade's things and pack them in boxes that I found in the shed. Every half hour or so, I looked in on Mama. She hadn't moved. Her arms were still draped at her sides. Her mouth was still open.

When everything was packed, I sealed the boxes. Where would I hide them? I had to put them somewhere Papa wouldn't look. I had to make him think I did as he asked. I started to cry again when there was a knock at the door.

I was glad to see Mrs. Frobischer and Shelby.

Without saying a word, Mrs. Frobischer hugged me. I went limp in her arms.

I was resistant to enter through that basket-handle archway. I wrung my hands as I walked past the sign that read simply, "DeCuir." How very typically Marionneaux—the same family still ran the local mortuary. All of it was too much. To begin with, the memory of George's L.A. funeral was still too fresh in my mind. I wasn't sure I could withstand another burial service even if it was one for a girl I'd only met once. But, I forced myself to go inside. Dove needed me. That's all that mattered. I had to stick by her side even though it meant a trip back in time.

The funeral home was virtually unchanged from the last time I had seen it. Despite the passage of seventy years, I swore the wooden chairs were the same ones upon which we sat when we said goodbye to my father. My mother was very brave. She did not cry—not then, but I had heard her later that night walking downstairs whimpering like a lost pup. We were all lost without Daddy.

My father had been a beloved member of the community. Everyone called him, "The Meat Pie Man." He was a local celebrity because of his kitchen and his heart—both were bountiful and productive. Almost everyone in our part of Marionneaux had attended my father's service—the room was filled with familiar faces from the Rue de la Marchands. Most of the businesses on D'Arbonne Street had closed for the afternoon.

Perhaps everything would have been different if my mother and I had been prepared for his death, if he had been diagnosed with some illness. Of course, I didn't want my father to have suffered through some terrible malady, but the accident that took his life was so unexpected that it left me unable to accept that he was gone. Maybe if it had been I who had found him the afternoon that he fell from that ladder, instead of my poor mother, I would have been better able to comprehend his passing.

I couldn't help but blame myself. I was supposed to help him that afternoon. I was supposed to stand at the foot of the ladder—to hand him roofing nails and shingles, and most importantly to warn him if our rickety old ladder looked unsteady or showed signs of splintering.

But, that was the day I was meant to get the final fitting for the dress I was to wear to an upcoming dance at the high school. I was so enamored of that crimson gown that, I'm ashamed now to admit, it preoccupied my every thought. Ours was not a life of gowns and formal occasions. Ours was a life of yeast and confectioners' sugar. That dance was to be my first, and that gown represented exciting new possibilities.

My father very sweetly released me from my commitment so that I could go to my fitting. Alone, he went about the business of replacing some missing shingles on our highly pitched roof. In fact, he had volunteered to fix the roof himself instead of hiring a carpenter so that we could save the money for that damn dress.

He went up on that ladder for me. And, without me to warn him, the ladder cracked as he had feared it might, as I was to warn him against. He broke his neck and died instantly.

When I learned that my father was killed, I couldn't comprehend it. But, later, when the reality struck me, I grew angry with myself when I wondered if I would still be free to go to the dance. I hated myself for my selfishness at that particular moment and I swore I would never give in to such feelings again. I remembered sitting at his funeral filled with the hot needles of desperate grief. Later, I wondered if it was grief over his passing or grief upon realizing my own flaws.

That was the beginning of a lifetime of awareness of my own imperfections and a lifetime of assigning guilt to myself as penance for those shortcomings. But, it was only the start.

How odd to remember my father's funeral. My teenage years were but a dim flicker seen through worn, threadbare fabric. Everything before George married me—made me his wife, his greatest project—was a dim memory.

Why, then, did the murder of a veritable stranger bring back so many memories for me? And, why did I feel a gnawing sense of culpability for the poor girl's death?

George would have said, "You can take the girl out of Catholicism, but you can't take the Catholicism out of the girl." Remorse, he once concluded, was my hobby. Did he know why? Perhaps he did. But, that was before. Or was it after? Drat! I forgot what I had concluded. Nevertheless, it didn't matter. Dove needed me to help her say goodbye to her sister.

Jade's funeral was so unlike my father's and George's had been. At each, the room was so full; people had to stand in the back. But, for Jade's service, the room was empty. The strangest thing about it was the absence of Mr. Ji. He did not attend his own daughter's funeral. I don't suppose I should have been surprised, seeing the way Dove had acted when we visited her the day of the murder.

Shelby and I had helped Dove carry Jade's things out of the house. I let her keep them in the backroom of the bookstore. I wasn't sure why she wanted to, but she seemed utterly desperate, so I agreed without question. As we brought the boxes into my shop, I had the uneasy feeling that one gets when one's being watched.

I glanced briefly over my shoulder. Augustin and Marie L'Ebène were seated across D'Arbonne Street at Le Café Savoureux de Bouchée. Marie weighed heavily upon her scooter, feigning interest in some speck on the handlebars. In a wrought iron chair next to her, Augustin had obscured his face behind the sickly orange-toned cover of some medical journal.

They didn't appear to be watching us, but I felt self-conscious nonetheless. I was about to alert Shelby to their presence, when a silver coldness settled into my stomach that made me feel certain that she knew they were there. A bluntness passed through Shelby and she kicked at a stone as we walked, her shoulders rigid with intentions, her head static upon her neck. She seemed so unlike her usual beautiful, petulant self for those few seconds that I dared not interpret her thoughts. I felt it inconsiderate to intrude upon whatever feelings she was entertaining. Instead, I watched her as we walked—hoping to understand her better so that I could be of better use to her in the future.

Perhaps she truly did not see Marie and Augustin. But, if she did, she opted to ignore them—maybe she was ashamed to be seen with us, maybe she feared their judgment, or maybe she simply hoped that she would be shielded from their stares for just a moment—lost in the crowd on D'Arbonne Street.

There were no such crowds at Jade's funeral. Along with the girls' father, Amelia Rittenhouse was also noticeably absent. One would have thought that she would have attended the funeral of an employee—especially one that was murdered in her own home. As we stood, bathed in a salmon light at the corner of that dusty, stale room, Shelby put her hand on my arm and smiled.

"Miss Rittenhouse never leaves her property." Shelby said quietly. How had she known what I was thinking? Perhaps I had muttered it aloud or perhaps Shelby had the same thought. She was brighter than she let on. Why did she hide her sensitivity and her intellect?

"It's because she's a witch," Shelby said—trying not to smile. "She stays in her mansion and stirs her cauldron."

A flicked my index finger at her shoulder and we both giggled a little despite ourselves.

Dove and Mr. DeCuir, the diminutive funeral director, walked Mrs. Ji into the viewing room and sat her down in the front row. The woman was utterly lifeless. I watched her carefully for several minutes just to make sure she was still breathing.

Once Mrs. Ji had been arranged in her seat, Dove took her place next to her mother. I sat to her right with Shelby next to me.

We were the only ones there for about half an hour. Mr. DeCuir paced nervously in the back of the room—anxious to get the service started. His must be a hectic business in a place like Marionneaux where the native population's primary exit is that of death. I was certain he was worried about the timing of the service after ours. I watched him pace.

Shelby surprised me. She had been very gentle with Dove with as little theatricality as possible—even occasionally glancing at Dove and reaching over my lap to pat her plump little hand. Perhaps she was even less like her grandmother than even I had realized. My doubts resurfaced when Shelby whispered to me, "at least they could have fixed the mother's hair better."

I shook my head. Shelby began to get a look of panic as she looked at the coffin for what I suspected was the first time. I wondered if she had ever been to a funeral before. Again, I felt warmly toward her for making the effort to support her friend.

Shelby leaned over and whispered to me. "I do wish Mommy and Daddy had come. At least they could have filled out the room a bit."

"Did you ask them?" I inquired softly.

Shelby nodded, "I did. Mommy said that she would rather eat her own hand than go to that…" Shelby paused, "Well, she didn't want to come. I asked Daddy, too."

"What did he say?"

"Only that he had no desire to go to a stranger's funeral." Shelby sighed. "He seemed very angry that I had asked him." Shelby looked at the coffin again.

"Grandmother L'Ebène was going to come. She likes funerals." Shelby rolled her eyes.

"Not surprising," I thought to myself.

"But, she didn't want to…" Shelby paused to choose her words carefully. "She didn't want to be with…"

"With?" I asked, already knowing the answer.

Shelby flushed with embarrassment, "Strangers, I guess." She opened her clutch, "just like Daddy had said." She punctuated the thought with a convincing nod, took out her compact and began rearranging her hair. I smiled at her. Perhaps she didn't understand that Marie was a bigot, perhaps she was ashamed of it, or maybe she was simply unwilling to accept it.

We waited a few more minutes and just as the funeral director was about to begin, a woman walked into the room. I immediately recognized her as the woman I had seen in the garden at the Rittenhouse Mansion. Without the misty blur of the garden, which had given her almost a fairy-like countenance, I saw that she was more troll-like than elfin. Her black and silver hair against her ashen skin gave her a harshness that I had not noticed before. She glanced at the closed casket and pulled her gray shawl over her shoulders.

"Who is that?" I whispered to Dove who had been preoccupied with stroking her mother's slack, ashen hand.

Dove turned and looked at the woman. She shrugged. "I don't know." Her hand quickly went back to grasp her mother's. Dove squinted and swiftly glanced at the woman again. She leaned into me and whispered. "She must be Agathe—the other maid at Miss Rittenhouse's."

"I see," I replied.

"Jade," Dove paused, "Once told me that there was an older maid that stayed in one part of the house. That must be her. I never saw her before today."

I caught Shelby studying the woman. She had a queer look on her face. "Everything all right?" I asked.

Shelby nodded and bit her lip. "Uh huh."

"You sure?"

"Yes." Shelby swallowed. "She's…she looks…"

Shelby never had a chance to finish her thought.

Mr. DeCuir cleared his throat, clearly impatient. "Shall we begin?" He asked in the deceptively gentle, singsong way that morticians have. I've never understood why they do that. I suppose it's meant to be soothing. At George's funeral, when the mortician cooed at me, I wanted to slap him. That would have amused quite a few people.

I was tempted again. But, I wasn't the sort of person who went around slapping random strangers—even though I might have been able to get away with it. After all, I was, "The Hollywood Widow." The nickname alone entitled me to slap a funeral director or two. Alas, no, Mrs. George Frobischer didn't hit people.

The room had grown almost unbearably hot and just as that little troll, DeCuir, began to speak again, I felt an uneasiness wash over me as if I was being observed. I looked over my shoulder. Someone else had entered the room. I could sense it. And, I turned slowly to see who had come in. A man about my age, perhaps older, dressed all in black. He was very tall and painfully thin. His wispy gray hair was long and wild and his waxen skin was the color of the room's stone floor.

He stood at the back of the room and looked directly at me—his face expressionless, but his eyes dancing. Where had I seen those eyes before? I looked at his hands…they were long and thin—like those frescoes of Christ in Judgement—the Pantocrator—that George and I had seen in Byzantine churches when we visited Turkey. The fingers were so long that they seemed to curl into themselves. No, I'm wrong. There was nothing church-like about him. He was straight out of a silent film. *Nosferatu.* He continued to stare directly at me.

The woman at the back of the room that Dove had supposed was Agathe glanced at me, possibly noting the rise of terror in my face and she turned sharply around to look squarely at the creature that stood behind her. She stifled a scream and rose noisily to her feet—the chair scraping against the stone floor.

She lunged for the man and he put his hands up as if he were shielding his face. He opened his mouth as if to yelp, but he made no sound.

Shelby and Dove quickly leapt to their feet, and I found that I had risen from my chair as well. We all faced the bizarre scene being played out at the back of the room—everyone except Dove's mother who sat with her eyes fixed on the casket.

The mortician drooled a weak warning.

"Who is that?" Shelby gasped; clasping her hands—fingers linked—behind her head.

All I could do was shake my head absently and continue to stare at the man's hands—like long talons. He swatted at the dark haired woman.

I knew those hands.

My eyelids began to flutter as I was dragged backward through time in a sea of crimson.

The shadowed river listens,
Waiting for the rain,
Lies lost in such sharp silence
Her beauty will wane:
She wears her hope like diamonds
All colors save but one
Diana's orb will free us
Reflected in the sun.

I was drowning.

When Mrs. Frobischer hit the floor, I screamed, and dropped down beside her, scuffing my shoe in the process. They were new shoes, too.

She gasped and sputtered and made the most unflattering noises as her eyes rolled back in her head. The funeral home man rushed to her side, asking if she was all right.

I looked up for a moment; both the tall, ugly man and the short fat woman were gone. I was glad they left because neither of them smelled very good and they had upset Mrs. Frobischer so.

I smoothed some stray hairs off of her forehead. Oh good, she had been using that moisturizer. Then, I arranged her skirt on the floor into neat folds around her legs. There was no need not to look like a lady.

The funeral home man rushed from the room and returned with another man—younger and bigger. He looked strong. I pressed my lips together.

The strong man picked Mrs. Frobischer up and carried her off. He told me to follow. I looked at Dove who had sat down again next to her mother. She nodded at me and waved for me to go. I think she was crying. Dove's mother hadn't moved. It was as if she hadn't noticed anything that had just happened. She might as well have been alone in the room with the casket.

Really, I was glad to be out of there. I felt very uneasy. I looked back at Dove's mother one more time.

Averill Cage at school says that Chinese people have crazy funerals and that they wear red and burn the dead body on a big fire. I don't think Averill would lie to me. Maybe that's why Mrs. Ji is so confused. Maybe it's because this wasn't a typical China-type funeral. But, either way, I was glad to be away from her for a little while.

I quickly followed the strong man and the little funeral man into a room off of the main hall. It was dusty and peach colored—filled with little sofas and ashtrays. It smelled very bad, kind of like Grandmother L'Ebène.

The strong man ordered the little man to go call an ambulance. All the while, Mrs. Frobischer gasped for air. But, her eyes had stopped rolling around.

I took Mrs. Frobischer's hand and held it. It felt cold. I was scared. She really needed to take better care of her cuticles. I thought about how I'd instruct the girl at the little spa to give Mrs. Frobischer a manicure.

Mrs. Frobischer began making noises. I wasn't sure if she was talking or just grunting. I couldn't make out what she was saying if she was talking. It almost sounded like, "Red." Suddenly, she took a deep breath and darted up into a sitting position. She exhaled slowly and grabbed at my sweater.

I smoothed her hair behind her ear. She was trembling. Her hair was really very soft for someone her age. Someone told me that old people's hair just gets thicker and thicker as they get older. It must have been Averill who said that. He also told me that your hair never stops growing—even after you die. Oh no. Was Mrs.

Frobischer sick? I didn't know what was happening. I thought about her hair growing.

She looked at me for a few seconds as if she didn't know who I was, and then slowly, as the color returned to her face, her eyes seemed to focus.

"Shelby," She said.

"Yes." I nodded.

She sat back…relaxing against the little orange-pink sofa.

"Did the ugly man scare you?" I asked.

"Ugly man." She repeated.

I nodded sympathetically. "The ugly man that looked like a monster."

She nodded, "Yes."

"Did you know him?" I asked.

"I'm not sure." She murmured. She was still shaking.

"What happened?" I asked.

"I was drowning," She whimpered.

I cocked my head to one side and looked at her. Poor woman must have hit her head. I inspected her forehead for bumps. I saw none. "No you weren't," I said patiently. "We're inside. There's no water here."

"I know," Mrs. Frobischer snapped. She blushed.

"They went to call an ambulance." I said, ignoring her outburst.

"No," She bolted upright again. "I'm fine. I don't want an ambulance. Go and tell them to stop."

"I don't think…" I began.

"Please," Mrs. Frobischer asked pitifully.

I agreed to do what she wanted. The two men seemed put out, but cancelled the call.

When I came back, Mrs. Frobischer was standing. She looked terrible, but I didn't mention it because of everything she had just gone through. She put her arm around my shoulders and thanked me for helping her. She seemed better. I took her arm in mine and we went back into the room with the coffin. Mrs. Frobischer apologized to Dove's mother. The woman didn't answer or indicate that she had heard Mrs. Frobischer. She just looked right through us as if we weren't there.

I thought it was kind of rude of her not to acknowledge Mrs. Frobischer. But, then I looked at Dove. Maybe her mother just didn't know what was going on. I wondered how that would feel.

We took our seats next to Dove. All I could think about from that moment on was the ugly white scuff on my new shoe. Well, that's what I chose to think about in the front of my head. Way deep in the back of my head, I wondered what Mommy would do if I were murdered. Would she act the same as Dove's mother? I didn't think so.

Jade is in that box. She doesn't like to be shut in. She doesn't like dark. A baby girl in the sun. On the green grass. The green grass. My baby girl. There is no more sun.

There is no more sun.

There is no more baby girl.

They will put her in the dirt. He made her dirty. Douglas. Made her dirty. Douglas made her dirty. She will be in the dirt. Like Mama.

Just like Mama.

Waiting for the rain

Only a picture now. A picture of Mama. A picture of Jade. Only a picture.

My baby.

My mama.

Where did they go?

Promises.

Where did the promises go? Lies, they became lies.

Lies lost in such sharp silence

I promised it would not happen again.

I knew it would.

I knew my baby.

I never knew Mama.

Mama is with Jade.

Jade is not alone.

Jade is in the box. In shadows.

The shadowed river listens,

My beauty in shadows.

Her beauty will wane

Get out of my way! Woman! Get out of my way. I must watch Jade. I must watch over her. I must watch until she is safe. With Mama. Safe with Mama.

They can't hurt her now.

He hurt her. He hurt her. Where is the sun? He took away the sun.

Diana's orb will free us

Reflected in the sun.

Get out of my way!

Jade was mine. She made us laugh. She made it bright.

Reflected in the sun.

She made music with her laugh. There is no more music. There is no more sound. No more sound for Jade. No more sound for me. Only silence until I can hold my baby. No sound until I can sing with Jade. And Mama. Mama loved me. I loved Jade. Love Jade. He loved Jade. Douglas. Hsin. Hsin loved me. Hsin loved Jade. Now, he loves no one. He made her gone.

Get out of my way, Devil! I must see Jade.

Dove! Dove! Move that devil. Dove! Look at her. I cannot look. Move her for your mother!

Dove. Will she miss my voice?

No, Dove will hug the silence. Like her library…bookstore, like her pictures. Silent.

Draw this for me, Dove. Draw it in lines—red and green and black. Draw it in white. Draw it in the silence of white.

Lies lost in such sharp silence

Dove came to us in silence. My miracle. My silent miracle. I was too old. Too old for a baby. They gave us to her. Too old. But, they let us keep her anyway.

Miracles come in silence. So do sins.

Such sharp silence

Dove will hug the silence.

I hugged Jade.

Douglas hugged Jade.

I will wait for her.

Waiting for the rain,

Darkness.

In darkness it is stagnant
In light only will grow
Proud branches strong and sturdy
Where darkness once did flow.

Jade. Green grass in the sun.

All colors save but one

There is no more green.

Only red.

Hsin Ji

I could not go. Niu need me, but I could not go. I already say goodbye. My Jade die long before her body. I lost her long ago. It didn't matter if her body died, too.

Niu is lost to me also. It's only a matter of time…

And Dove?

Will she be like her mother?

Will she float on her dream? Or will she drown in quiet?

Drowning. All I could say is that I was drowning. Of course, I knew, even at the time, that saying such a thing made no sense. And, yet, that is what happened.

As I clawed my way out of that suffocation and struggled back into the salmon light of that small mortuary room, I had to be careful to control my arms which had filled with an energy all their own.

I can recall the one occasion of my married life when I had sprouted thorns. I was at the dentist, getting a cavity filled—my jaw uncomfortably open for what seemed an eternity and with the sound of running water filling my head. As the dentist and his assistant worked away—hands plunged into my mouth, I felt that I could not breathe. The world was growing dim and my only thought was to save myself. My arms took charge of themselves then, too.

I didn't even know I had done it until much later that night when I was sitting across from George at dinner and suddenly remembered the whole incident.

George laughed when I told him. He promised me that the dentist would not sue us over one scratched cheek.

That night, we went to Ciro's and danced. I loved him so terribly much. George called me a baby tiger and we laughed, but I was inwardly terrified by my behavior and swore to myself that I would never do something like that again.

Luckily, I was able to control my arms as Shelby came into focus. Afterwards, she had been kind enough to see me back to the cottage. The girl has a heart under her coating of sugar.

After Shelby left, I lay down on the sofa in the front parlor. I didn't shut my eyes. If I could have avoided blinking, I would have. With dry eyes, my mind wandered.

Long ago, George and I had amused ourselves with staring contests. It was an excuse to look at one another. We took any opportunity we could find to look at one another.

I remembered one particularly nice Sunday afternoon spent with Martin Gable and Arlene Francis. We were sitting outside by the pool. Arlene was talking at great length about vacuum-packaged cold cuts and how John Charles Daly always loved her post-theatre finger sandwiches. When Martin and George came out of the house to join us, the world around us was erased. There was no one else. Only George. I couldn't take my eyes off of him. At that point, we had been married for quite some time, but he was still my great love.

Arlene noticed our unbreakable stare and joked that if we didn't blink soon, our eyes would fall out. I told her she could vacuum pack them. Everyone laughed. We laughed a lot then.

I always felt safe, caught in George's stare. Now, I found myself uncomfortable if anyone looked at me too long. More trapped than uncomfortable—much like when that horrible creature had looked at me at the funeral.

I tried not to think about him. What else had happened that day with Martin and Arlene? We ate hotdogs. I remembered Bette Davis in *Now, Voyager;* "June has prepared some very special canapés for you." They *were* very special canapés. We all laughed. Arlene loved hotdogs—grilled kosher hotdogs.

Lying there on my couch, I almost felt the warmth of the sun on my shoulders as I remembered that lazy Sunday afternoon in 1964—eating hotdogs and being washed in the love of George's stare. I took a deep breath. I finally felt safe enough to shut my eyes.

I slowly lowered the lids. Behind them I saw George in his white swimming trunks and navy blue and white striped sweater. He was eating a hotdog and talking. He was talking to Martin Gable, but he was looking at me. I felt my heart flutter. I felt warm and safe.

I could almost hear him talking.

"Yeah," He was saying, "Kilgallen is a bitch. But, she's like a damn bird dog with a story."

"It'll catch up with her," Martin responded.

"Oh, fellas!" Arlene chuckled. "You're just threatened by a strong woman."

I felt myself laugh.

"Shaddup!" Martin joked, standing up and mimicking a caveman; "Me no like."

George almost fell off of his chair.

He looked at me again. I felt the warm sun.

I looked over at Martin. He was taking off his shirt…not a pretty thing. “Let’s go for a dip.” He said.

The sun wasn’t warm.

“Good idea,” George said brightly. He had stopped looking at me.

“We girls will sit here and admire our athletes,” Arlene joked.

I was cold. George had stopped looking at me.

The scene grew pink. I had looked away from George. Someone was in the distance—watching. I couldn’t see him clearly. The scene was growing darker. He was a long burgundy stain on the pinkness of the background. I heard the sound of George jumping into the water. Splash!

“No!”

The scene was a wash of red.

Hands scratched and grabbed at me through the red—long thin fingers cut into my arms.

I tried to scream. But there was no sound. Red silence.

I tried to open my eyes, but I felt paralyzed. I felt as though someone was sitting on my chest, holding me down and growling—snarling without sound.

I was trapped in the red! I was drowning. Drowning in the red. Garnets! There was a girl! She was carved and sliced! I couldn't see her face! Help me! Help her! I tried to scream, but the sound caught in my throat as if someone had shoved cotton in my mouth.

Hands…clawing! Where was George?

The red was filling my lungs—it closed in on me like the sides of a box. Walls of deep red like the hallway in the Rittenhouse Mansion.

I couldn't fight the red. I felt my body go weak. I couldn't fight the silence.

Yes! Yes, I can!

I tried with all my might to wake myself. And, finally, I was able to break through the silence, to break through the red.

I bolted upright. I was alone in my little living room—still wearing the black dress I had worn to Jade's funeral.

The house was quiet. I wiped my forehead.

I knew I had to go back to Amelia Rittenhouse.

Amelia Rittenhouse

Foolish imbecile! Disgusting waste of meat!

Unwin was standing right in front of her! *Temper, old thing.*

There's absolutely no reason that she couldn't have convinced him to go with her from DeCuir's funeral home. Agathe has always been a disappointment to me—no matter how many chances I've tried to give her, she fails me—every time. Why have I kept her for all these years?

I should never have taken her back. *You had no choice.* When I saw what a failure she turned out to be, I should have cast her aside again. I should have left her where she was. But, now, I can't. Not only am I at the mercy of her ineptitude, I am at the mercy of her knowledge.

I've been feeling weak ever since Unwin escaped. My heart seems to have moved to the middle of my chest and always feels as if it's bubbling. *It wants to leave you, too.* I can barely stand, let alone speak. And, when I am made to speak to Agathe, the result is always a rage that makes the bubbles burst faster.

Why would Unwin leave me? Doesn't he realize that he isn't safe outside of this house? Doesn't he realize that I am the only person that can protect him? Someone has to protect him from the parasites! They'll destroy him! They'll consume him.

I suppose he didn't think about it when he left. I suppose it's best that he did escape. Otherwise, he would have been exposed.

How can a body feel so weak and yet have such a pulsing energy in the arms? A bizarre…slow, fast, slow, fast, slow, fast shooting of energy—like a neon tube. Is it possible for one's life to shoot out of one's fingertips? *If one is blessed with life to shoot.*

In the time that Unwin was missing, I didn't want to leave my room. For the first time in decades, I made Agathe open the windows. I don't like the smell of the outdoors, the sounds, and the light…*the things that could get in*…but I hate the presence of death more.

When I smelled the fetid soup of the damp earth through the window, a disturbing picture flashed before me...a memory, a nightmare.

I was standing at the Bayou Vin Atténué, watching Unwin. Two bodies lay at his feet. One was wriggling the other was not. I couldn't see the faces on the bodies, but I could see that they were women—the living one dressed in a scarlet gown, the dead one—nude except for a necklace of garnets. Surely the corpse was the Asian girl. Jade, I mean. A familiar voice sounded behind me.

"Shall I tell them, Amelia?"

Amazing how one question can change the course of the entire world. I turned to check. I was alone. It was just my memory. *You can't fight it, old thing.*

I took a deep breath and got up to shut the window. I would ask Agathe to fetch some air freshener when she returned. I could not bear to have the windows open any longer. *Don't let the marauders in. Don't let them know.*

The windows had always been open when I lived in California. I wanted to be as close to the outside world as possible. I was daring then—reckless, careless. *Foolish, drunk, wasteful.* I challenged whatever was out there to come and get me. Taking my own life wasn't an option—not directly.

However, I concluded that if my death was an accident or at someone else's hand; my sin would not be compounded. Perhaps it would even erase my sin. Sins, I mean. *Doesn't it take a lifetime to erase a dictionary, Amelia?* The people that needed my money to survive would be provided for after my death. I was most assuredly not abandoning my responsibilities. I couldn't drink enough to forget them, and I couldn't drink enough to die.

When I departed Marionneaux to start anew in California, I was 21 years old. I felt as though I was as old as I am now. Unwin was safely locked in the house and the baby…*the babies, Amelia, don't forget the other one.* Fine, the babies were gone.

I had to leave. I didn't think I could take another minute here in this house. They'd eat me up soon enough if I stayed. Unwin would be better off alone, I thought. I never wanted to return. I fled. *Coward…just like your father.*

That day had been so much more frenzied than the day almost two years earlier when father had taken Unwin and me with him to China. We were to learn the family business. Father was so proud, so confident. *Like you, old girl?* He had hoped that we would manage the mines one day. And, the trip to China was just the beginning.

It was the beginning of many things—not the least of which was my abrupt entry into womanhood. Father and Unwin had done such a good job of taking care of me that I felt almost ready to approach a new life. The trip to China was to be the start of it all.

I would exact ownership of my name once again. I would be proud to be a Rittenhouse! I was to be the strongest, boldest woman in our family history. The family hadn't had a strong female since old Ulrika Rittenhouse. *And we know what happened to her.*

Everything had been resting on my shoulders. I was to be the future. Me and Unwin! I haven't failed! The business has grown exactly as father hoped it would. He told me his dreams that day we left.

Father had a lead on some new mines in China. He said the gems in those oriental hills would rival any other mine he was working—"more than just garnets," he promised.

"But, garnets have never failed us," I laughed.

Father put his big, hairy arm around Unwin's shoulders. "One day, my boy, you'll be one of the richest men in the world." Unwin blushed. Father looked at me, "And you'll be one of the most comfortable women." I don't think anyone else has ever looked at me with love—except maybe mother, but she has been gone so long I can't remember the soft caress of her maternal eyes. Even without mother, we were a family—Unwin, father and me—more so at that moment than ever before. Why didn't it last? *What's missing you old fool? The fortune was to be Unwin's. Why did you take over?*

I had to take control! I've always been the one to rebuild after the parasites leave us wounded!

I wouldn't change a thing I've done! *Wouldn't you? Don't you dream?*

Yes, even I dream sometimes.

I wish I could go back to that day some seventy years ago when we left for China. Unwin was a strapping lad of twenty—handsome and tall with broad shoulders and an unruly crown of jet-black hair. His smile melted many a heart, my own included. I wished I had been as attractive as he was. But, I made up for it in other ways—ways my brother could never match. We were as close as any brother and sister could be. And, we couldn't wait to explore the orient together. Everything looked so bright that day. It would never look bright again.

I've learned to function quite well in the dark. I've made a kingdom out of darkness! I've done all that I could despite the destruction all around me!

The world fell apart again when we returned from China. In one night, one terrible night, our lives swallowed us all up. I should never have let it get so far out of hand. I should never have insisted that Unwin listen to me, take my hand in his and follow me home. We should have told the truth. I should have protected him better—differently. But, since father had died while we were abroad, it was really Unwin who should have been protecting me. *Weak, weak, spineless…*

Looking back, now as my heart bubbles and my arms pulse, I curse the day I ever left Unwin in the house alone after that awful, dark night. It was a selfish thing to do.

But, it can't be erased.

My time in California is one big blur. I danced, I drank, I…well, I did anything I could do to forget what was waiting for me in Marionneaux and, of course, what was waiting for me in New Orleans. *Slut.*

Oh, the parties! Norma Shearer was a bore with those eyebrows. But, she taught me a thing or two about alcohol. *You let them feed off of you.*

I fed off of them! I gobbled up life! *While Unwin starved.*

I never abandoned my family. I'm a Rittenhouse! We take care of our own. And we stand up for ourselves!

I tried my best to avoid Rosa Frobischer. She had seen everything. Yet, she didn't remember. How I envied her that. How I had hated her. I hated her for many reasons.

I hate you Rosa!

Hate. That's what I've become…a withered sack of hate. *Ugly, ugly, ugly!* I am thoroughly ugly—the embodiment of everything disgusting. *Withered sack of hate!* I'm vile! *Calm down, you're not so vile, old girl.* I did my best. *It's just that you're rotten, Amelia.* I have to snigger when I think of it—the epitome of decay in the finest house on La Colline Cramoisie.

If Unwin actually spoke, I'm sure he would agree as well. I wondered if Agathe would find him. I knew she'd agree, too.

It was all too similar to forty years ago. That time, no one had to die for Unwin to get out of the house. Agathe was probably only thirty at the time. She only had just started to work for me. It was easier to forgive her for letting Unwin outsmart her. *Forgiveness equals weakness!* This last time, it was unforgivable. I've often wondered if she did it to get even with me.

Forty years ago, when Agathe called me and told me that Unwin was nowhere to be found, my arms went numb—a feeling that I grew to miss. All I could do was come back to Marionneaux. I'd had to find him myself. If you want something done right, do it yourself! That's what father always said. *He didn't mean you.*

I knew where he would be—the one place Agathe didn't look.

I left the airport and headed directly to the cemetery. I found him exactly where I thought he would be. He hadn't had a chance to say goodbye and it had eaten at him for thirty years. I thought after that, he might get better. He didn't.

At the time it seemed as though everything was so complicated. Forty years later, looking back, it was quite simple. All I had wanted to do was protect him. I even failed at that. *Failure!* I realized it as I guided him out of the cemetery that day.

He didn't go back to the cemetery the second time. At least, I didn't think so.

Unwin Rittenhouse

Poor girl. She's so pretty. Fatter than her sister, but pretty. They're all very beautiful. Black hair. Skin like porcelain.

She talks to graves, too.

I touched the tomb. The seal around Jade's vault was still a little wet. The top was rough. It felt like sandpaper. Her name hadn't been engraved on it yet either. I wish I had brought some chalk. I would have written her name on it. I would have written "Jade Ji" right across the top in yellow chalk. No—white chalk. Maybe I would have drawn a picture on it, too. It was so plain. Really, it was just a plain concrete box above the ground. It could have held anything—pipes, a gas meter. I knew, however, that it held my sister.

I could have drawn an angel on it. The angel could have had Jade's face. But, I guess that would have just washed away the next time it rained.

The day was sunny, but I didn't feel very warm. I was the only person in the cemetery. I looked around. I felt very alone, but at the same time, I felt as though someone was watching me. I was reminded of Jean Louise Finch in *To Kill a Mockingbird* being watched by Boo Radley. Maybe it was Jade watching me from heaven.

I had asked Mama if she wanted to go with me. I thought maybe she'd want to go to the cemetery. She didn't answer. She didn't even move.

I read in the newspaper once about a family in town. We go to school with one of their sons, Averill Cage. They have a wax museum in New Orleans. Actually, they have museums all over the world. They make sculptures out of wax. That's what Mama was. She was a wax figure. Only, she breathed. But, breathing isn't talking.

Papa won't talk to me either even though he can. He just won't.

Only Mrs. Frobischer and Shelby talk to me.

I tried talking to Jade.

"I'm going to plant some flowers here," I said pointing to the cement rimmed flower boxes on either side of her vault. "Maybe Gerber daisies. You like those. Or roses. Don't you like roses?"

I paused as if she would answer. I suddenly felt very stupid. It was like talking to Mama.

"There's a cypress tree. I wonder if there's a nest in it. I'll have to look."

I wished I had taken the time to draw Jade's sweet face one more time—her delicate smile and smooth skin—just once more before she died.

"I cleaned out your room," I said more softly, "Papa wanted me to…" My voice caught in my throat. "Well, I took all of your things to Mrs. Frobischer's shop. She's going to keep them for you. She's a very nice lady. She likes to take care of people. She won't admit it, but she does."

I looked out past the cypress tree by the ridiculously large sundial. "Time waits for no one." I thought I saw someone moving in the shadows. I rubbed my eyes.

"Yes, Mrs. Frobischer is going to keep them for you. All except your rubellite pin. You're wearing that." I wondered if she realized it. Did she realize anything?

"Papa moved all your furniture out of your room." I mentioned. I didn't tell her that he had burned it all out back by the chicken coop. He would have burned everything if I'd let him.

"Jade," I said, "There are so many questions."

Yes, there were many questions. I had been thinking about the things I had found in Jade's top drawer. Why did she have an empty jewelry box? Who was Douglas? What about the red stones?

"Like," I continued, "Where did you get that necklace?"

After Papa moved all of Jade's furniture out of the room, he instructed me to rip up the stained carpet. He didn't actually tell me to do it; he left me a note with his orders. The note ended with, "I know this is not girl's work, but your size makes you able to do it." I did as I was told.

I pulled up the carpet. It had gone very easily, actually. It was so old and worn (and rotten in some places) that it came up easily from its staples. It was like pulling up a cotton blanket. The dust made my head hurt. But, somehow that didn't seem to matter. I rolled the carpet—awkwardly—and dragged it out for Papa to burn.

I wasn't very good at things like that. Just because I was big, didn't mean I was strong. I sure wasn't graceful. Jade was graceful. It made me mad having to do work like that. I wanted to throw things. I wanted to break things. But, I didn't. I kept working.

In the process, I accidentally knocked over the little, pale green vase that Jade had loved so much. I reached for a silvery green fragment and ended up cutting my finger. My blood stained the rough, white, broken edge of the pottery.

After sucking at my finger for a moment, I picked up the remaining pieces and threw them away. No one would miss them. I felt bad, though. I felt like maybe I wished it to happen. I felt like maybe I had done the same thing to Jade. I was mad at her when she moved out. Maybe I wished for her to be broken, too. Maybe I did it without even knowing. Maybe it was my fault. Maybe.

I tried not to think about it. I tried to do like Jade always did. I figured if I just worked and didn't think, I'd be okay. Just like Jade.

After I tossed the unwieldy roll into the backyard, I went back inside and mopped the raw wood floor with a damp rag. Crawling around like that hurt my knees. But, the pain in my legs kept my mind off of the pain in my heart. I tried to make the floor as clean as possible. I didn't let myself think of anything but that dirty floor.

It had discolored for years underneath that filthy carpet. As I crawled around, I felt one of the boards dip under my knee. One board was weaker than the others. I thought, at first, that it was rotten and just gave under my weight. But, once I looked harder, I could tell the board had been sawed and one half of it was just wedged back in.

I felt around the top of the sawed half. A little hole had been drilled into it. The hole was about the size of a finger. I guessed that the hole was to be used to pull the board up. I stuck my finger in and hooked it under the board. I pulled. The cut half came up very easily.

Inside, on a wide beam, I found a dusty velvet sack about the size of a bag of coffee beans. I opened it. Inside was a necklace of stiff, white, shiny metal. It was thick and heavy. I squinted at it like it had just fallen from the sky. It was made up of large, rectangular red stones with three clear stones that looked like diamonds stacked in a vertical line on each side. I counted them. There were twenty-six red stones and eighty-one clear ones. I couldn't have imagined that it was real.

How could Jade have had something like that? It had to have been fake. It looked too expensive to be real. I put the necklace back in the bag. That's when I remembered the little black jewelry box I had found in Jade's bureau. There was no way that the red necklace would have fit in there. It was too big.

Once I read a book about a missing treasure. This French guy looked all over his house for some rubies that were lost. He tore up the attic. But, they were right under his nose the whole time. The rubies were sewn into a dress. No, wait, that wasn't a book. It was a movie that I saw on TV with Mrs. Frobischer. *Gaslight*. That's right. I remember because the French guy tried to make the pretty woman go crazy. I felt very bad for her. But, she won in the end. She got the rubies. She got the handsome detective. And, she didn't go insane.

She was lucky.

I thought about showing the necklace to Mama. But, why? She would have looked right through me. There was no way I would show it to Papa. I was beginning to always get the feeling that he wanted to hit me.

I thought that maybe I could take the necklace to Mrs. Frobischer. She would have been able to tell if it was real just by looking at it. She had all kinds of necklaces and rings and bracelets and pins. They were all different colors and metals. She knew a lot about jewelry, I'd have bet. She could easily have told me what the stones were.

But, I thought that maybe that wasn't a good idea either. Mrs. Frobischer had begun to look very tired ever since Jade's funeral—ever since she fell. Besides, she didn't need to be bothered with such things.

I held the black velvet bag tightly in my hand, and then pulled it open again for one last look at the necklace. I had never seen anything like it before. It certainly was beautiful. I thought I might wear it to Shelby's party.

A cracking of sticks in the shrubbery around the cemetery's sundial, reminded me that I was wasting the time I had meant to spend with Jade whether she knew I was there or not.

"Did you know that Shelby is having a party?" I spoke to the vault, "A big one for her sixteenth birthday. It'll be very formal. I've never been to a party before—not any party—let alone a fancy one in a big house. I remember when I was a little girl, I would watch you get ready for all the parties you went to. Remember? Sometimes you'd let me help you with your hair."

But, even that wasn't the same. Jade went to parties that we held at the restaurant. She went as a hostess—to work—not as a guest. Maybe I was the first in my family to ever be a guest at a party.

Again, I saw something near the cypress. Eh, it was probably just the play of light on the leaves.

I still felt stupid talking to my dead sister. But, as stupid as I felt, I felt more sad.

I sang the poem she had loved so much:

Down deep below the surface
Weary roots do drink
The water rich with Heaven:
Closer than we think.
In darkness it is stagnant
In light only will grow
Proud branches strong and sturdy
Where darkness once did flow.

"Goodbye, Jade." I said as I stood up. "I'll always miss you."

I sighed. I had always missed her anyway.

As I walked home, I tried thinking about Shelby's party. I wondered if she was as excited about it as I was. I wondered if she knew how lucky she was.

Shelby Halifax

How exactly am I supposed to plan a grand party by myself? Sometimes it feels like I am the only person in the house. The servants haven't even been much help to me. For God's sake, what do we pay them for? Oh, but to be fair, Therese has been some help in organizing the servants to do the few things that they bother to help me with.

I wouldn't dare tell this to Mommy, but really, I sometimes feel as if Therese's making fun of me with her eyes. None of the others take me seriously either. They don't want to take orders from me. When I'm sixteen all that will change! They'll realize that I'm a grown woman and then they'll listen to what I have to say.

Averill, at school, says that if I want the servants to do anything I want, I should catch them doing something they're not supposed to and then threaten to tell on them. It's not such a bad idea, but I really don't want to waste my time watching the servants that much. I don't think I'd really be that interested in what they do. And, it's not like I have lots of extra time to spy on them anyway. All my afternoons are busy getting ready for my party. Besides, it doesn't seem very nice. Then again, it seems like something Mommy might do.

The party planning is supposed to be Mommy's job. But, every time I try to talk to her about it she waves me away. Daddy will listen to me, but he has very little to say about it. What do men know about pretty dresses and party decorations? All Daddy knows about is golf. And, he's even bad at that. Oh, that's not very fair. I've just been upset lately. A lot of things have been on my mind. Not just the usual stuff either. Not shoes or boots or nail polish. Lately, I worry about different stuff. I don't like it. On top of all my party stuff, I've been thinking about so many different things. Dove mostly…

Dove, bless her heart, has been very helpful. But, I haven't wanted to bother her with the details of my joyous celebration. It doesn't seem right no matter how eager she is. After all, she just buried her sister. Sometimes, I'll let her listen to me or go through the catalogs with me while I try to find the perfect flowers or party favors. Sometimes, I'll even let her pick something out. Of course, I'd never actually order anything she picked. Her taste is so awful. Is that mean to say? But, if it makes her feel better to be involved, than I guess I can take the time to let her think about something fun. She is my best friend after all.

As much as I would never have thought it could be true, Mrs. Frobischer has been the most help to me. I guess really that shouldn't surprise me. I'm sure she must have planned all sorts of elaborate affairs when she was in Hollywood.

Just the other day, while Dove and I were at the bookstore, I was talking about the party. It seems to cheer Dove up so. Mrs. Frobischer told me all about the parties she had been to in California. She told us all about all the old movie stars and their beautiful dresses.

She mentioned the lady who beat her kids with hangers…oh…I can picture her in my head…her name was…Crawford. Yeah, Crawford. She told us how this Crawford woman had arrived at one party dressed all in gold satin decorated with amber colored beads and how when she walked, the sleeves flowed out behind her "like sunshine." I liked the way that sounded. I thought I'd ask

Mommy to get me a gold satin dress beaded with little amber sparkles. I wondered if I was old enough for it.

I went home that afternoon and cornered Mommy in the morning room. As usual, she was lying on the chaise. She was still in her robe and nightgown even though it was four in the afternoon. I wanted to ask her why it was all right for her to walk around the house in her nightclothes, but it wasn't for me. She never used to do that before. But, she never used to drink during the day before either. Well, not that often anyway.

"Mommy," I said cheerfully, hoping that if I was extra sweet, she wouldn't shoo me away, "I know what kind of dress I want for my party."

Mommy nodded and tilted her head up to take a sip of her bourbon.

I waited. Honestly, how long does it take to drink from a glass anyway. She acted like it was some kind of magic potion or something the way she sipped it so slowly. Oh, how disgusting! Some of it dribbled down the corner of her mouth, just like a baby.

Well, I had never actually seen a baby, but that's how I imagined they'd drink. I pictured a baby drinking bourbon from a glass and then sort of just falling off to one side. I tried not to laugh. It wasn't right to think such silly things. Mommy would not approve. She always told me there was a time and place for everything. And, right then wasn't the time to be laughing. Right then, I guess, was the time to drink bourbon because Mommy showed no signs of stopping any time soon.

After a few minutes, I realized she wasn't going to participate in the conversation. So, I kept right on talking. "I want a gold satin dress with amber beads."

She chuckled and took another sip of her drink.

"Mommy?" I said.

She finally looked at me.

"Did you hear me?"

She nodded and chuckled again.

"Mommy?"

"I heard you!" She finally said. But, it wasn't the tone of voice I had hoped for.

"What do you think?" I asked innocently.

"I think you're too young for satin." Mommy snapped.

I had been afraid of that.

"What should I wear?" I asked defensively. "My pink pinafore?"

"You little…" She began, but cut herself short. She took another sip. "No, I'm having a dress made for you."

"Really!" I exclaimed. I was so happy. She had been thinking about the party after all! "Tell me about it!"

"Oh, you'll love it!" She sloshed. "It's green. Pale green silk."

"Silk," I thought. I'm too young for satin, but not silk. I'm sure there was some sort of huge significance that I was missing.

"Green?" I asked.

"Oh yes…a lovely sage-y green." The "s" sound on sage-y was very elongated.

I scowled. Green was not my favorite color.

Mommy sat up and glared at me. "You'll love it."

I sighed. "Okay." There was no sense in arguing. I had wanted her to be involved, after all.

"Where's Daddy?" I asked, trying to change the subject.

"Probably gone for pork dumplings," Mommy laughed sloppily.

"Huh?" I had noticed that Mommy and Daddy weren't talking as much as usual—not that they had ever talked much. But, I had noticed that they glared at one another a lot and when they did talk, it was more shouting than talking.

"Are we having Chinese for dinner?" I asked.

Mommy just laughed. I didn't know what was so funny about what I said. I wished Mommy and Daddy would try to get along—at least as well as they had up until a few months ago.

"Do you think Daddy will like my dress?" I asked, hoping to make her smile.

"Oh, he'll love it." Mommy howled and scrunched her face up. "I picked it out with him in mind."

I nodded—unsure. When her face relaxed after she twisted it all up, I noticed that Mommy had begun to look a lot older. She was actually beginning to look a lot like Grandmother L'Ebène. That was unfortunate. Grandmother L'Ebène always looked a lot like a Halloween mask to me. She always wore too much make-up and too much jewelry. In fact, she reminded me a lot of Mardi Gras.

Grandmother L'Ebène would wear a gold satin dress beaded with amber. That was just the sort of thing she'd wear—a big, giant, shiny circus tent, all hiked up over her scooter, her ugly, raisin-y, purple hands barely moving under too many rings. Yes, she'd wear a gold satin dress. I was suddenly glad that I wasn't going to get one.

Mommy had stopped paying attention to me. So, I continued to think about Grandmother L'Ebène. I didn't like her very much. I hated to admit it—even to myself. I don't know much about how families are supposed to work, but I know that you're not supposed to dislike the people in your family. I tried to remember if I had ever liked her. I must have once. But, she's always had such vicious things to say about Mrs. Frobischer. That makes me mad. Mrs. Frobischer has probably been nicer to me than anyone else ever had. Except maybe my Daddy. And, even he wasn't so nice all the time anymore.

Why aren't more people like Mrs. Frobischer? I guess if they were, it would make Mrs. Frobischer less special.

But, it seems to me that people could spend a little more time being nice to one another. I knew I had a lot of room for change there. I wasn't always as nice as I could be. I knew that, but I also knew I had to do things a certain way or else Mommy and Grandmother would shout at me. I figured I could secretly be a little nicer to people, be a little more like Mrs. Frobischer when I wasn't at home. But, why isn't Mrs. Frobischer nicer to herself? That's where she could learn a thing or two from Mommy.

I looked at Mommy. One of her eyes was shut, one of them was open and she was breathing noisily. Like that, she really did look a lot like Grandmother L'Ebène—all except her eyes. Mommy had Grandfather L'Ebène's eyes. They always had that same cold glint. Daddy's eyes weren't like that. Daddy's eyes were sad. Luckily, I take after Daddy's side of the family with their more defined features and longer limbs. The only characteristic of Mommy's family that I have is my dark hair—just like Grandfather L'Ebène's.

I thought it was quite beautiful on me—the dark hair in contrast to my white, luminous skin. But, sometimes, I wished I had Daddy's sandy-colored hair and tan complexion—his healthy "all American" look. Sometimes, I wished I was a lot more like my Daddy.

Daddy broke my train of thought as he came into the room glancing quickly at Mommy and putting his briefcase down.

"How's my girl?" He asked.

"Which one?" Mommy slurred, opening her eye.

"Shelby," Daddy answered curtly.

“I’m fine,” I nodded, “We were talking about my dress for my party.”

“Oh, no, don’t tell him, sweetie,” Mommy oozed, “You’ll ruin the surprise. And, you know how much your Daddy loves surprises!”

“No he doesn’t,” I argued without even thinking. But, it was no use to argue even though what she said wasn’t true. Daddy didn’t like surprises.

“Yes, he does,” Mommy growled.

“Voletta,” Daddy sighed.

“What’s the matter, Douglas?” Mommy teased him; “Do surprises scare you?” She was being cruel. I wasn’t sure what about, but I could tell by the way she was talking that she was being mean. I didn’t want to hear it.

I walked out of the room, then. I decided to go upstairs. I wished it were already my birthday. I wished I were at my party. Isn’t it funny how we wish our lives away?

At the landing I heard a glass break and Mommy shouted.

Yes, Mommy was a lot like Grandmother L'Ebène.

Marie L'Ebène

All I want is a lousy, stinkin' match. This Virginia Slim isn't going to light itself. At least my daughter's servants are more together than mine. She's got that going for her.

I don't know how Voletta can stay there. Shit, I know why she does. She's my daughter, after all. And, she does take her mother's advice. And, why shouldn't she? I've gotten us this far, haven't I?

Luckily, she lives like a queen. But, I don't know where she finds the strength to live with a man that cheated on her—especially when Douglas' mistress was a foreign girl. Ew! Can you imagine?

Voletta surprises me. I never thought she had my tenaciousness. But, everything I did, I did for her and her sisters. I'm sure Voletta can understand.

"A match please, Cosette." Shit. How long does it take? I could have rubbed my legs together and made fire quicker. I'll have to tell Augustin to dismiss that girl when he gets home.

I've gotten Augustin fairly well under control now, but it took some doing. His retirement seems to have softened him a bit, too. He has his woodcarving to keep him busy. He says it's the closest thing to being a surgeon that he can do. I think he misses his work. But, now he has so much more time for me and, obviously, his daughters, too.

In fact, he seems to be paying a lot more attention to the grandchildren. Crap, he's even picked out his own present for Shelby's birthday. I went through his desk, but I wasn't able to find a receipt. I'll figure out what it is, though. I always figure everything out eventually. I always get what I want. I got Augustin, and I've gotten to keep him.

I just got in the car and drove. I knew…know…what I did was wrong. But, Jade was everything that Voletta wasn't. She was sweet and natural—innocent without a real cruel bone in her body. She was beautiful.

Beauty isn't something that I find regularly throughout the day. I spend half of my life sweating over the pulsating innards of my fellow man. Mine is an existence of flesh and bone, of saws and scalpels. Jade was my contact with the celestial. Jade was my small taste of heaven.

The world is an ugly, dirty place. I don't know—maybe if I had chosen a different profession. No one insisted that I become a surgeon. But, I had all of these romantic notions about saving people's lives. Now, I wonder why I ever wanted to do such a thing. Most people aren't worth saving. When did I start to feel that way? Most definitely, it happened shortly after I married Voletta.

I sometimes look into the faces of the people I see on the streets and wonder when I'll be seeing them in the operating room. The sickest thing…no, it's merely one sick thing…is that if someone really gives me a hard time—let's say an inept clerk—I will invariably imagine some time in the future when I'll hold their life in my hands. I think to myself how I'll get even. I always feel exhilarated and dirty all at once after that—rather like going home after an evening spent with Jade.

Jade—so gentle and pure. I sometimes hated myself for soiling her pristine soul. But, sometimes I hate myself anyway. I always have. Maybe that's why I became a surgeon—to compensate for social standing, to lessen my guilt. God knows, I didn't have to work. When you're a Halifax, especially a Douglas Halifax—heir to the Halifax Pharmaceutical fortune, you don't have to work. But, I wanted to prove that I was a real man.

So, I followed in the footsteps of one of my more illustrious ancestors, Fuller Halifax, and studied to be an actual doctor. Fuller tended to the Yellow Fever victims in New Orleans. He was a great man. I wanted to be a great man, too. At the same time, I wanted to make my own way in the world. Maybe that's why I married Voletta L'Ebène. Maybe I used her as much as she used me. No, not possible.

But, perhaps that's why I let myself fall in love with Jade. Oh God, that makes me all the more responsible for what happened.

I had seen Jade on D'Arbonne Street many times from afar—just enough to fantasize about her. The day we finally looked in one another's eyes, she blushed, I blushed. She had my heart from that moment on.

We had to meet secretly, of course. It was difficult for both of us to get away. But, we managed. When we were together, I felt real pleasure for the first time in my life. She was my pleasure.

I managed to get to the jewelry store without Voletta finding out—I don't think. Her network of suburban spies is all knowing. I couldn't spend too much. If I did, Voletta would have questioned where the money went. I must account for every dime I spend. But, Jade was as happy with those little pearl earrings as she would have been with a five carat diamond. Poor thing. She never knew better.

We both had been so careful, but in Marionneaux, nothing is secret for long. I wondered how much her father knew. She always worried about Voletta. I always promised she'd be safe—swore I'd protect her. I failed.

But, I was desperate. I couldn't let anyone take my Jade away from me. I was willing to do anything to preserve what we had. Anything!

I wanted to spend the rest of my life with her. I never got the chance. They won after all.

I only wish I had been there when they found her.

I hate it that she was alone.

She hated to be alone.

Who doesn't?

Now, that my sweet Jade is gone, what is there to live for? Shelby I suppose. I worry a lot about Shelby. I just hope she doesn't end up like her mother and that she grows up being more Halifax than she is L'Ebène.

Please, God, if you exist, make sure my Shelby always remembers who she is.

Agathe Le Banni

Now I know who I am. I always thought I knew and I have to say I had some ideas on the subject. Now that I know for sure, it's a little bit of like ordering cake and getting a dish of fish bones. Sweet Holy Mother, I was hoping for someone with a heart. I can't say I'm nose wide open with the truth.

Lawdy, I had no idea where I'd find Unwin. I'd looked all over Marionneaux. To be truthful, I didn't care none if I found him or not. That first time, I had cared all right. I looked all over for him. I just couldn't find him all by my own self. It took Amelia to find him, then. I sure felt a hell of a lot better when she did. I cared then—not just about Unwin, but about a lot of things. But, that was forty years ago.

After forty years locked up with a damn ugly thing like Unwin Rittenhouse, a girl just stops caring—what with no one to talk to—him just starin' at me all day, all quiet. All that time lookin' at me, but I don't think he ever actually saw ME once. Always felt like he was lookin' at someone else. It's better that way.

Why would I have wanted to find that Unwin? I don't feel nothin' for him even though I know I should.

The one time I was sure he knew that I was a real person was when he gave me that little piece of paper with them two words written on it. That paper answered all my questions. I didn't even thank him. But even if I did, would he have understood me? I should have been more loyal to him. I just couldn't.

How could I? All I could worry about was me. I'm all I really got. Maybe I always did worry about myself more. No one else ever did. I knew I'd be okay. And, I knew soon enough that I'd get everything that was due me. Amelia knew I was on to her even though I didn't say a word. And, then I read her old papers. Now, all I have to do is wait.

No one knows how horrible sick it was to find Jade all cut up like that. Even though we never said two words to one another, I still felt bad for her. Made me think about her poor Mama.

Nobody wants to see a young girl die that way. I'll say, though, that it's just as well that the killer got to her before he got to me. Of course, if anyone ever found out what all I know, I'd be next. I have to be the first to do somethin' about it. That's why I wrote those letters. The Lord don't like ugly.

But, I had to find Unwin. No time to think about murder.

It had been too many days since I'd last seen him. I'd taken to sleepin' under the damn bridge just so I didn't have to go back to face Amelia. "Let her figure I was out lookin' all night" I thought. Hard times make a monkey eat pepper, don't you know.

No way was I goin' back there without Unwin.

Maybe no way I was goin' back there anyway.

I cried for Agathe.

So many years alone with her. So many years of silence.

So sad that she had to die, too.

III
Digging

Alleluia! My first reaction was relief. I didn't have to worry about her revealing my secret any longer. No one can tell me that Agathe had been anything but a burden from the very start. *Convenient.* She had been more trouble than she was worth. I won't allow anyone to tell me otherwise. Hear me? No one! *Who would try, Amelia? Who's left?*

She was useless! Not only that, but she reminded me of him—his face staring needles into me from behind that dark hair. Those greedy, hungry eyes feeding off of me—everyday. *You can still feel him. Can't you, Amelia?* I felt many emotions that night.

That concentrated feeling of relief overwhelmed me and mutated into a hideous guilt. I began to feel that pressure in my chest again. *Thump, thump, pop!* I took a deep breath and settled into my leather chair. I felt as though I was breathing through mud and my lungs rattled when I inhaled. I was too old for all that exertion.

I thought of Unwin…still out there in Marionneaux somewhere with no one to protect him. My brother—roaming like some sort of stray—no one to feed him, no one to take care of him—alone.

My heart beat loudly. Who would take care of me? With Jade and Agathe both dead, I would have to fend for myself. *How will you do that, old girl?* With the exception of the previous night, I had not been out of the house in forty years. Who would shop for me? Who would feed me? Unwin and I were in the same predicament. Perhaps Agathe's death hadn't been such a good thing.

I ran my hand over my face—my skin felt thin like wrapping tissue. My hand wandered down to my neck and stopped there, the fingers curling around my own throat—loose folds of skin pushed up and dropped over my fingers like wet crepe. I tilted my head up—the skin did not become taut—before I relaxed my hand. *Easy now, don't hurt yourself...more than you already have.*

I began to let that guilt consume me like flames on kindling and the remorse licked at my soul—remorse because Unwin was still in trouble, still lost. Remorse because Agathe had died alone, unloved, unconnected. Remorse because I felt no grief upon her passing!

She wasn't so bad. *You've changed your mind?* She did waste her life to look after Unwin. She devoted more to him than I ever did. *Not true, Amelia. Aren't your responsible for his damnation?* But... *Didn't you damn Agathe, too?* I gave her a roof over her head and food in her ample belly! I gave her that when she had nothing. All she did was take my food!

I had always convinced myself that the free room and board was reward enough for...everything. *Was it?* Looking back, it was more of a punishment. I should have let her be free. She should have been able to live. Her genes weren't her fault.

I gasped. That bitter electricity shot through my arms again while the rest of me went loose and my bowels turned to liquid. The constricting steel band of fear tightened around my heart again and it made me cold—ice cold in the summer. Just like Agathe, just like Jade. Just like Mingmei. My heart beat furiously. I wondered if Agathe's did before she died. *Thump, thump, POP!* Did

Jade's? Did their hearts beat like mad as the blood pumped through the slices in their skin? Were they afraid?

I was afraid. Afraid for Unwin, afraid for me, and as much as I tried not to be, I was afraid for Rosa Frobischer. She was still the biggest threat to all of us.

George had written a murder picture once called, "Maid to Die." Secretly, I had tittered at the title, but he seemed proud of it, so I said nothing. The story involved an ancient woman in a large house—your typical gothic/horror fair—where every maid that worked in the mansion met with a rather gruesome end.

There were, of course, a dozen suspects, but the murderer ended up being the mistress of the house. The revelation of the culprit was supposed to have been surprising because the woman was so incredibly old and frail that one would never consider the possibility that she could have the strength to lift a Bible, let alone wield a hatchet—the murder weapon.

The picture was not one of my favorites, but oddly enough was one of the biggest box-office successes of George's career. At the time, I wasn't sure what exactly it was about the plot that made me disinclined to love it. After all, I usually loved anything that George wrote. But, "Maid to Die," didn't sit well with me. I tried to reason that it may have been the actual film that I didn't like—the casting, the sets, maybe even the wardrobe. But, I knew that it wasn't the film I didn't care for. It was the script.

No, it wasn't especially grisly. In fact, the majority of any gore was merely implied or discussed briefly in passing dialogue. Thinking about it decades later, I realized that I felt sorry for the young women that had been victimized. I felt that to trivialize their passing by making it into a spectacle was in poor taste. How silly of me to mourn fictional people. But, wasn't that George's job? To make us care for those that never were? Perhaps the script was better than I had realized. Regardless, audiences ate it up with an unusual hunger.

The night of the opening of "Maid to Die," we celebrated with Mickey Rooney and Deanna Durbin (of whom I was never fond). And Deanna asked George what made him decide to have the old lady be the killer. George answered, "She wasn't what she seemed." Deanna acted as if that statement was the most brilliant phrase ever spoken by man. Pity I spilled my drink on her.

But, it made me think of Amelia Rittenhouse. She appeared to be as strong as an ox despite her over ninety years of life. Maybe she wasn't what she seemed either.

Of course, as exhausted as I was, nothing seemed to be what it should.

I had spent the better part of that day fighting my sleepiness. I didn't want to give into it and wind up having another red dream. The fear of being trapped in that in-between world—that horror world—again was so great that I would have stayed awake for the rest of my life to avoid it. Sleep, however, was proving to be too powerful and I was beginning to feel rather like a fly with two out of six legs stuck to a spider's web.

That's why I had turned on the television—I hoped the distraction would keep me awake. I thought of George. And, I was pleased to see one of his films was on—even if it was one I didn't like.

"Maid to Die" proved to be just the distraction I needed, and I soon began to forget about my worries for a bit. During commercials, I made a mental list of other starlets upon whom I should have spilt drinks.

I supposed that imagining such behavior didn't necessarily make me the sort of person that would decisively engage in the ostentatious and jazzy behavior of a prima donna .

While George had expressed a theory that my subconscious desires had compelled me to do so, spilling that glass of wine on Deanna really had been an accident—an unfortunate and messy twitch. Wasn't it?

I let myself giggle as I remembered. Deanna was mortified. Honestly, judging by the reaction of those around us that night, it was quite funny. However, do I recall feeling some teeny tiny sense of triumph? Well…

Could George have been right? Was it true that I could have had that much moxie hidden away somewhere within me? Wouldn't that have been humorous and fitting?

Maybe so, but I couldn't allow myself to think it was true even if I enjoyed the idea of some hidden part of myself involuntarily making me do something as pretentious as dousing a B-list movie gal with cheap house wine.

Ah, well…regardless of the veracity of George's theory—fantasizing about doing bratty little things like that doesn't hurt a soul. I giggled again. Oh no…another tear.

The warmth of my nostalgia was quickly chilled when the film was interrupted by a news report. The reporter's words pricked me like knife points and when it was over, I was surprised to find my mouth hanging slack and my hands curled into fists.

A woman had been found dead in an alleyway behind D'Arbonne Street. She had bled to death after sustaining multiple, deliberate cuts all over her body. The woman was identified as Agathe Le Banni. Before I had a chance to process the name, the broadcaster said, "Miss Le Banni was employed as a maid by Amelia Rittenhouse of Marionneaux, heir to the Rittenhouse mining fortune."

Miss Rittenhouse had no comment.

Another one of Amelia Rittenhouse's maids—sliced to death.

I lay very still for a few minutes and tried to remember my first meeting with Amelia Rittenhouse upon my return to Marionneaux. It had been so brief that the house made a greater imprint in my memory than the woman who had so unceremoniously booted me out. Again, I remembered the red walls, and then Amelia's faded red gown and, of course, the dreams that followed. I was being shredded by garnets.

Why would I inflict that upon myself again? A sensible person would not. And, yet, I knew I would.

I debated with myself about what was driving me to go back to the house at the highest point on La Colline Cramoisie. Why would I go back to that terrible place? Yes, part of it was that I felt sorry for Dove. She would always have to carry around the burden of her unanswered questions. But also, I felt sorry for myself—also weighed down by questions and by an intrusive silence of self-doubt that haunted me like a yawn before a hurricane.

I had no one to protect me anymore. If I didn't want to live out the rest of my days in agony, I had to begin another quest. Or start a new one. I wasn't sure which. George would have known.

I felt as though a piece of myself was missing—a piece that was integral to making me the whole that I had vowed to become after George died. And, somehow, I was drawn to the unmistakable redness of La Colline Cramoisie and the gray canker upon it—the Rittenhouse Mansion. I fully believed that my nightmares were more than indigestion and old age. I had to listen to what they told me. I had to answer my own unspoken questions. For Dove, for Jade and for myself—for all of us, I had to be brave. Surely, surely, I could do it. "'Atta Girl, Rosie." Well, surely I could try.

•••

The next morning, I put on my short sleeved, pale gray cotton dress with the black print of irises, pinned my black shell brooch to the collar and set out immediately for La Colline Cramoisie and the Rittenhouse Mansion.

I turned the knob to ring the front bell. As I had expected, no one answered. My inclination was to walk away—defeated. I had never been taught to be the kind of woman that just walked into people's houses. Thornless roses never pricked. What would George have done? He would have walked right in. I would do the same. I now have to be both George and Rosa. The thorns are for the rose's own protection, after all.

I smiled, remembering the incident with the dentist. There were some thorns in me—somewhere.

I tried the large brass knob and found the door to be unlocked. With my shoulder to the heavy wood, I pushed the door open and entered the room. Surrounded by red, I called out, "Amelia! It's Rosa Frobischer!"

I heard her bark from a darkened corner—washed in a maroon shadow. "Get out!"

I used neighborly concern as a pretext—still unsure of what I was doing, but confidant in my purpose. "I heard about poor Agathe Le Banni and thought I would see if you were all right."

She laughed, but still sat. "You? Suddenly, you have cares outside of yourself."

She was feisty. Was that true? Was that what people thought of me? I tried desperately to ignore her.

"Amelia, I hope you're all right…" I said in an oddly convincing way, drawing upon decades of training by observation in Los Angeles. I was shocked by the ease with which I could be so shallow. "…considering what's happened. I was so sorry to hear about Agathe." That much was true.

"I'm not." She growled.

"You're not?" I asked in mock disbelief.

I had expected her to say that. I walked closer to her. Her eyes shone yellow through the dusty crimson haze of the room—not from jaundice, but more from the lupine heart that I was certain beat in her chest. There was no doubt that she had once been the she-wolf that danced upon tables. However, at that particular moment, bathed in scarlet shadows, she looked a bit like the discarded skin of an over-ripe tomato.

"No," She said flatly. "People die."

"Amelia, surely, both of your maids…well, surely, you must…" I ceased that bumpy train of thought. "But, Jade, she was such a young woman." I opined.

"Young women die, too." She said. I had the feeling she was trying to shock me into leaving.

I sat down next to her in the tawny corner. As I did, I looked at the landing where I had seen the shadow that first day. There was no such shadow then.

"But, don't you care? A young woman is dead. Her mother is crushed with grief." I said quietly.

"People get crushed," She said huskily.

"Yes, but for a mother to lose her child…"

"What do you know of it? How many children do you have, Rosa? All you ever knew was your husband. There was no one else in the world."

She pinched her lips together as if in self-punishment for admitting that she did, in fact, know exactly who I was. I pretended to have not noticed.

"I know enough to realize that a mother always is ruined when a child dies before she does." I answered, looking directly into her eyes.

"Not always," She laughed loudly. "Not when the child is worthless."

"Worthless," I nodded my sarcasm. "Was Agathe worthless?"

"Ultimately." She shrugged.

"Would her mother think so?"

"I couldn't tell you," She blanched.

"Every life is precious." I argued.

"Not once they expire." She snarled. "And sometimes, not before."

Her logic confused me. "Amelia," I began.

"Get out of here," She snapped. "With your talk of grief. What do you know of grief? Real grief is misplacing someone—a living person—and being helpless to care for them. When someone dies, there's nothing you can do. But, when they're simply lost, then you mourn!"

I nodded and opted not to press the issue any further.

"What do you want from me?" She asked as the house creaked loudly. She paused to listen to it.

"Answers." I said plainly. "Jade's young sister is my friend."

"Is that all?" Amelia hissed. "Or do you want answers to something else?"

"Yes," I decided not to lie. The red walls seemed to close in on me. "Otherwise, I wouldn't be as bold as to inflict this visit upon you." I continued with the truth. I felt naked before her.

"The past is like a useless girl," Amelia growled. "It should die, too. Let it die and stay that way. Remember, resurrecting the dead helps no one." She strained her neck forward as if trying to hear something in the distance.

"There's a difference. In order for something to be resurrected, it must be buried first." I added harshly. "Buried and honored!" I was reeling with the queasy intoxication of a previously unknown courageousness.

"And how do you expect me to honor two women I hardly knew?" Amelia Rittenhouse answered, "Do you honestly expect me to rend my clothing and tear my hair? Is that why you came here? To convince me to mourn my servants. I have other things to mourn."

I felt trapped, my courage faltered, so I opted for truth once again. "I was hoping I could get your help in finding out who killed these two women."

"Why?" Amelia shuddered.

"For their families." I admitted, "For me."

"Their families?" She croaked.

"Yes, so that their families can bury the pain along with their daughters' bodies." I answered in a dry, strained voice. "Everyone has that right—a right to bury their pain along with their dead."

"Sometimes," Amelia smiled, "One ends up burying oneself in the process."

My throat began to feel tight.

"Or lifting themselves up in relief and by the good memories." I cleared my throat. "Surely you must know something that could help us figure out who did this. Some little thing that only you could know. Don't you owe it to Agathe's family if not Jade's?"

"Agathe's family? The girl had no family. She was an orphan. She was unwanted. Her passing affects no one."

"I assume she worked for you for years," I began.

"She was, to me, just a machine. She could not be anything else. It would have distracted me from what was important." Amelia replied dreamily. "Yes, yes, I know."

To whom was she speaking? I continued, "But, don't you want to make sure whomever did this is punished? Isn't that important, too?" I tried the argument of justice—or revenge. I thought she would appreciate that.

"I'm not interested," Amelia said as her eyes wandered to the opposite corner of the room. "There's enough punishment in this world without my help."

"But," I argued.

"It's over! It's all in the past. It can't be changed. Let it be!" She paused and hugged herself. "I will. I will!" Her sallow eyes darted around the room. "Remember your past with George," She added in an eerie quiet, "And leave me to do with my past as I please."

I nodded, feeling again some foreign valor, "Fine, but what about the present? What about Jade's sister, Dove? Should she go through life always wondering why her sister had to die? Should she grow up under a cloud of dark secrecy?"

As I blinked, I saw that damn red behind my eyes and with each crimson flash, my nerve wavered. I clamped my eyes shut momentarily, hoping to clear the scarlet. However, when I opened them, I was still engulfed by it.

I tried to continue. "Doesn't she have the right to find a reason for what happened? Doesn't she have a right to dig for answers so that she can rest knowing the truth?" I became angry. "You know what happened to those two women! I think you owe it to their families to tell the truth!"

"The truth?" She laughed again, suddenly with me again, "Rosa Frobischer is preaching to me about truth! That's rich. Truth is reality and everyone's reality is different."

"Truth is truth," I spat. Red…red…red. I struggled to make the panic yield to strength. "And, I'll keep digging until I find it."

"Marionneaux isn't the sort of town you want to dig in—all this bayou land. You might hit water and drown trying." Amelia Rittenhouse laughed.

I saw myself out before my throat closed completely.

As the door shut behind me, I was able to breathe again. "I don't care what you say!" I shouted at the door.

I stumbled as I walked down the stairs and spread my arms to balance myself. I felt like a baby bird trying to take flight.

I was shaking with anger and felt as though I was perspiring through the thin material of my gray dress.

I would show her. I'd make sure whoever killed those women would be punished—to free myself, to free Agathe, to free Jade and Dove…and her poor mother. I could do it. I was Rosa Frobischer! Wasn't I?

Amelia Rittenhouse

That Frobischer woman needs to be stopped! She's getting too close. *Stop her! Block the door!*

I tried to dissuade her from pursuing the topic further. I thought perhaps if I offended her enough—or frightened her—she'd let go. I don't think she will. Suddenly, she wants to rip open old wounds. Doesn't she realize that it'll kill her? Doesn't she realize that she should just let go of this?

Where did she get that fight? *Worry more, Amelia, about your own fight.* But, this is the same woman whose main purpose for living was to stand next to George Frobischer and smile. Suddenly, she's seeking justice? There is no justice. If there were, I'd…I'd just like to see some evidence of it. I wish I could, but that's a mission I had forsaken long ago. *Quitter!* Sometimes I wish I hadn't. But, wishing never did any good either. God knows, maybe it could.

I wish Unwin were here.

I wish I had some of Rosa's innocence.

I wish I had a drink.

I wish I were completely numb.

No, it still doesn't work—wishing.

Quitter!

Shelby Halifax

I wish nothing had ever changed. The last day of school before summer vacation and I come home to find Mommy passed out on the chaise in the morning room. Now, it isn't like I expected a tickertape parade and a cannon salute, but you'd think it wouldn't have taken too much effort to pour me a glass of lemonade and to sit up for just one afternoon. At first, I thought she was dead. I felt terrible that the feeling made me feel good. And, I felt even worse when I was disappointed that she was still breathing.

But, she'd been so awful and—bitchy—(there I said it and I'm not sorry) for weeks. Like, when she did talk to me all she did was make fun of me and tell me I'm too much like my father. I'm glad I am. It's better than being like her. I guess she does have the added benefit of being drunk all the time. At least she doesn't have to feel anything.

Averill Cage, from my science class, he says that his mother drinks during the day, too. But, his mother isn't at all like Mommy. Averill's mom is sweet even though she's kind of spacey and dumb like she's not ever sure what's going on. I sometimes wish Mommy were a little more like that—just nice and quiet. She could still be drunk all the time if she wanted to. I was beginning to realize that there wasn't much I could do about that part of it. I didn't want to talk about it with anyone if I didn't have to.

I tried to go on as if nothing was wrong. I didn't want the servants to get suspicious and start talking. I had a feeling that they knew that Mommy was not well. But, why confirm anything?

I was hoping to have had some celebration in honor of my graduation from ninth grade. We usually celebrated at the end of the school year—well, at least Daddy and I did. But, since everything else had changed, I figured that I shouldn't be shocked when that tradition changed, too. I wish I had known why everything was different.

I looked for Daddy. He wasn't home yet. Maybe he was operating on someone. I admired him for being able to save people's lives. Or maybe he had been playing golf. I didn't envy him that.

For lack of anything better to do, I went up to my room and tried to busy myself with my dolls. Nobody had to know I was still playing with them. I picked the Chinese girl doll. Again, she seemed to be laughing. I remembered the day that Dove's sister had been killed. I ran a finger across the doll's face. I felt better again, but still not terrific.

I was feeling a little sick and wilted from the damp heat and thought I would change my clothes. I was sure my hair was all frizzy. Maybe I could find a cute hat, too. I put the doll down on the floor and went into my closet.

As I was changing my clothes, I thought I heard the door to my room creak open. But, when I listened again, I heard nothing and figured that it was just the house settling after the change in temperature or the all the wetness in the air which always seems to make the doors and windows swell.

When I came back into the bedroom, I was shocked to see Grandfather L'Ebène standing outside the closet door. I wondered how long he had been there. I blushed.

"Where did you come from?" I asked sharply.

"Is that any way to talk to your favorite grandfather?" He asked with that glint in his eye—the same glint Mommy always had when she was sober.

"Sorry, grandfather," I muttered, looking down at the floor. It was then that I noticed that he had stepped on my doll. Her head was smashed.

"My doll!" I shouted and went to her, picking up the pieces of her head.

"No matter, darlin'," Grandfather L'Ebène cooed.

"You crushed her." I sighed.

"There are always more just like her," He smiled thinly.

"But, you brought this doll to Grandmother such a long time ago and she gave it to Mommy!" I said, feeling as if I would cry.

"The world is filled with China dolls." Grandfather L'Ebène answered, still smiling. "No use getting attached to one."

I frowned

"Besides, you're too old for that. You're getting to be a woman." His voice was thick with honey.

I put the pieces of doll down on the bed, "It's just she was so pretty."

"Not as pretty as you," He winked at me. "Look at you with your long dark hair. My hair was that color once."

"I know," I nodded.

"You're just the prettiest girl I've ever seen—next to your mama when she was a li'l one." His teeth looked slick when he smiled. "That's why I want you to have this." He took a square jewelry box out of his pocket—it was wrapped in gold tissue.

"For me?" I asked.

"Yes, something pretty for the prettiest girl in town." He handed me the box. "But, you gotta promise not to open it until right before your party."

"Why?" I asked, taking the box.

"Cuz it's something real special for you to wear on your big night."

"All right," I sighed. I put the box down on the bed next to the fragments of doll face.

"Is that all you have to say?" He asked. There was that glint again.

"Oh. Thank you Grandfather." I added.

I held my breath while he hugged me. I didn't want to smell him. He always smelled like he'd just been working in the yard. He walked out of the room without another word—only turned back and winked at me. Winked and glinted. I could hear him singing softly as he walked down the hall, "Down deep below the surface, weary roots do drink the water rich with Heaven…closer than we think."

I sat down on my bed and looked back and forth between the doll shards and the box. Normally I would have torn it open the moment the door shut behind him. But, I didn't really care.

Thank God Mrs. Frobischer called me just then wanting to know if I'd like to go with her to city hall.

I did. I would have gone anywhere with Mrs. Frobischer. Really, to get out of the house at that moment, I would have gone to hell with the devil. There, I said that, too. And, I'm not going to take it back.

I wiped my face. What a hot day! I walked through the alleyway behind D'Arbonne Street. I wasn't really in so much of a hurry. I heard one of the meat merchants say it was hotter than hell. I wondered how he knew.

One time, I looked through the copy of *The Inferno* that they have at the library. This one had pictures in it. All those people swirling around were scary to me. I remember I went home and I tried to draw my own pictures of it. I couldn't finish them. When I saw that I drew Mama's face on some of the people, I had to tear the paper up. That day was hot, too. I remember I sweated a lot. I didn't like it.

Mrs. Frobischer doesn't like to sweat either. I guess that's something else we have in common. I liked having things in common with Mrs. Frobischer. I just liked Mrs. Frobischer. I wondered if she was at the shop.

Walking further down the alley, I passed some men unloading crates of seafood. The men watched me as I walked. Their faces dripped with sweat. Their hands looked rough and dirty. I looked back at the men, but not so they'd know. I looked out of the corner of my eye at them.

Some were in aprons; some in T-shirts stained at the armpits, others still with no shirts at all. Their leathery skin was dark from the sun and oily from their work. How would I draw them? So many different browns to draw…with thick salmon tongues, filthy hands in dark ochre blending into the black and rusts of lobsters and begging to be seen against the fleshy gray mess of crawfish. Thinking of the color made me excited. I felt like I could go on forever thinking about those colors. The earthy colors of toil. But, there was no time for drawing—or perhaps just no energy.

The whole alley smelled like rotten shrimp. The scent was even stronger by the dumpster where I had tossed in my school notebooks. I even threw away my drawing pads. I didn't really want to think about anything. Not even colors. Not for a long time. Mama didn't. Why should I?

To be fair, I didn't really know what Mama thought or if she thought at all. And, I certainly couldn't say what Papa was thinking. I hadn't actually seen him in days. He was at the restaurant before I got up in the morning and stayed there until after I went to bed.

When I got home, I fed and cleaned Mama first and then the chickens and went to my room.

I was tempted to go to Mrs. Frobischer's bookstore. But, I answered my own question. I saw the "closed" sign on the door as I walked home. I had a craving to look through the boxes of Jade's things again. Something inside me wanted to read the love letters from that man—Douglas. I knew I shouldn't but I wanted to anyway. Probably better if I didn't. I didn't feel too much like thinking.

I wondered what it would have felt like to be beautiful like Jade was and to have a man write me love letters. I didn't think anyone ever would. Shelby, on the other hand, was as beautiful as Jade had been.

She already was getting notes from boys. Sometimes it made me mad when she would read them aloud to me. One boy, Averill Cage, wrote the most often. His writings were…what's the word? T.S. Eliot would have called Averill's notes, "hollow." But, the sheer volume of them was evidence enough of Shelby's popularity and beauty.

I pictured Shelby and thought about what she might wear to her party. I didn't have anything near as beautiful as any of Shelby's clothes to wear. But, I did have the red necklace that I had found under the carpet in Jade's room.

When all my chores were finished and I was sure Mama was safely arranged in her bed, I quietly shut my door and crept to the spot where I had hidden the necklace. I had tucked it neatly in a hole in the web-like fabric of the box spring under my bed. I reached up and felt the soft velvet of the bag—gently pulling it out and undoing the cord that cinched the sack shut.

I was really gentle with it. I treated it like I might treat a baby bird. I knew they were rocks and I couldn't hurt them. But, they were precious. And, Mrs. Frobischer always says you have to treat precious things with care. She says that's why she has to make sure she treats me nicely.

I liberated the necklace from its velvet cocoon and laid it out on my quilt. Looking at it, I knew why Keats wrote the way he did. I understood why Vermeer painted like he did, too.

One time, I saw copies of Vermeer's paintings in a big art book. They were so beautiful that I couldn't understand how he could make things shimmer like that with just paint. I really couldn't see how anything could shimmer like that in real life either. But, then I saw that necklace.

I softly brushed my fingertips over the rocks and felt the faintest shiver through my arms from their hard coolness.

I carefully picked the necklace up and went to the mirror, holding it in front of me.

"Oh, it's beautiful," I purred as if someone—some man—was presenting me with the necklace. It felt silly to make believe like that. But, it felt nice, too. Maybe that's why Jade had that far away look in her eyes.

I draped the necklace in front of my throat. I was afraid to fumble with the clasp. I turned toward the window with my back to the door. Yes, I would wear it to the party. If I couldn't be beautiful myself, at least I could wear something beautiful.

I shut my eyes and imagined my grand entrance to the party. Even Shelby would be impressed.

Suddenly, I felt a pressure on my neck and a quick scratch as the necklace was ripped off of me. My eyes popped open and I spun around.

"Papa!"

"What are you doing?" He screamed.

"I…"

"Where did you get this?" He shook the necklace in my face.

I rubbed my neck where a scratch had begun to swell from the scraping of the necklace against my skin.

"You whore!" He threw the necklace at me. "You're a whore like Jade!"

I trembled and shook my head.

"You wear your grandmother's necklace!" He was so loud; I thought my head would burst.

"Are you a whore like she was, too?" His voice seemed to shred his throat. "Like your mother!"

At first I didn't even know what had happened. I didn't feel the sting until a few seconds afterward. I knew that the back of his hand had left its imprint on my face. All I knew was that I ran. I ran as fast as my fat legs could take me. Even a block away I could still hear him screaming.

I just ran.

George always walked so fast that I sometimes felt that he was trying to beat his own shoes to the finish line. Shelby was moving just as quickly that afternoon and I panted as I ran to keep up with her as we walked to the town hall. What had gotten into her? I didn't think she'd ever do anything that would overheat her or mess up her hair and yet there she was striding the banquette so purposefully that she seemed as if she were on her way to put out a fire. Perhaps the dear girl was on some sort of quest of her own. If only she'd have confided in me. Maybe I could have helped her. She had such a determination that she frightened me a little.

"So, what are we doing?" She asked without any emotion to her voice.

"We're going to the city hall," I tried to smile.

"I know that," Shelby muttered. "Why?"

"Can you keep a secret?" I asked.

"Of course, I can," Shelby said with no small hint of irritation.

"We're going to try to find out who murdered Jade." I said softly.

"And the other woman, too?" She asked.

I nodded.

"How are we going to do that?" She asked through clenched teeth.

"I don't know yet." I sighed.

When we arrived at the town hall, we followed the signs up the stairs, through the Records Department, to the office of the Marionneaux Cultural and Historical Center where we were greeted at the desk by a large, healthy black woman. Her nametag identified her as Eulabel Watkins. She was quite handsome—her gray hair wrapped in a silk scarf that matched her brightly colored blouse. She looked to be near my age. I smiled at her. I was at once surprised and relieved. How nice that for a change my first instinct wasn't to be suspicious of someone. This woman made me feel safe and I knew from the start that she and I would be great friends.

I grinned widely at her, "Hello, Eulabel. I'm…"

"You're the Hollywood lady," Eulabel chuckled.

I laughed, "How'd you guess."

"Only new person ta come in here. Hadda be you. 'Sides, you look like they say." Eulabel smiled.

"How's that?"

"Old and rich," Her laugh was like the beating of drums.

I blushed and Shelby smiled for the first time that afternoon.

"So wha'choo doin' here, Miss F.?" Eulabel asked.

"I'm just looking for some recent historical information about Marionneaux," I answered vaguely.

"Like wha'?" She asked without visible suspicion.

"Oh, old newspaper clippings. Things like that." I said without looking at her. Why wasn't I telling her the truth? George always said I was a terrible liar. I think Eulabel would have agreed.

"Wha' for?" She asked.

I looked at Shelby. "My young friend and I were thinking about writing a book based on local history."

"Oh, folks ain't gonna like dat," Eulabel said softly.

"Oh, you misunderstand. It'll just be based on people here. Not about them exactly," I lied.

Eulabel nodded and smiled a pleasant half-smile. She looked at Shelby.

"Dat true, Missy?" She asked the girl.

Shelby's eyes widened and she looked at me.

Eulabel laughed again, "No, I see it idn't."

I blushed again. I was caught. I may have trusted her more than most, but I realized I still didn't trust her completely. That's why I didn't tell her everything from the start. I was embarrassed and wanted to hide. What a bad combination—to be a terrible liar *and* to be mistrustful of everyone at the same time. Perhaps that had been my problem all along, I thought. Of course, that was before. Now, I know differently. I just hoped this new woman wouldn't judge me too harshly for my ruse.

"Now, woman," Eulabel continued. "Whatchoo wantin' a know. I'll tell ya. I like you. You got a look about ya reminds me a them ladies in the old movies. Like Bet' Davis or tha' other one who couldn't walk 'n' talk a' the same time."

"Olivia D'Havilland?" I asked.

"Tha's the one," Eulabel laughed. "I know you up t' somethin'. But, it don't bother me none. I'll tell ya what you want t'know. But, ya gotta promise me not to tell anyone who told ya."

"I promise." I said, leaning in closer to Eulabel.

"Some o' dem folks 'round here need some settin' straight anyway. I have da feelin' you just the lady to do it." Eulabel grinned.

I grinned back.

Shelby smiled, "She is."

I felt better—at least momentarily. "I'm trying to find out a little about," I looked over my shoulder. "Amelia Rittenhouse."

"Oh wheeeeee!" Eulabel squealed.

I hoped no one would notice. But, the others in the office seemed used to her outbursts. "My, my, my but you did pick a fine subject!" She chuckled.

I smiled uncomfortably.

"I'll betcha there's lots to tell about her—crazy ol' bitch. But, she's one of the few that's actually good at keepin' secrets around here. I will tell ya what I know, though."

She leaned over the counter again.

"You was here a long time ago. Right?" She asked.

I nodded.

"You remember the brother?" She asked.

I shook my head, "No."

"His name wa' 'Unwin.'" Eulabel laughed and looked at Shelby, "Sounds like "onion" don't it?"

Shelby couldn't help but smile.

Eulabel continued, "Well, there was the brother, Unwin. He was supposed t'be the next big thing—takin' over his daddy's business—you know, them jewel mines and what not? Anyway, they all go to China for awhile—the brother, the old father and that Amelia. I was just a girl at the time—younger than you," She looked at Shelby.

"When they come back from China, the father is dead—right. So, then, there's all kinda weird stuff. People sayin' that that ol' Amelia was a big ol' slut back then."

Shelby blushed.

"But, anyway. One night, the cops get a call that someone hears screams by the bayou. So, they go and look. When they get there, they find this dead Chinese woman. She's all cut up and her body is half tossed into the bayou. Well, the water is all red with blood from this cut up girl. She been killed just like that girl in the Rittenhouse mansion a little while ago."

"Who did it?" I asked, feeling very weak and light-headed. In the back of my head, I heard the chant of the poem that Agathe had been half-singing—

The shadowed river listens,
Waiting for the rain,
Lies lost in such sharp silence
Her beauty will wane...

My mouth tasted of copper.

"You okay?" Eulabel asked me, patting my shoulder from across the counter.

"Mrs. Frobischer," Shelby took my elbow.

"I'm fine," I nodded, gripping the brown marble edge of the counter. "Go on. Who did it?"

"No one knows." Eulabel sighed. "But, they think it was the brother—that Unwin the Onion. Y'see, the police see him leaving the bayou that night. There was marks in the mud like another body been dragged."

I nodded—when I blinked, I saw the red. Even when my eyes were open, I saw the red. I knew I was sweating horribly and I was beginning to get very angry. I tried to hide it.

"Who was the girl?" I asked. Shelby still had a hold of my elbow.

"No one know at first," Eulabel said quietly for effect. "She was all cut up. The water was all red with blood."

"You mentioned that," I said as pleasantly as I could muster.

Lies lost in such sharp silence.

Eulabel nodded, "Sure you okay?"

"Yes, yes," I said—trying to mask my impatience. "It's just your story is so interesting."

"You a funny lady," Eulabel grinned. "Anyway, the girl—she was all nekkid. 'Cept she was wearing this big necklace—all red stones and diamonds."

She wears her hope like diamonds
All colors save but one
Diana's orb will free us
Reflected in the sun.

I shuddered and my body jerked as if someone had shoved me. I held onto the counter harder.

She wears her hope like diamonds

Red stones—garnets—cutting garnets like my dream. Cutting, wet with red water.

Lies lost in such sharp silence

Her beauty will wane

Shelby put her arm around my waist.

"So, they bring the Chinese lady to the morgue, but by the time she get there, that big necklace is gone. Then, they find out who she is. Name is *moo-ming* or *ming ming* or somethin'. I'm not good with them foreign names. I'll stick to the people I see on D'Arbonne Street."

My body drooped and I tried to make it look like a nod. I don't think Eulabel bought it.

"So, did she have any family in town?" Shelby asked. "The dead girl?"

"You just like your old friend," Eulabel's laugh drummed its tattoo. "Not real family…well, she have a little baby, though."

"Oh?" Shelby asked. "Does she live in town still?"

I was glad Shelby had taken over. I felt as though I was drowning again. All I could see were the sparkling garnets.

"I don't know what happened to the baby after that. There's all kinds of stuff people say, like that Unwin the Onion took the baby and ate her. But, that's not a nice thing. I bet she grew up pretty, though. I seen pictures of the dead girl. She was a beauty in that exotic way that they have. Pity that she got all cut up."

Shelby blanched. "Cut up," She repeated.

Eulabel smiled. "I knows it, child. It's too much like what just happened up in that big house. I been thinkin' 'bout it, too. Ya know? Kinda hard not to think about it. Too much the same not to have somethin' to do with each other."

Shelby nodded.

"Isn't that weird?" Eulabel stopped smiling.

Shelby shivered, "What about Unwin," She couldn't help but smile, "…the onion?"

"No one knows," Eulabel sighed. "He just gone and disappeared. Folks say they see him—every few years wanderin' 'round like some ghost. But, you know how folks can be. It's like that monster in Scotland…Nessie. Folks sees what scares 'em."

"The necklace," I managed to gasp. "What happened to the necklace?"

"Someone took it, I guess. Or it fell off when they were takin' the body away." Eulabel said. "It never did turn up."

I managed to thank Eulabel for her time.

I don’t remember how I got home.

Unwin Rittenhouse

I liked the way the mud felt between my fingers. It was soft and smooth. I didn't know why I thought I could find it after so long. But, the digging felt good. I didn't find the necklace. I found something much better. She was so beautiful. Her skin was smooth—like the mud only white. Her hair was so black like the night sky. I really…I don't know how she got hurt.

I ran as far as I could after Papa hit me. I didn't know where I was going. I went to Shelby's house. Her father told me that she had gone out somewhere with Mrs. Frobischer. He looked at me so strangely—like he knew me. The funny thing was, I felt like I knew him, too, even though we had never met. He had never been there on the few occasions I had visited Shelby at home. Her mother was always there. When she wasn't drunk, she always looked at me like she hated me. I couldn't understand why. But, Shelby's father didn't look like he hated me. I wished my own father were more like him.

It was getting dark. I knew if I didn't go home, it would only make things worse with Papa.

Once, I read this book about a dog and this mean guy. Oh, I already told you about that book. Didn't I?

I know I should have told him about the necklace when I found it. But, I was just trying to keep him from getting upset. I guess no matter what I did, he was going to get upset anyway. How could I have been so stupid?

I don't know why the necklace made him react that way. He called me a whore. Just like my mother, just like Jade—just like my grandmother—he said. That made the tears fill up my eyes. How could he say that about Mama, about Jade? I never knew my grandmother. She had died long before I was born. I guess the necklace had been hers. But, I seriously didn't think she had been a whore.

I walked slowly back home. I took the time to look at all the shops on la Rue de la Marchands. I walked by Mrs.

Frobischer's store—hoping that she and Shelby had stopped there on the way back from wherever. The store was dark.

I turned the corner at D'Arbonne Street. In the distance I could see the Bayou Vin Atténué. I could smell it better than I could see it. I was so tempted to go there—just go and sit there and wait for everything to get better.

But, I knew it wouldn't. I walked home.

I was glad to see that Papa wasn't there. The house was dark and quiet except for the radio that we always left on in Mama's room. I felt bad, leaving her alone for so long. I peeked into her room. She was sprawled out on the floor. Her eyes were open.

I figured she had rolled out of bed again. She did that every so often. I decided I would go warm up her soup before I put her back in bed.

I went in the kitchen and got the pot of soup out of the refrigerator. I had made it before I left for school that morning so that all I would have to do later was heat it up. I tasted it. It was bland, but it didn't matter. Mama never complained. Besides, she hardly ever ate anymore anyway.

I went into Mama's room and stepped over her. I didn't bother saying anything. I had stopped that long ago. She never spoke. Really, she didn't even seem to be listening when anyone talked to her. I had given up trying. Her silence hurt me too much.

I read an article once that said that if you talk to your plants, they'll grow better. I drew a picture after I read that. It was a picture of my head. But, my body was a plant. I was all wilted up and brown…and red.

I arranged the pillows the way I figured she would like and went to pick her up. The room was very warm, but Mama was so cold. She felt very heavy and didn't bend the way I thought she would when I reached down to pick her up. I tried lifting her again and her head tilted back a bit.

That's when I saw her neck.

I lowered her gently back to the floor and stared at her throat.

It was scratched and bruised—a ring of purple against the gray of her skin. I recognized the pattern immediately—the rectangles in between the three round bits.

I sat down next to her and held her cold hand.

At least she was with Jade.

We sat in silence for a long time—me just holding her hand.

But, the silence seemed wrong.

I sang, instead. Once, she would have liked that.

Down deep below the surface
Weary roots do drink
The water rich with Heaven:
Closer than we think.
In darkness it is stagnant
In light only will grow

Proud branches strong and sturdy
Where darkness once did flow.

Shelby Halifax

I just can't believe it, but Mrs. Frobischer had another one of her attacks. I guess I could say that she was much more elegant about it this time because she didn't fall down and spit all over the place. We walked home quietly together, my arm around her waist. I didn't like the way she felt in my arm. It wasn't like when she hugged us. She felt cold and rigid.

I brought her home and helped her stretch out on her little sofa. She didn't want to go to bed. It all made me think of Mommy, draped across her chaise. But, even sick like that, Mrs. Frobischer was a thousand times nicer to be around than Mommy.

I understood why she was so upset. That lady at the city hall had told us a lot of stuff—all of it was gross and sad.

To think that Dove's sister and some poor forgotten girl had both been murdered the same way—seventy years apart. It was just so strange. Seventy years was a long time. The first woman, if she had lived, would have been old enough to be Dove's grandmother. I wondered if she had been someone's sister, too.

I didn't have a sister so I couldn't understand what Dove must have felt when it happened. I imagined how I would have felt if Dove had been killed—she was the closest thing I had. I couldn't stand the thought. Then, I imagined what it would feel like if Grandmother had been murdered. I didn't think I would have minded and I felt bad about that, too.

The evening was warm and slightly cloudy—a typical Marionneaux summer night. And, as it grew darker, I wasn't really in a hurry to go home. I knew that it was getting near to the time that Mommy's third round of drinking started and I really didn't care to be included in the drunken antics that always followed. I was in no hurry to see it or smell it.

Averill, this boy I know, well…he says that when someone drinks a lot, the best thing to do is to stay away from them until they sober up. He also says that the second best thing to do is to drink, too. That's what Averill does. He says he sneaks some of the liquor away from the wet bar when his mom and dad and the staff aren't looking. But, I don't think I could do that. I tasted Daddy's whiskey once. I didn't like it because it burned my throat and besides, alcohol makes you age quicker. No, I'd just stay away from the house for a while.

Of course, I could have gone home to keep Daddy company. But, he didn't notice me much anyway. So, I figured why bother?

I thought about "Unwin the Onion" and I laughed. But, the more I thought about it, the less funny it became. Eulabel had said that he was Marionneaux's very own Loch Ness Monster—people seeing him when they wanted something to be afraid of.

I had seen him. I was certain that he was the ghastly man that had walked into Jade's funeral and upset Mrs. Frobischer so. He had to have been that weird man! But, why, why would that horrible person have gone to Jade's funeral? I tried to talk to Mrs. Frobischer about it a little bit. I think she agrees with me. I hope we never see him again.

I pictured him in my head—tall and thin, face like a stone mask with his crazy hair. And, his hands—those long, long fingers. I felt a little sick to my stomach and I wanted to sit down, but there wasn't any clean place to sit, so I just kept walking. I turned past D'Arbonne Street and walked to the Bayou Vin Atténué.

I figured if I went to the place where the murder had happened, I might be able to deal with it and clear my head. I didn't want to spend too much time thinking about such awful things. Thoughts like that just aren't good for the complexion. But, is making yourself forget good for anything? I'd have to ask Mrs. Frobischer. She knows about those sorts of things even though she doesn't think she does. If only she had been around when I was little.

As a little girl, I enjoyed watching the water at the bayou and I could still remember times when its surface sparkled like gems in the light. But, it didn't look like jewels that night. That particular evening, the moon was just a fuzzy glow behind the clouds. The light was very dim and it made everything look a little funny. It was oily or yellow or something like the time when Therese spilled salad dressing on Grandmother L'Ebène. It was that kind of yellow and it reminded me a little of the color of our house.

Even though the place smelled yucky, it was a lot more pleasant than going home. At the bayou, at least, it was quiet. The only sound was the scritch-scratching of the tree limbs on themselves in the weak breeze.

As I looked out at the bayou, a maroon shadow cut into the oily, salad dressing yellow film on top of the rusty looking water. I thought maybe another cloud was blocking the already low light. I looked up. No, the clouds looked the same. Maybe it was a tree that bent funny in the wind. But, the wind wasn't that strong. I looked around again. It was not a tree even though I wished really hard that it would be.

He was even more grotesque than I remembered—his long, snake-like fingers caked with mud.

He saw me.

He smiled.

He walked to me—arms outstretched.

He still smiled.

I backed away—not wanting to let him out of my sight.

My heart pounded.

My shoes slid in the mud.

I felt my breath burst out of me as my back hit the ground.

I saw red.

IV
Family

Shelby's sixteenth birthday fell on a Saturday. The three of us were to celebrate it quietly by ourselves. There was to be no big party—not then. That would have to wait until we returned. We had been in New Orleans for five days.

New Orleans was more or less near our parish. Marionneaux wasn't that far from the Crescent City. But, Mama and Papa never had taken me. They never would…

I read about New Orleans a lot. Some of the novels about New Orleans are vampire novels. I used to really like vampire novels. A lot of the other things I read about New Orleans make it seem like it's a dark, exotic, mysterious place. I guess, it is, in a way. But, I thought it was more colorful than anything else.

I sat in the lobby of The Hotel Rainier and studied the jewel-like tiles in the ceiling mosaics. They sparkled with a light that I had never seen before in Marionneaux. In fact, the whole of New Orleans had a light of its own. Everything had a spark of purple, green and gold. Sitting in that elegant hotel lobby surrounded by all the ornate decorations, I remembered my parents' rotting house behind the restaurant even though I didn't want to. Who would have thought that I would have ended up in a place like The Hotel Rainier?

I found it a weird but welcome change of scenery. I wished I had packed my oil pastels and gotten some more drawing paper. It sure would have been a challenge to copy those colors! But, I only had a few minutes to pack.

There wasn't enough time to think of things like oil pastels. I barely had time to pack the regular things like toothpaste and socks. Mrs. Frobischer promised she would get me anything else I needed when we arrived in New Orleans.

Mrs. Frobischer and Shelby were due to meet me in the lobby before our celebratory day out. A day in the city was to be our way of keeping Shelby's birthday. I left the suite that Shelby and I shared while she dressed. My attempts at light-heartedness had failed. Neither of us was feeling particularly jolly. And, in all honesty, Mrs. Frobischer seemed out of sorts as well. But, we each tried to keep one another's spirits up.

I don't know why I didn't stay up in the suite with Shelby. It's just I hated watching her try to use that green hat to hide the large bandage she got at the emergency room. She winced each time the hat brushed against the wound. It was too much for me to bear.

Like always, Shelby was tardy getting downstairs. That can always be expected. But, I found it odd that Mrs. Frobischer was taking so long. I was beginning to get cranky and hoped that I could cheer up. I didn't want to ruin Shelby's birthday. We all needed something special and perhaps our outing to the antique shops in the French Quarter would be just what we needed.

Growing bored with the mosaic tiles, I turned to the gold elevator doors with their design like rays of sunshine, and watched the people come and go from the hotel. Some were in a hurry; others seemed to have all the time in the world. I found both sorts to be annoying. Why waste a life always rushing from one place to another? But, also, why have a life if you have nowhere to go? I wondered which the better avenue was.

The quiet rage I had been feeling since I found my mother's rigid body on the floor of her bedroom began to burble and boil again. I felt that strange weakness in my arms again—weak and strong all at once. The feeling was horrible like my body was eating and digesting itself from the inside out. It made me feel helpless—much like I had that night—the night that Mama…

I tried to keep my eyes from spinning in my head by studying a family that had just come out of the elevator—a mother, a father and their grown son. The young man looked to be in his late twenties or early thirties. He was carrying a white terrier, who, cradled like a baby in his arms had fallen asleep. Nice, pretty dog—just like I had always wanted.

They didn't see me watching them; they were too wrapped up in themselves—in their own stupid joy. I looked at each of their faces. The mother was a pretty, petite woman with waist length brown hair and happy eyes; the father, darker in coloring, was a distinguished looking man with glasses. Their son didn't look more like one of them than the other. With his straight nose, lighter skin and dark brows, he resembled both of them equally. They were smiling and making quiet jokes to one another. The whole time, the younger man stroked the sleeping pup in the crook of his arm.

I wanted to storm across the lobby and tell them off. I wanted to say, "How dare you be so happy? How dare you be together right here where I can see you? My mother is dead. My father is nowhere to be found! I have no one!"

The young man with the dog glanced at me. His brown eyes burned me. Could he know what I was thinking? He smiled. No, he could not know.

The white dog woke up and licked his nose. He yawned a big dog yawn. I think the dog looked at me. Maybe of all of them, he knew best what I was thinking. Maybe he had been lost once, too.

It had been surprisingly easy for Mrs. Frobischer to convince the city to let her have temporary custody of me. I only had to spend one night in a foster home. I wished she could have taken me home with her on that awful night that I had found Mama—that night when the police told me that they thought my father had killed her, that night when they grabbed me by my arms and carried me out of my house. That night…

Later, I was glad that I had been blinded by hot tears as I was evicted from my own home. At least I didn't have to watch my life grow smaller in the distance.

I spent the first night of my renewed grief in a stranger's house. I wished I could have gone with Mrs. Frobischer. She would have comforted me. She's good at that. She took my small life and made it bigger. That's what she does. She makes thing grow. She talks to plants.

Why wasn't I happy, then? Is it okay to be sad when you're supposed to be happy? I guess when you've seen the things I saw, it is.

Maybe it would have been better if I hadn't gone home at all that night. I would never have seen what I did. Maybe I should have gone straight to Mrs. Frobischer's house. I could have waited for her. And, I could have been with her when she found Shelby bleeding in the mud at the Bayou Vin Atténué.

Rosa Frobischer

The battle I had with child protective services lasted for six solid, sweaty, agitating hours. At the end of it, I was told that I could keep Dove until they found her father. So, I figured, that essentially meant forever as I didn't suppose we'd be cursed with an appearance by Hsin Ji anytime in the foreseeable future.

I wasn't certain if the police had told Dove that they suspected that her father was the one who strangled her mother that night. I didn't want to mention it. But, I was sure that she suspected it herself.

As I sat, putting on my make-up, in my room in The Hotel Rainier, I felt more at ease than I had since I moved back to Marionneaux. The panic, the suffocation, had all but been erased from the moment we arrived in New Orleans. So had the red.

I couldn't help but shudder when I thought of the awful wave of sickness I felt at the bayou that night—like thousands of bricks crashing down on my head. That night, I seemed to function with a mechanical strength I never knew I had possessed. Did George know I was that strong? Probably, so. George knew everything. He wouldn't have been astounded. But, I was. Those few weeks were awash in surprises for me—discoveries not only about myself, but also about others.

For instance, Shelby's increasingly capable protectiveness. When we had met, I'd never have guessed she could show devotion to anyone other than herself.

However, I later recalled that after our visit with Eulabel, Shelby brought me home without a modicum of complaining. While not jovial, she endeavored to be upbeat and tried to keep my mind from wandering. I hadn't shared with her all of the images that had flashed through my head. I didn't know if she would understand. I didn't know that I really understood myself.

She stayed with me until I was able to pretend to be calm. We talked a little bit about what Eulabel had told us and about the strange happenings at Jade Ji's funeral. Shelby, bless her, wanted to discuss it all more. I could tell she was struggling to figure it all out. But it had gotten too late, and I wanted her to go home before she got in trouble.

I had been fighting to keep myself from falling asleep and was lying motionless on the loveseat when Douglas Halifax called me. He was worried. Shelby hadn't come home yet.

I don't know why I thought that she would have gone to the Bayou Vin Atténué that night. A bayou is the last place you'd expect a girl like Shelby to go. But, given everything that Eulabel had told us earlier in the day, I suspected that Shelby's natural curiosity would have gotten the better of her. I was right and I thank God that I was! Normally, I would never have gone to that bayou. In fact, it was the last place in the world I wanted to go, second only to Amelia Rittenhouse's palazzo. And, yet, for Shelby and Dove, I've been to both places.

By the time I got to the bayou, Shelby was alone—splayed out in the mud, like some Baroque painting of a recumbent Christ after the "Deposition From the Cross" that George and I might have seen in Rome or on the walls of the Rittenhouse great hall.

My heart, I thought, would stop beating when I saw that. I was immediately suffocated the closer I got to the bayou, and when I saw Shelby, the deluge of red began again. I fought through my own thoughts and made my way to the girl. She was barely conscious.

I asked her what had happened and she told me that she had slipped in the mud and gashed the back her head on a rock. But, the swirl of footprints in the mud told me otherwise. They indicated that she had been struggling to get somewhere. While we waited for the ambulance she admitted what happened. She had seen Unwin Rittenhouse.

I believed her, partly because I was convinced I had seen him once myself—at Jade Ji's funeral, and partly because I knew Shelby wouldn't lie to me. No one else, however, took Shelby seriously. The police told us that no one had seen Unwin Rittenhouse in seventy years and that he was more than likely dead. Her parents' reaction was much the same. When they met us at the hospital, both Voletta and Douglas Halifax dismissed Shelby's claim as the fanciful imagination of a clumsy teen. In fact, Voletta's attitude toward everything that night was so ambivalent; I wondered why she even bothered to come to the emergency room at all—especially smelling of bourbon as she did.

Douglas was more sympathetic—taking his daughter's hand and making her promise never to go off on her own again. I could tell that his mind was processing everything that Shelby had told him. If anyone were ever going to believe her, outside of myself, it would be Douglas.

Unlike his wife's, Douglas' eyes showed that he loved Shelby. But, even that love for his daughter was clouded by the obvious animosity between him and Voletta.

Ever charming, they took their daughter home without offering to give me a ride. As I walked back to my cottage, I saw flashing police lights at the other end of D'Arbonne Street. I was in no hurry to go to sleep and find myself in the grip of my own terror, so I walked further to see what was going on.

When I became aware that the ambulance and police cars were parked outside of Dove's house, I quickened my pace. I arrived just in time to see them carry out the body in its black bag. Dove was screaming as two officers held her by the arms. I tried to stop them, but they insisted they had to take her to a CPS foster home. I promised Dove I would fix it. I did. "'Atta girl."

I thought it would be best for all of us to get away for awhile. So, I proposed the trip to New Orleans. It was easy to get the Halifax's to agree to let me take Shelby along. In fact, they seemed glad to be rid of her. And, since Shelby's Sweet Sixteen party was being postponed in light of everything that had happened, I pitched the trip to Shelby as being a birthday treat. She, too, seemed relieved and responded with a great deal of enthusiasm.

The day after Mrs. Ji's funeral, we left for New Orleans. Luckily, I had run into Eulabel again on La Rue de la Marchands and asked her if she knew of anyone who could watch my shop while I was away. She recommended her sister—an English teacher who needed some summer employment to help with the bills until school started in the fall. With everything packed and in order, Dove and I boarded the limousine and off we went to pick up Shelby. I knew that hiring a car and driver for such a short drive was folly, but I thought it would please the girls as well as give me a peace of mind since I have never enjoyed driving even the shortest distance.

I hoped the trip would do them some good. However, I suspected that Dove's mind would always be at the Marionneaux cemetery with Jade and her mother while Shelby's thoughts would remain dizzy in the mud at the bayou.

Shelby immediately perked up when the limo delivered us to The Hotel Rainier. The sumptuous décor appealed to Shelby's refined tastes perfectly and she immediately began to relax. She even stopped fidgeting with the bandage beneath her green cloche hat.

Dove, on the other hand, had absolutely no reaction whatsoever. I was beginning to fear that she would retreat into silence as her mother had. But, she soon began to relax a bit, too—if only just to make us feel better.

We had no real plans or itinerary. On our first night, we all stood in my room looking out the window watching the lights. The central spire of St. Louis cathedral rose up on the horizon and seemed to invite us down to smell the food and become lost in the crowded streets—in that swirl of people that embrace you the moment you step out onto Bourbon Street. New Orleans has a way of winding its beauty and hospitality around you like the vines of the volutes and scrolls of the black wrought iron that decorate the buildings on either side of the narrow streets. I prayed that the atmosphere would work its magic on the girls. They both needed so desperately to be embraced.

The only definite plans that we had made were for the Saturday of Shelby's birthday. I was to take the girls to Café Du Monde for a brunch of beignets and then shopping on Magazine Street. I had promised Shelby that I would buy her anything that she wanted—anything at all—as my birthday gift to her. George always used to do things like that. He would make these extravagant gestures as a way of masking his insecurity. I had learned it from him.

Shelby seemed to be looking forward to the day a great deal. Dove pretended to be as well. But, her eyes told me differently. Maybe she would find something to make her happy. But, I didn't think they sold what she was looking for on Magazine Street.

As I started for the door, the phone rang. It was the front desk patching a call in.

"Mrs. F.?" I recognized Eulabel's voice immediately.

"Eulabel, is something wrong?" I asked.

"Well," Eulabel stalled.

"Come on, now," I said, trying to cover the fear in my voice.

"Looks like someone gone and broke in last night," Eulabel said.

"Into the bookstore?" I asked.

"Yeah," Eulabel said. "My sister wanted me to call you. She was scared you'd be mad."

"It's not Yolanda's fault," I sighed, "So, how bad is it?"

"Now, that's the funny part. Looks like just a broken winda…nothin' missing." Eulabel said.

"Nothing?" I asked in disbelief.

"Nope. All the cash is still here. No sign that anything was taken." Eulabel answered.

"Well, imagine," I said softly. "Just get someone to fix the window. You can have them invoice me. I'll pay the bill when I get back."

"Yes ma'am."

"Thank you Eulabel," I said before hanging up.

"That's not right," I said to myself.

I fixed my hair and went to the elevator. I was late meeting the girls. I decided not to tell them about the phone call. I didn't want to upset them more than they already were. But, it seemed that Dove, Shelby and I weren't the only ones searching for something.

Shelby Halifax

I didn't want to disappoint Mrs. Frobischer. After all, she'd gone out of her way to take Dove and me to New Orleans with her. She'd even hired a limo to take us! Not only that, but, she'd gotten us the most beautiful rooms in The Hotel Rainier.

Even though it was my birthday, I didn't feel much like celebrating. I didn't feel much like doing anything. My head still hurt—even after over a week. I have a feeling it's because I haven't been sleeping very well. Every time I shut my eyes, I see that awful man coming toward me.

No one believes me—except Mrs. Frobischer. I think Dove believes me, but I don't think the old man's name means anything to her except that he's related to Miss Rittenhouse. We didn't tell her what the black lady at the historical center told us. I thought about telling her more, but it didn't seem right. Besides, she just doesn't seem very interested in talking about it. She doesn't seem very interested in anything at all. Unlike me, she can't even pretend to be happy. Poor thing.

I really do feel bad for Dove —so much had happened in such a short amount of time. It would have been nice if more people had come to her mother's funeral. It was the same few people that had gone to Jade's, but with one less. We're kind of the only family that Dove has now. No one knows where her father has gone.

Although I won't say this to Dove, I was actually glad that her father had gone away. I don't know if he killed Mrs. Ji or not, but I do know for a fact that he struck Dove. The red handprint on her face only went away completely a couple of days after we arrived in New Orleans. I can't imagine what that must have felt like. Daddy would never have hit me. But, at least she's healing.

I wish I could have said the same for myself. It took twelve stitches to close the gash in the back of my head. I was sure it would scar. But, thank goodness, my pretty hair covered it. They were afraid it would become infected because I had been lying in the mud for so long. But, it didn't. The bandage was ugly and I was beginning to get very tired of wearing hats all the time. How could I not? I didn't want people staring at me as if I was an escapee from a war movie.

Fixing the hat just right seemed to take extra long on the day we were supposed to go shopping. Really, I just wasn't trying very hard to be quick. The night before had been particularly restless and getting out of bed and getting ready seemed to be taking longer than usual. After I was satisfied that the bandage didn't show, I went downstairs to meet Dove in the lobby. She sat on the eggplant-colored borne in the middle of the room and was making angry faces at the passers-by. She seemed particularly put out by one family with a dog. I could understand how she felt. Sometimes, I watch other people and get a little jealous, too.

When Dove saw me, she raised her eyebrows and widened her eyes—I think to give herself the look of someone who was in a good mood. It didn't really work, but I thought she was sweet to make the effort, so I pretended that she had fooled me.

"Happy Birthday," Dove said as happy-sounding as she could.

"Thank you," I smiled. "Where's Mrs. Frobischer?"

"Not down yet," Dove muttered.

"That's not like her," I said, "It's more like me." I thought a joke at my own expense would make Dove feel better. I know how insecure she is. But, oh, that hat itched!

Dove faked a smile and then looked down at the patterned carpet. "You know, I really do want you to have a happy birthday."

"I know." I smiled—for real.

Dove did, too.

"So what do you want for your birthday?" She asked me.

Averill says that the other kids at school are jealous of us because we can have anything in the world that we could ever want. He says that because our families are rich and we live in great big houses on some of the best real estate on La Colline Cramoisie, we're the luckiest people in town. I usually think Averill is right about these things. But, about that, I'm not so sure. What did I want?

"Breakfast," I shrugged.

Dove looked at me funny.

I glanced up at the fancy, curvy gold clock that hung over the concierge desk. I wondered what was taking Mrs. Frobischer so long. I also wondered what Mommy and Daddy were doing right then. It was Saturday, so the chances that Daddy was in surgery were slim. He was probably out golfing. Mommy, if not hung over, was probably drinking her breakfast with Grandmother L'Ebène.

Yeah, the two of them were probably sitting on the veranda making snide comments about the tourists that drive up and down La Colline Cramoisie to look at all the fine old houses. Either that, or Mommy was still drunk from the night before and was throwing up and yelling at Therese.

I was beginning to feel that Mrs. Frobischer and Dove were more my family than my own mother and father. I couldn't help but think how Grandmother and Grandfather L'Ebène would react if they heard me say that. Mommy certainly wouldn't care.

Out of the corner of my eye, I caught Dove watching me still. I looked right at her.

"What were you thinking about?" She asked.

I hesitated, "My mother."

Dove flinched. I knew I should not have said anything about mothers.

Her eyes got glassy and she looked up at me, "Me too." She paused, "Mine—not yours."

Thank goodness, we didn't have to finish the conversation. "Good morning! Good Morning! Good Morning!" Mrs. Frobischer sang as she got off of the elevator.

"Hi," Dove and I said in unison.

"Happy birthday, my dear!" Mrs. Frobischer said, kissing both my cheeks.

I smiled.

She offered a hand to Dove who took it and stood, then she offered a hand to me. We walked out of the hotel together. It was fun to walk hand in hand. I didn't remember ever doing that before.

Maybe we were a family.

"Does family mean nothing to you?" I shouted at Voletta. "Shit, you little ingrate! Do you know how much we've had to sacrifice to make a life for you and your goddamn ugly sisters?"

"Stop bellowing, mother! Please!" She shrieked and covered her ears with her hands just as she did when she was a child. I see that forty some odd years of life and a decade's worth of plastic surgery haven't made her anything more than she was when she was a baby.

Little bitch! She was still throwing tantrums! The sleeve of her peignoir dragged through her orange juice and vodka. She was disgusting! Augustin would have been ashamed and angry. "What's the big deal?" She moaned.

"You let *my* granddaughter go with that Frobischer woman!"

"So! I'm glad to be rid of Shelby for a while. She's too much like Douglas." Voletta argued.

"Don't you know what kind of person she is?" I continued, hoping I could make some kind of impression on my puerile daughter. I was so disappointed; she usually had more of her father's sense. "I don't come to visit for a week and you've given my granddaughter away!"

"No one gave Shelby away. She'll be back." Voletta squealed. "She's fine. She's with her two little friends."

"She's with the Asian girl, too?" I was horrified. "What will people think?"

"They'll think," Voletta paused to sip her drink, "that she takes after her father!" She laughed sloppily.

"Really, you disgust me sometimes;" I frowned, "Is it too much to ask for a fucking match? Really, Voletta!"

"Mother, don't smoke in the house."

"Why not?"

"It stinks."

"You stink, you little shit." I shouted again for their maid before I tried to reason with Voletta again. "If you're not going to think about the reputation of this family, I am!"

Voletta took another swig.

"What would your father say? Do you know how this will hurt him?"

"It won't hurt him," Voletta belched.

"Oh, but it will. And you know how your father gets when he's hurt," I pouted.

"Yes I know," Voletta leaned forward, taking a gulp of air presumably to calm her stomach. "All I know is that I didn't want Shelby here for just a few days. It kills me to hear her talk about 'my daddy this, my daddy that.'"

I continued, "And speaking of Douglas, where is he?"

“Don’t know,” Voletta shrugged. “Maybe he didn’t come home last night. He wasn’t in his room this morning.”

It was worse than I thought. I had to act quickly. Maybe Voletta was right. Rosa Frobischer’s absence had already proven helpful. And, with the girl gone, too, it was the perfect time.

Eulabel Watkins

Poor Mrs. F. I have gone and screwed this up. I should have done told her the whole truth. I knew I should have, but I didn't want to make it worse for her. She's got her hands all full up with them two girls. Last thing she needs is to be worried about the bookstore.

Yolanda is blaming herself for this. But, it isn't my sister's fault. She did as she should have—made sure the door was locked and everything. How was she to know someone was gonna smash right through the window?

I just want Mrs. F. to have a nice time with them two poor, sad girls. I want them to be able to forget about all their troubles back here in Marionneaux. But, I should have told her that them boxes in the backroom have been rummaged through. And, I should have told her about him—the Loch Ness Monster—right there in the beam of my flashlight.

I put my hand in front of my eyes. The sunlight was so bright, it hurt. The man with the top hat helped me up into the carriage before he climbed back up himself. I felt fat and awkward. Mrs. Frobischer sat with her back to the mule and Shelby and I sat across from her on the opposite bench.

I had never been on a carriage ride before. They were offered in Marionneaux at Christmastime during the annual parade. But, my family could never afford one. And, besides, the town wouldn't look any different behind a donkey than it did on foot.

Shelby seemed more interested in looking at the people than the buildings. I enjoyed watching her face light up when we passed the front of St. Louis Cathedral and she saw all the street performers on Jackson Square. Some were singing, some juggling, some drawing, others posing as human statues. I tried to look at the pads and canvases of the visual artists that we passed. Bold lines and bright colors seemed to be what they all had in common. As I looked around at them; I wondered where they found the freedom to draw that way.

People watched us as we passed by on our carriage. Shelby pretended not to see the stares of the people on the banquettes. Mrs. Frobischer truly seemed not to notice them. I found myself meeting their stares. I looked directly into the eyes of those that were watching me. Some flinched and turned away, some held my gaze until the carriage rolled past. I wasn't used to looking people dead in the eye. Doing that felt good and bad all at the same time. Such were the politics of a carriage ride through the Quarter. It was sure interesting and even I had to admit that it was very enchanting.

I felt like Cinderella for a few minutes. That was the only one of my books that I could think of where someone rides in a carriage. I read a novel once where a lady gets run over by a carriage. She was killed. I looked at some of the people on the banquettes. I wondered if any of them would ever be killed by a carriage. I'd feel bad for them if that happened.

Mrs. Frobischer didn't really seem to be paying attention. She was biting her bottom lip as if she were deep in thought.

Soon, I found I was enjoying listening to the driver. He told us a lot about the history of the French Quarter. I listened hungrily to everything the driver was saying. All the stuff he talked about was like the things I read about in my books.

I was beginning to think that Mrs. Frobischer was right when she said that life goes on and that it's our duty to live it well. But, then we drove by St. Louis Cemetery No. 1. I remembered Mama and Jade in their side by side vaults. How was I going to pay all those bills with Papa gone? Mrs. Frobischer has already done so much. I couldn't ask her to help me pay bills. I had to do it myself. But, how?

Was I going to be a poor orphan like Oliver Twist? Would I have to sleep in a coffin?

"This is St. Louis Number One," the mule driver was saying, " This here is da final resting place of many important people from Naw'leans history. Not da least o' which is Marie LeVeaux, the famous voodoo queen."

I looked at Shelby and smiled. We had had the same thought.

"Just a little too similar to my grandmother," Shelby chuckled.

Mrs. Frobischer chuckled, too.

We felt lighthearted for the rest of the ride.

Once the carriage returned us to where we started, we walked to Café Du Monde and sat at one of the tables outside behind the pretty wrought iron rail.

After studying the short, but tasty menu, I looked up. There was the family of three from our hotel sitting directly against one side of the rail. The younger man looked nervous. His terrier had been tied to the other side of the railing. And, while the dog didn't seem to mind (he was greedily licking powdered sugar off the entirely sugarcoated floor), the man couldn't stand to be separated from his pet even by those few inches.

I wondered what it would feel like to care that deeply about something. I wondered if I ever would. I wondered if anyone would about me.

My good mood was fading and Mrs. Frobischer could sense it.

"After this, we'll go to Royal Street for some shopping," she said.

Shelby smiled, "I can't wait."

"And, of course we'll go to Magazine Street, too. It's too far to walk, so, we'll take a cab. In fact, why don't we start there?"

I took my little pocket guide book out and looked at it. "There's a mansion near there." I pointed to the book. "It says it's near Magazine Street."

"What's special about it?" Shelby asked. I thought maybe she didn't want her shopping interrupted.

"It says it's the house of 'The Elegant Ogress.' It says here that she is thought to have murdered…" I couldn't finish it. "Never mind. I don't want to go there anyway."

Mrs. Frobischer crossed her legs and stretched her right foot at the ankle for a couple of seconds before turning to me.

"You know," She began, "I was thinking. Just because it's Shelby's birthday doesn't mean that she has to get all the presents."

I felt rude, but all I could do was stare at the family with the white dog. I didn't know there were still real families. Why didn't I see the one that was sitting right next to me?

Mrs. Frobischer either didn't notice or tried to ignore me. She continued, "Since Shelby can get whatever she wants today, I think, in honor of her birthday, you should, too."

"That's a great idea!" Shelby chirped, also probably trying to cheer me up.

I don't know what came over me. I knew better, but I couldn't help myself. I shouted, "So, are you going to buy me a new mother and father?! What about a sister?! Jesus, Mrs. Frobischer!"

With that, I ran off. The terrier barked at me.

Unwin Rittenhouse

The broken glass was so shiny and smooth. I just had to pick a piece up and hold it. It reminded me of father and how he would study the stones in the light—holding them this way and that. I tried to do it, too. But, I looked foolish doing it.

I could smell something. It reminded me of Agathe. It smelled like earth.

I had to put down the glass when I heard the noise.

I didn't mean to make the lady scream. Pretty old black lady…

Why did she have to shine that light in my eyes? All that did was make me angry.

I squinted and shook my head as I watched Dove run off—raising my hand to shield my eyes from the afternoon sun. I didn't think she'd make a scene like that. That was more my thing than hers. She had done a good job of it, too.

"I'll go," I nodded at Mrs. Frobischer.

I ran after her. My head hurt—the bump, bump, bump of my feet on the pavement made my wound throb. I found the pain was making me angry and it was all I could do not to shout at Dove when I found her.

Luckily, I didn't have to run far. She had darted into an enclosed shopping area behind the Café Du Monde and was sitting on the edge of a fountain with her head in her hands. I quickly took a deep breath to calm myself down a little and to make the pain go away, Then I walked slowly to Dove. I felt rather like I was approaching a wounded stray—slowly and quietly so as not to frighten it away.

When Dove noticed me, she bent at the waist and put her head on the concrete edge of the fountain—sobbing loudly. That's just not attractive on anyone, really. But, even still, Dove looked better than most when she did it. She looked…I don't know…different somehow. She lifted her head so that she could see me.

I pointed to the fountain. In its center, were whimsical sculptures of jazz musicians in black silhouette—like puzzle pieces.

"Let's toss a nickel in the water," I said opening up my purse and pulling out a coin. Dove watched me cautiously. I tossed the nickel into the fountain and listened as it plunked into the water—settling onto the cobalt blue tile.

I sat down next to Dove without even brushing the water beads and dust off the edge of the fountain. I knew it would ruin my slacks, but I didn't care. Some things are more important than clothes. I continued to look at the cutout musicians.

"What're you doing?" She asked sharply.

"I'm waiting to see what they play," I said, pretending to be really serious, "I did tip them after all."

"Idiot," Dove said. But, she laughed afterwards—that was all I wanted.

"If I'm an idiot, what does that make you?" I asked.

Dove sat up and wiped her eyes. "That makes me a fat, ugly orphan who's mean to people when all they're trying to do is be kind. It makes me cruel. An unlovable, mean, fat orphan. No wonder God decided to take my family away."

"Huh?" I scoffed. "God doesn't punish people—not the God I learned about from my Grandmother Halifax. I don't know about whatever oriental god you worship."

Dove scowled and then giggled a little, "I was raised Christian. Catholic, in fact. My father converted when he came to America and married my mother. She was already Catholic."

"Well, there you go," I nodded. "Who knew you people could be Christian. Averill says that you worship gods with lots of arms."

"That's the Hindu."

"Oh. Well, anyway, God isn't punishing you. And besides that, you're hardly unlovable. Mrs. Frobischer loves you." I paused, "And, I do too."

Dove smiled.

"Look, Dove," I began, "What's happened to you is really lousy. You feel alone. You've lost your mom and your sister. God knows where your father is. But, you've got me and Mrs. Frobischer."

"I doubt Mrs. Frobischer will ever talk to me again after the way I yelled at her." Dove sniffed.

"Oh, you'd be surprised," I grinned. "Come on."

I was happy when Dove stood and followed me back to the café. We paused at the gate to pat a West Highland White Terrier that wagged its tail when it saw us. It wanted so badly to lick Dove's hand that it cried out. The three people with the dog laughed at his excitement. Dove bent down and gave the dog a big hug. Playing with the dog seemed to make Dove a little calmer. We thanked the people and went on to the patio.

Mrs. Frobischer sat nervously brushing powdered sugar off of her black skirt. She didn't get all of it. When she saw us her eyes lit up. We sat down next to her.

"I'm sorry if I seemed insensitive," Mrs. Frobischer said softly, "I was just trying to…to…distract you."

"I know." Dove nodded. "I guess maybe I've been doing that myself—a bit too much. I haven't given myself a chance to deal with what happened to Jade and my mama. I haven't even let myself think about it too much. Every time I do, I try to think about something else—a book or a movie or some picture that I drew. I'd rather think about anything, but...."

Mrs. Frobischer looked off into the distance, "I'm sorry. I should have let you talk about it more. I just…well, that's what I do. I try to make things better. I try to take people's minds off of what's wrong in their lives." She began to cry. "That's the way I was…I mean, that's what I've learned to do when something is wrong."

"No, no," Dove said. "You've been wonderful. I shouldn't have yelled at you."

"I shouldn't have been so insensitive," Mrs. Frobischer began.

"Oh for the love of corn!" I interrupted. "Everyone's sorry. Now, can we get some more beignets?"

Both Dove and Mrs. Frobischer looked at me first with shock and then with amusement.

"Yes, let's," Mrs. Frobischer smiled—waving for a waiter.

"And, then I want to go shopping. It is my birthday after all!" I pouted—partly for show and partly out of sincerity.

"We'll do just that—very shortly," Mrs. Frobischer smiled.

"And damn it," I began, "I'm hot." I took off my hat and gently fluffed my hair—running my index finger over my bandage. Mommy would have a fit if she saw me exposing my bandage. I didn't care what people thought.

I'd earned it.

Amelia Rittenhouse

"What did I do to deserve this?" I thought to myself as I lay on the marble floor. *You have to ask?*

I looked up at the scarlet walls. How father had loved this house! I shut my eyes. Father had loved me, too. And Unwin.

"Unwin! Come home to me!" I cried out. I knew he would not.

Everything could have been different.

I might have been a good mother. *Like a snake, Amelia?* But, instead, I drank my life away. I drank Unwin's away, too. And, Agathe's…and…and…Jade's. Yes, Jade's, too. It's all related, isn't it?

Maybe if I had pursued a normal life. I could have married. I could have raised…

I couldn't sit up.

Can't even raise yourself, Amelia.

So, I continued to stare up at the gilt coffers of the ceiling and found my thoughts lost in the prisms of the chandeliers—how they sparkled like diamonds…father's diamonds. Every color. *Nature's artistry.*

With bellies full of beignets and hot chocolate, the girls and I flagged down a taxi on Decatur Street and ventured toward the bustle of Magazine Street. We were to visit there before taking another cab to the costlier shops on Royal and Chartres.

I was pleased to see that Shelby had removed her velvet cloche. The weather was too warm for her to wear it. I had worried that she'd have gotten overheated. I was surprised that she didn't stop once to fix her hair in the reflection of the shop windows.

I wasn't surprised, however, when Shelby paused to marvel at the displays in the windows of the Bijouterie d'Antiquité. She was immediately enraptured by the sparkle. Her excited stare told me that she would find her birthday present among the shelves of estate jewelry.

I was pleased that Dove also seemed interested in the jewelry store. Without a word, we entered. The shop smelled strongly of cigarette smoke and was filled with the sound of sentimental string music. It reminded me of evenings spent with Vivien Leigh during the production of *Street Car.*

We were immediately greeted by a small birdlike woman with beige hair who appeared to be in her late seventies. She wore an aubergine pantsuit with a rather ostentatious amethyst and fiery opal pin on the right lapel.

"Hello, hello, hello, ladies!" The woman chirped—waving her hand in a circular motion. Light reflected off of a substantial alexandrite ring—sending shocks of purple, green and hot pink around her head like fireworks.

"Hello," I nodded.

Dove and Shelby stood next to me with mouths agape. I don't think they had ever seen anyone quite like her.

"Can I help you find anything?"

"Well," I said, putting my hand on Shelby's shoulder, "Today is this young lady's birthday."

"Oh! Félicitations!" The woman tittered. "You're looking for something special, then?"

"Yes," I nodded.

"Goooooood," the woman grinned, "My name is Clémence."

I don't know why I felt compelled to introduce myself. The woman had put such effort into her pretension of friendliness; it seemed only right that I should respond somewhat in kind.

"I'm Rosa. Rosa Frobischer." I said, putting my hand back on Shelby's shoulder and the other on Dove's. "And, these are my…" I stopped myself. They weren't my daughters, but that's what I was going to say. Daughters! Really, they could have been my great granddaughters. But, they weren't that either. Both girls looked up at me. "Friends." I continued, "These are my friends, Shelby and Dove."

"Ahhhh, Dove," Clémence chirped obsequiously, "Such a pretty name. Where are your wings, little bird?"

Dove shrugged.

If Clémence noticed Dove's less than enthusiastic response, she certainly didn't let on. She continued with her ingratiating welcome speech, "And, Shelby, you are the birthday girl?"

Shelby nodded.

"You are sixteen?"

"Yes!" Shelby answered with pride.

"Oh, such an age. Such an age." Clémence murmured. "You just look—right. Take your time. There's some spiced lemonade in the back and little cookies." She certainly was eager. "Let me know if you see anything you like."

"She can have anything she wants," I said loudly—shocked by George's voice coming out of my mouth. Why did I feel the need to impress this woman?

George referred to his flamboyantly generous moments as "being a sport." He always felt kind of ashamed of himself afterwards—he never said so, but I could tell. Why did it take George dying for me to see how much a like we were?

Clémence grinned, "Such a generous friend! Just holler if you need me."

The store was enormous and we took our time looking at the rows of cabinets that lined the walls. Frankly, Shelby was too young to wear any of the pieces in the place. But, she and Dove both seemed so mesmerized by the sheer sparkle of it all, I let them be.

Clémence left us alone and busied herself with polishing a 1930's era diamond and sapphire bracelet—such that Gloria Swanson would have worn. All the while she polished, Clémence hummed absently. The tune sounded vaguely familiar…like a variation on one that I had known before.

Shelby stopped in front of a low cabinet in the back of the store. She motioned me over.

"Mrs. Frobischer, look!" She pointed to a ring—a cluster of garnets set in platinum to resemble a rather enormous flower. "It's beautiful!"

I couldn't help but shudder. My mouth went dry and I felt the beads of perspiration forming on my forehead and dripping down my cheeks. Or were those tears?

"Did you find something?" Dove came up beside us.

Her reaction to the ring was similar to mine. However, she had the good sense to simply walk away.

I continued to stare at the red stones while Shelby went on about the ring's beauty. My focus was so deep that I didn't even hear Clémence approach us from behind. I jumped when she spoke.

"Ahhh yes. Those are Mozambique Garnets. Total carat weight is 15. Do you like it?"

Shelby nodded, "Yes. Could I see it?"

"Of course, dear child," Clémence cooed, "Of course it can be sized if it doesn't fit." Looking at me, she added, "The girl has excellent taste. We just got this ring in. It's from a local woman's estate. Crafted in 1965—very nice. These things come back in style every few years. Now, let me go get the key to this case."

I dabbed at my forehead and eyes with my handkerchief while Clémence went to fetch the key—humming all the way. Shelby couldn't take her gaze off the ring and Dove stood next to me looking toward the front of the shop.

In seconds, Clémence returned—smiling and singing. With the lyrics, I recognized the tune…

She sang:

Down deep below the surface
Weary roots do drink
The water rich with Heaven:
Closer than we think.
In darkness it is stagnant
In light only will grow
Proud branches strong and sturdy
Where darkness once did flow.

My back stiffened. It was that little tune that had been haunting me.

"Something wrong?" Clémence asked. She had noticed that not only had I taken on a look of shock, Shelby and Dove had as well.

"That song," I managed to choke.

"Oh you like it? It's from a poem called 'The Shadowed River" by a woman named Columbia…Columbia Navarre," Clémence explained. She started to sing again:

The shadowed river listens,
Waiting for the rain,
Lies lost in such sharp silence
Her beauty will wane:
She wears her hope like diamonds
All colors save but one
Diana's orb will free us
Reflected in the sun.

All three of us gasped as she sang.

Clémence Couvillion

Now if that wasn't the strangest thing. Some woman—a tourist—came into the shop with these two girls. Don't know if they were her grandkids or anything like that. One of them was Chinese. Well, one of the girls—the white one—wants to see one of the rings from old Marly Terrebonne's estate—a big tacky garnet number.

Anyway, this Rosa woman—Miss Moneybags—says to let the girl have anything she wants. So, I go get the key. I have to say I was in pretty good spirits—looked like I was going to make a few sales. So, I was singing like I do when the mood strikes me and I'm feeling on top of everything, you know.

Well, if it don't beat all. All three of 'em just kind of went all pale like they had just seen a ghost. I didn't know what the hell had happened.

So, the woman, this Rosa Frobischer woman, asks me what I'd been singing. Well, I had to think for a second. I sing that little thing all the time, so I don't really think about it when I'm doing it.

It was that little tune that the girl used to sing…the one by…Oh! What's it? The words are from some half-black, poetess lady from Natchitoches...oh right, Columbia Navarre. Well horse feathers…there was another name that I couldn't remember before. Oh! Cage…Columbia Navarre Cage.

Anyway, I told this Rosa about that Columbia mulatto and all three of them just stared at me like I was talking in Chinese. Well, okay, not Chinese, the little oriental girl would have understood me. But, some language—Oh, I don't know—Russian. They're looking at me like I'm talking in Russian.

Well, at this point all I want to do is slip a little something in my lemonade and go read my novel. It's so good—one of them with the stable man and the lady of the…well now, I've gone and made myself blush.

But, I didn't get my refreshments because they all looked like they were gagging and it kind of made me not thirsty—if you know what I mean. So, I asked them if there was something wrong. Well, the Asian girl walks to the front of the shop and looks out the window and the white girl…you know she had the biggest, ugliest bandage wrapped around her head…maybe she was terminal or something and this was one of those "Make A Wish" deals…anyway, the white girl turns around and stares at the Terrebonne ring.

So, it's just me and Rosa Frobischer talking.

She said nothing was wrong, but she looked all shaky like and I asked her if she wanted to sit down or wanted some of my famous lemonade. She said no she did not want to have a drink or to sit down—but, don't get me wrong—she was still friendly about it.

She asked me where I had learned that song. I thought that was very strange, but I didn't let her see that's what I was thinking.

So, I told her the truth. I told her how I had learned the song from that girl that Mama had taken in when I was a twelve. Lordy, I haven't thought about that in years. I was so upset what with my being on the verge of woman-hood and Mama taking some unwanted orphan pauper. And, what a sickly looking thing she was—ooooh, came with nothing at all except ratty little piece of paper with that tune on it and a blanket. Didn't even have a last name! The folks at the orphanage made one up for her…Le Banni. A strange name if you ask me.

This Frobischer woman's eyes got about as big as saucers and she said she wanted to know more about Le Banni. I told her everything I knew. Figured it couldn't hurt anybody.

I told her how Mama raised the girl up to be strong and how it turned out, the girl wasn't half bad once she grew up. And she certainly was a help to us here in the store. We used to joke with her that she musta been a jeweler in another life or maybe her real mama or daddy worked with jewelry. She was a natural. That's when she wondered who her own mama and daddy was. We never kept it a secret that she was adopted.

At least she had a talent for taking care of jewelry because the girl grew up uglier than a mud fence—short as a goose and with the strangest, blackest hair you ever saw. The more she thought about it though, the more ornery she got, and I knew that she needed to find out about her real mama and daddy.

So, I decided, I'd help her find out. Mama said it was all right for me to take Agathe up to the orphanage on the shore of Lake Pontchartrain where we got her. We asked the people there—they had some kind of record of the mother, but not the father.

We went back home Agathe was all kinds of upset. But, I told her I'd help her contact her real mama. So, we found out the real mother's address and wrote a letter to her. Took a couple of years, but I knew when we got that envelope from Marionneaux that it had to be from Agathe's birth mother.

And, it was. In fact, she invited Agathe to come and stay with her in her big mansion.

I'll never forget the handwriting on that letter—big, loopy letters. And the most gigantic signature you ever did see all scrawled out on the bottom…

I'll never forget it. Or that name.

Amelia Rittenhouse.

What bites me is that I didn't even make a sale.

"Jade used to sing that song," I panted to Mrs. Frobischer. We hurried out of the jewelry store and into a cab. For the whole ride, we all sat really quietly. And soon, we found ourselves back in the French Quarter. We were swallowed up in the crowd on Decatur Street.

Mrs. Frobischer looked at me and cocked her head to one side. "Really?"

"Yes." I nodded.

"I don't suppose it would be uncommon for people from the same town to know the same song," Mrs. Frobischer said slowly. She was speaking more to herself than to me or Shelby, I thought.

Shelby put her hand to her head, she looked tired and uncomfortable, "It's true. My grandfather L'Ebène hums it, too."

"The woman who wrote the words was from Natchitoches which isn't too awfully far away from Marionneaux," Mrs. Frobischer continued. "So, I'm sure that many people throughout these parishes know the song or at the very least, the words."

"Do you really think so?" Shelby asked. "I haven't ever heard any other people sing it. How do you know it?"

"I heard Agathe Le Banni singing it when I first visited Amelia Rittenhouse," Mrs. Frobischer answered hurriedly. We stepped away from the rush of the crowd and ducked under the awning of the French Market. She stopped for a minute and bit her lip; "Do you think that's where Jade learned it?"

"No," I shook my head. "Mama," I gulped, "Mama used to sing it, too—long before Jade moved out to work for Miss Rittenhouse."

"Wow," Shelby exclaimed as we settled down a bit, "Old Lady Rittenhouse had a daughter."

"That she gave up for adoption," I continued.

"And, it was Agathe." Mrs. Frobischer added.

"I don't understand," I began, "Agathe worked as a maid for Miss. Rittenhouse. Why would she do that? Especially if she knew that Miss Rittenhouse was her mother."

Mrs. Frobischer shrugged, "I don't really know."

She paused and looked at me before she began again, "Didn't you say that Jade often complained because Agathe was only responsible for taking care of a few rooms in the house while Jade had to clean the whole mansion?"

I nodded, "Yes."

"None of it makes sense!" Shelby exclaimed, still holding her head. "Agathe was…you know, the same way that Jade was. The same exact way!"

"Murdered," I said softly.

“Yes,” Shelby sighed apologetically, “I didn’t want to say it.” She took a deep breath. “I don’t see what the connection is between your sister and Amelia Rittenhouse’s abandoned daughter—other than the fact that they both lived and worked in the Rittenhouse Mansion. Who would want to kill both of them.”

“Can I tell you something?” I said suddenly. I had never planned to say it out loud, but I had to get it out.

They both nodded.

“When Jade was killed, something deep in the back of my head made me think that…” I took a deep breath, “That my…father killed her.” I paused and exhaled before I continued, “You see, something strange had been going on. He and Jade hadn’t been getting along. And, then, after my father hit me and called me a ‘whore’ just like Jade, and then after my mother was killed and my father disappeared, I was almost certain that my father had done it. I can’t understand why he would have, but I think—thought—he did.”

“Thought?” Mrs. Frobischer asked.

“Well, I can’t figure why my father would have wanted to kill Agathe, too.” I said.

“Maybe she saw him—you know.” Shelby said quietly.

“Could be,” I nodded.

“Could be,” Mrs. Frobischer agreed. “You see, all this time, I thought that Amelia Rittenhouse did it herself. Both Jade and Agathe had worked for her. But, knowing that Agathe was her daughter changes things.”

Mrs. Frobischer's eyes wandered.

"What's wrong?" I asked.

"I was just remembering a conversation I had with Amelia about grief. That's all." Mrs. Frobischer answered. "But, your mother's death," She looked at me quickly, "doesn't fit in with this. Amelia never knew your mother, I don't think."

"But, about that third murder," Shelby said uncomfortably.

"My mother," I said firmly, "You can say it."

Shelby sighed, "But, your mother wasn't killed in the same way as the other two. She was strangled. So, maybe someone else…" Shelby stopped talking and put her hand to the back of her head. She shook as her fingers touched the stitches beneath her bandage.

"I think it was Unwin Rittenhouse," Shelby finally said.

"Who?" I was beginning to feel like I could throw up. I thought I'd heard Shelby say that name before. But, I wasn't paying attention when she did. I was confused. Nothing made sense.

"The guy that scared me at the bayou," Shelby was still shaking.

Mrs. Frobischer nodded, "Amelia Rittenhouse's brother. The rather frightening man that showed up at Jade's funeral."

"Him? You think he killed Jade and his niece AND my mother?" I asked.

"He killed a Chinese woman once before." Shelby nodded.

"He did?" I gasped.

"Oh, we hadn't told you." Shelby looked down at the ground.

"We didn't want to upset you further." Mrs. Frobischer added. "Besides, no one was really sure that Unwin Rittenhouse is still alive."

"Until we all saw him," Shelby rubbed the back of her neck.

"And, there's no evidence that he actually killed that girl seventy years ago. The police saw him at the crime scene." Mrs. Frobischer said. "Listen, let's get a muffaletta and we'll tell you everything we know."

We got our sandwiches and Shelby and Mrs. Frobischer told me everything that Eulabel Watkins had told them the day my mother had been killed.

I sat quietly until they were finished.

"What was the girl's name?" I asked.

"Eulabel couldn't quite remember," Mrs. Frobischer sighed. "She said it was Ming something."

"Mingmei?" I yelped.

“It could have been” Mrs. Frobischer said after widening her eyes, “Why?”

“Mingmei was my grandmother’s name.”

If only I could sleep. Just a little.

The cemetery was empty. The pretty stout girl wasn't there. No one was talking to the graves. I went in.

Jade Ji—I knew her. She walked past me all the time. I think she knew I was watching her.

Niu Ji—that's a new grave. Oh, oh, yes. Mingmei's baby. I remember, yes. She's sleeping now, too. Sleep well, baby.

Oh, Mingmei.

She was so soft.

Why?

There she was. The vault next to Niu.

Mingmei Sun.

My love.

She was sleeping.

Douglas Halifax

I awoke on the couch in my study calling for Jade—my love. I ran my hand across my stubble and shivered, reaching for my shirt. My T-shirt was drenched with sweat. I smelled pretty foul and was glad that Voletta wasn't in the room to criticize me about it.

I would not have noticed right away that someone had come in while I was sleeping had it not been for the fact that one of my shoes had been overturned as if someone had tripped over it in the dark. At first, I figured it was Therese—unaware that I had taken to sleeping there the past few weeks. Even my private bedroom was too close to Voletta's. I could smell her through the door that connected the rooms. That's why I started sleeping in my study. I figured no one would bother me there. I was wrong.

It certainly couldn't have been Voletta. She had learned to tolerate me the first time, but not the last. She would never have voluntarily come anywhere near me.

I got up stiffly and lumbered for my desk—searching for some aspirin. That's when I noticed the neat pile of letters on the blotter. Jade's letters—the ones I had written to her.

My first thought was that Jade's father—that awful Hsin Ji—had done it. No one had seen him since Niu was killed. But, how could he have gotten in? I suppose nothing is impossible.

All I can be certain of is that this won't be the last time someone tries to get to me.

It's my duty not to let them.

Shelby must never know.

I have to protect my family. All of it.

Rosa Frobischer

The night after we had spoken to Clémence Couvillion, I found I couldn't sleep. I kept trying to sort everything out.

Amelia Rittenhouse's daughter, Agathe Le Banni, had been murdered in the same exact way that Jade Ji had. Amelia hadn't given any indication that Agathe was her daughter—she had shown no grief nor motherly concern. But, I supposed, what could one expect from a woman who had given her daughter up for adoption only to bring her back thirty years later to work as a maid? Furthermore, during all that time, where was her missing lunatic brother?

I thought about Unwin Rittenhouse as he was at Jade's funeral—this fantastic creature with little to no resemblance to the human being he must have been once. I tried to remember my time in Marionneaux as a girl—before George. Surely I had seen Amelia, if not Unwin Rittenhouse. They were both older than I by a few years, but we must have passed one another on the streets. We must have had mutual friends.

Why hadn't I heard of that first murder seventy years before? It couldn't have been long before I met George by pure chance on D'Arbonne Street. Certainly, I'd remember a murder. It happened right there at the Bayou Vin Atténué—only a short distance from the little house that I shared with my mother. I had been Shelby and Dove's age at the time. Surely I would have heard gossip about the murder of a Chinese woman. Both were such rarities in Marionneaux.

I tried to imagine Unwin Rittenhouse as he was then—a young man—standing over the lifeless body in silhouette against the tawniness of the bayou. And could that dead woman really have been Dove's grandmother? Perhaps Unwin Rittenhouse had killed Jade after all. And what of Dove's mother? Did Unwin Rittenhouse murder women of three generations of the same family? If he had, why? Had he killed his own niece, too?

And Hsin Ji—Dove's father—where was he? Had the mental strain of losing Jade, hitting Dove and seeing his wife killed been enough to make him flee? Or was he even aware that his wife, Niu, had been choked?

Oh, I had so many questions. What was it that George always said about questions? Yes, he used to say that the only way to understand anything was to ask questions. He said that the more queries we presented, the more we learned. And, the more we learned about other people, the more we learned about ourselves. I certainly had enough questions, but I sure as hell wasn't learning a thing about myself. Or maybe I was.

Over the previous weeks, I had done many things that I never thought I was capable of doing. Maybe my questions were leading me to find myself after all. Maybe I was about to meet that mysterious Rosa Frobischer.

Would our meeting be grand and stagy—in Technicolor and Cinemascope? Would I be sitting in some smoky room in a tasteful tweed suit? Yes, perhaps I would, and some woman in a gorgeous, low-cut gown with strappy pumps would come up to me and say, "Rosa, I'm Rosa. Nice to meet you." That's the way George might have written it. And, wouldn't it have been a blockbuster? Joan Fontaine could have played me. Or maybe even Kitty Carlisle. Yes, I think Kitty would have played me.

Too many thoughts made my chest feel heavy and my heartbeat quickened to be free of them. There would be no sleep that evening.

In many ways, I was glad not to have slept. Being awake afforded me protection against the nightmares I had been having. I didn't think my eighty-six year old heart could have taken another night of being trapped within a mound of sharp red stones. Another night of being slashed to shreds within that garnet hill before suffocating in its crimson thickness—the minerals slowly becoming fluid and filling my lungs, my eyes forever fixed in a scarlet stare.

The nightmares had gotten progressively more graphic and more frequent following the murder of Agathe. Beyond that, they had become almost unbearable upon the news of Niu Ji's strangulation.

I could almost imagine what she must have felt as she was choked to death—struggling, gasping for air…I had felt it many times after those flashes of red. But, even then, the feeling was so familiar—too familiar.

Yes, staying awake all night was preferable.

I hoped, at least, the girls were sleeping.

My eyelids felt heavy. I tried to fight it. My mind began to replay scenes of the day. Beignets. St. Louis Cathedral. The carriage man. The russet sunset over the Mississippi River. The shops. Oh, we hadn't gotten a present for Shelby. Magazine Street. The jewelry store.

Heavier and heavier—swimming in pink.

Clémence Couvillion.

Down deep below the surface
Weary roots do drink
The water rich with Heaven:
Closer than we think.

We should get a present for Shelby. That ring. That garnet ring. Clémence Couvillion and Agathe.

I tried to fight the sleep.

In darkness it is stagnant
In light only will grow

The garnet ring—sparking scarlet. Garnets—sharp and cutting. Sharp and cutting…

Red.

It flooded my lungs—hands reaching for me through the red—thick horrible. Long fingers grabbing at me.

There was a girl! I could see her through the redness! She's dead, oh, she's dead. Naked. Poor girl. Naked accept for that necklace. Garnet necklace.

I heard screaming. It was me.

I woke myself with my own shouts.

Dove had said her father had hit her after he saw her wearing a garnet necklace she had found in Jade's room. He hit her and she ran—leaving the necklace behind.

Dove said the marks on her mother's neck looked like the impression of the necklace on her skin. That garnet necklace! Could it have been the same one that had been found on her grandmother's dead body seventy years before?

More questions. Would they really bring me closer to myself? Was I bold enough to ask them? Would that necklace be the clue I needed?

If so, where was it? And what did it have to do with the residents of the mansion on La Colline Cramoisie?

I had to find out.

But, first, I had to find Dove's father. I had to see for myself what he knew.

Another thing I never thought I'd be daring enough to do.

"Dove," I muttered—half asleep. "Dove." I squinted in the darkness. "Telephone is ringing."

In the bed next to mine, Dove was sleeping a heavy, angry sleep. She was rolling around, thrashing, groaning and talking. The telephone was ringing.

I sighed and almost snorted in my grogginess. Luckily Dove was asleep and no one heard me do it. I'd have been terribly embarrassed if I'd been awake enough. My head throbbed.

I guessed I'd have to answer it—figuring it was Mrs. Frobischer, restless after one of her nightmares.

I fumbled for the phone.

"Hello," My voice was raspy. Ugh, I sounded like Mommy.

"Dove?" A man's voice asked.

"No." I grumbled.

"This is the room 412." The man asked. He had an accent.

"Yes," I sighed, "Dove is sleeping."

"Oh,"

"Who is this?" I growled.

“This is,” the man began, “Hsin Ji.”

I quickly woke up. “Mr. Ji? Where are you?”

“I want to talk to Dove.” Her father barked.

“I’ll wake her.” I said excitedly.

“No, no!” He shouted.

“Why not?” I snapped. “She’s been worried sick about you.”

“Don’t take such a voice with me!” He commanded.

“Excuse me?” I snarled. “How dare you tell me what to do?”

“Silence. If it weren’t for you—your people…” He trailed off.

“What about my people?” I asked sharply. Dove still hadn’t woken up.

“Nothing,” he answered flatly. “Tell my…tell Dove that…”

“What?”

“Is she well?” He said after a moment.

“No. She is not well.” I began and then I said something that I shouldn’t have, “Not since you killed her mother.” I knew it was the wrong thing to say.

“I?” He said softly.

“You did, didn’t you?” I challenged him.

“Tell Dove she will be in my heart,” he said instead of answering. Then, he hung up.

I did not tell Dove any such thing. Why should I have upset her further? I didn’t even tell her that he called. At the time, it seemed like the best choice. But, I know now that you can’t keep a father from his daughter forever.

Hsin Ji

Hateful girl! Devil! She accuses me?

All I want is peace.

I look to make peace with Dove who I raised. And, that girl, she is cruel to me. Maybe it is too late for Dove.

Jade—my baby once. It was not too late to make peace with her.

Who thinks there would be people in a cemetery in the middle of the night?

Who thinks to find a monster asleep on top of grave?

I did not expect it.

But, there he was.

That Rittenhouse man.

I thought he was asleep.

I slept soundly in the limousine for the entire ride back to Marionneaux.

Before we left, we met for a late breakfast in the Toile Room at the hotel. Mrs. Frobischer was already seated at a small table in the corner. It was partially hidden by a very pretty yellow and blue patterned drapery that had been pulled to either side. She smiled at us, but we could tell that she hadn't slept again the night before.

I read a story once about a boy who didn't sleep well. He was wide awake one night and he discovered a hidden door that took him to a different world. He was able to sleep in the other world, but, once he fell asleep there, he wasn't able to get back home. Maybe it was best if Mrs. Frobischer didn't sleep. I didn't know what I'd do if she ever got lost.

At each of our places, she had placed a small box. Both were wrapped in white tissue and tied with a thin, sheer white ribbon.

"What's this?" I asked.

"For you, a little souvenir of our trip," Mrs. Frobischer said with weary cheer. "And for Shelby, a belated birthday present."

Shelby immediately grabbed for her present. Then she let her arm casually rest on the table. I thought it was really mature of her to show restraint like that. Right then, she looked very grown-up in her canary linen pantsuit. Her black hair was pulled back and tied with a peach-colored silk scarf. The fabric flowed over her bandage, but not enough to hide it.

"Go on," Mrs. Frobischer laughed, "It's all right to be excited."

Shelby giggled and looked sixteen again.

She reached for the package again, this time opening it very carefully. Inside was a gray velvet box. Shelby opened it and gasped before taking out a pendant on a white gold chain. The pendant was diamonds set in the shape of an open heart.

"Do you like it?" Mrs. Frobischer asked.

"Oh, very, very much!" Shelby answered, standing to kiss Mrs. Frobischer on the cheek. "It's exactly what I wanted."

"I'm glad," Mrs. Frobischer nodded before passing two fingers over her tired eyelids. "I think it's better suited to a young woman than anything we saw yesterday. You see, George gave me that before we married. I wasn't much older than you at the time. It was the very first gift that he gave me. I brought it with me on our trip to wear myself, but I realized when I opened the box this morning that it really should be worn on a younger neck." She winked.

"I don't know what to say," Shelby said. She was still staring at the pendant. She looked so happy.

One time, I read a book about a really rich girl that had the whole world at her feet. But, see, she wasn't happy. So, she dressed up like a peasant and went out. She met some poor people and helped them with their chores for a day. They didn't know who she was. At the end of the day, they gave her a pretty flower to wear in her hair. Then, she was happy. When I read the book, I pictured the girl's happy face. In my head, she looked just like Shelby looked that morning at breakfast. I wish I'd taken the time to draw a picture of her face just then.

Mrs. Frobischer looked happy, too. Well, she looked happy and a little sad all at the same time.

"You've already said all that's necessary." Mrs. Frobischer nodded. She helped Shelby fasten the clasp at the back of her neck. It did look very pretty on Shelby who seemed to sparkle more than the diamonds.

"Now you," Mrs. Frobischer nodded at me.

I thought about acting as excited as Shelby had, but I didn't want to appear to be fake. I didn't know what to think. No one had ever given me an expensive gift before. I thought about Jade's rubellite pin that Papa had given her and then I remembered the empty jewelry box that I had found in Jade's drawer. Was it from her boyfriend? What was his name? Ahhh, yes…Douglas.

"Hurry up!" Shelby squealed.

I undid the wrapping and found another velvet box—this one a dusty green.

"Mrs. Frobischer," I began, on the verge of tears. I didn't deserve such a thing—whatever it was. I wasn't like Shelby…or Jade. I wasn't pretty. It wasn't even my birthday. Mrs. Frobischer was wrong.

"Go on," Mrs. Frobischer repeated.

I wiped a tear from my cheek and opened the box. Much like Shelby, I gasped when I saw what was inside.

"That was also a gift to me from George." Mrs. Frobischer explained. "That was the last gift he ever gave me before he died. I thought you might like to have it."

I looked back at the box and the ring it held. I had never seen anything like it before. It wasn't gold or silver like all the other rings I had ever seen. It was smooth green stone.

"Is it?" I asked.

Mrs. Frobischer nodded.

"Jade," I sighed.

At the top of it, a bright yellow oval-shaped stone had been set in—rimmed in yellow gold. I took the ring out and held it between my index finger and thumb.

Mrs. Frobischer smiled a tired smile. "The bezel set stone—that's what that kind of setting is called—is a yellow citrine." Mrs. Frobischer stopped and looked closely at me. "Do you like it?"

All I could do was nod.

"I hope it fits," Mrs. Frobischer laughed, "Being as it isn't metal, it can't be sized."

"Should I?" I asked to no one in particular.

"Yes, yes!" Shelby chirped.

I tried the ring on my ring finger, but it was too small for my thick digit. Luckily, it fit perfectly on my pinky.

"Whew," Mrs. Frobischer said exaggeratedly.

I fought back tears, "But, these were gifts from your husband. They're special to you. Why would you give them to us? They're too special."

"Nothing's too special for my girls," Mrs. Frobischer said firmly.

For once I didn't mind being called "girl." Not when it meant that I was somebody's girl after all.

We both hugged Mrs. Frobischer and ordered breakfast. All three of us ate far too much.

After we checked out, we waited under the hotel's canopy for the limousine. As we stood, I spun the ring around my finger.

The family with the white dog came out of the brass and glass revolving door and asked for their car. The dog wagged his tail at me. I smiled. He sat and looked at me—his fur bright white. The valet brought their car around—it, too, was white. They got into their car and as they pulled away from the curb, they looked at me. All three smiled. Maybe they did know what I was thinking. The dog wagged his tail as they drove off. I smiled, too.

Our limo pulled around the corner next and immediately after climbing in, I began to fall asleep while Mrs. Frobischer and Shelby looked out the window.

“Mrs. Frobischer,” I began drowsily. “Thank you.”

“Yes,” Shelby touched the diamond heart. “I still don’t know what to say.”

“Well, you could both do me a favor,” Mrs. Frobischer said.

“Anything,” Shelby answered.

“Please call me Rosa.”

“Rosa,” I repeated before I fell fast asleep.

Shelby Halifax

I watched Dove sleep as we rode back to Marionneaux. She wasn't twitching and mumbling as she had the night before. I was glad of that. I thought about waking her up when she started to drool a little because it sure wasn't the most lady-like thing in the world, but I didn't want to bother her.

She looked so peaceful leaning against the limousine's window. She seemed pretty. Yes, pretty. Why had I never noticed that before? I wished I could be as pretty as Dove.

I felt, in fact, quite ugly. I should have told Dove that her father had called the hotel the night before. I decided I would make it up to her somehow. It's not like I lied to her about it or anything. I just didn't tell her. There's a difference. It didn't make me like Mommy. I did it for a reason. So, why was that all I could think about?

Mrs. Frobischer—Rosa—seemed lost in her own thoughts, too. We didn't really talk at all for most of the ride. It was nice not to talk. I never thought I'd enjoy being quiet. But, sometimes, quiet is nice, too. Sometimes if it's quiet enough, you can hear things without people having to talk.

Mrs.—Rosa—looked a little worried. I didn't know how to thank her for the beautiful pendant she had given me. Maybe I didn't have to—like she said.

We arrived in Marionneaux too quickly. I was in no hurry to get home and M—Rosa—sensed that. She invited me back to her little house with her and Dove. We were to stop by her bookstore first. She told us that a window had been broken and she wanted to make sure that it had been fixed.

As we drove up D'Arbonne Street, Rosa looked out the window at the Rittenhouse estate high atop La Colline Cramoisie.

"Would you girls mind if I made a quick trip?" she asked.

Dove, who had finally awakened, said that she didn't. I agreed.

The limo would drop us off at the store and Rosa was to run an errand. She didn't tell us what. And, we didn't feel the need to ask.

Once Rosa looked at the window and found that it had been fixed to her liking, she got back in the car. We waited for her in the empty bookstore. It was late Sunday afternoon and D'Arbonne Street was quiet and empty.

I looked over at my usual place at the wooden table by the magazine racks. I didn't feel much like thumbing through any magazines. None of it seemed important. Rosa said it was because, I "no longer felt the call to immediate triviality." She was right, but there was more.

Really, I had too many questions and the answers wouldn't be found in magazine articles about hairstyles. My eyes followed the rows of books that stretched to the back wall of the shop. All those words…maybe they would tell me what I wanted to hear.

I looked at Dove and thought about telling her about her father's phone call. She actually looked relaxed and happy. Why ruin it? See, I really did have a reason.

"You gonna call your boyfriend?" Dove teased me. I liked seeing her so comfortable, even if she was picking on me.

"Averill isn't my boyfriend!" I played along with her. She did remind me, though. Averill had asked me to call him when we got home.

"Maybe I didn't mean Averill."

"How many boyfriends do you think I have?"

Then, she looked worried like she just remembered that we had a science test or something that she forgot to study for.

"I want to go in the backroom for a second. Wanna come?" She asked.

"Sure. What for?"

"I just want to have a look at some of Jade's stuff." She said softly.

I had forgotten that we brought Jade's things over from the Ji's house.

"Okay," I said.

We went to the back and Dove opened one of the three small cardboard boxes. She got a funny look on her face.

"Dove?"

"Someone's been in this box," She said in a tiny whisper.

She quickly began to rummage through the contents of the box.

"Where are they?" She panted.

"Where are what?" I asked nervously.

"The letters. Jade's letters!" Dove wheezed.

"I don't know. Which letters?" I asked, beginning to feel quite frightened.

"From that man—her boyfriend! They're gone!" Dove dumped the contents of the box on the floor and sat down next to the pile—frantically searching.

"I don't know," I repeated. "What did they say?"

"I never read them," Dove gasped. "Not really—just enough to tell they were from a man. He signed them, 'love…Douglas.'"

I felt very cold.

"Douglas? Did he sign his last name?" I asked shrilly.

"No," Dove stopped looking through the things on the floor, "Why?"

"It's just," I said, trying to catch my breath, "My father's name is Douglas."

V
Facets and Shells

Douglas Halifax

Jade and I never met at the mansion. She was always afraid that Old Lady Rittenhouse would catch us. I can't say as though I blamed her. Just the very thought of Amelia Rittenhouse makes me feel edgy to this day.

When I was a boy, my friends and I used to walk by that old gray husk of a house on La Colline Cramoisie and peer through the wrought iron bars of the fence. We'd take turns making up stories about the disgusting creatures inside. Of course, everyone had heard the rumors about the missing brother. In our childish minds, he was a combination Phantom of the Opera and Frankenstein's Monster—lumbering absently around Marionneaux looking for his lover's finger or something. As I grew up, I had dismissed the existence of Unwin Rittenhouse as fantasy. I had come to find I was wrong. And, also I had come to realize that the creature we invented in our boyish snickering wasn't too far from the truth.

One feeling I never could shake, no matter how old I got, was the idea that Amelia Rittenhouse was a witch—a real caldron-stirring, wart-growing, pointy-hat-wearing witch complete with giant crystal ball, green skin and a basket for Toto. Even as a grown man—a doctor no less—every time I walked to the crest of La Colline Cramoisie, I felt a shiver go up my spine when I reached the Rittenhouse place. Now, I realize that it was a premonition of things to come.

That's why I was particularly upset when Jade told me she was going to live there. I didn't want her around that spooky woman. I got a bad feeling about it. Turns out, I was right.

At first, when she told me she was moving out of her parents' house, I was elated—I would finally be able to be alone with her. I thought that maybe we could recapture all of the time we had lost. I couldn't control my joy—I would finally be able to escape Voletta again. She'd never divorce me. In a way that was good. I didn't relish the idea of leaving Shelby to be raised by her mother. Voletta—sober—was always the cruelest living thing I had ever met. But, as she began to drink more, she surpassed even herself on the evil scale. She takes after her parents.

I met Voletta when I was seventeen. She was stunning! Her hair was the color of onyx and just as shiny. Her skin was flawless. She was bright and funny—she could talk to me about anything from art to football and seemed to love the same things I did. She also seemed to love me, too. I came to realize shortly after we married that she could have cared less which man she took to the altar as long as he came from a good family and had a good earning potential. I fit the bill. And, I paid for it.

We married when I was twenty-one. Looking back, I'm surprised that she was able to keep the charade of pleasantness going for that long. I'm also surprised that I was so stupid as to fall for it. Within a year of our marriage, we were sleeping in separate rooms. That's when she bleached her hair. I had no choice but to move to my own room. She used to hit me in my sleep! She'd wake me up by slapping my bare shoulder and give me the litany of my faults. I tried to please her, I really did. I tried to be the man she wanted me to be. I had honestly begun to think that she was right—that I was the problem.

One afternoon a week, I left the hospital with some of the other guys and went to lunch. These were my favorite times—just me and people that actually liked me. I was able to smile and laugh. I felt like a man—no, not just a man. I felt like a human. We would always drive to the old Marionneaux Square and walk around—just being jerks and making jokes—always looking for a place to eat.

I had seen Jade on D'Arbonne Street several times. One of the guys had elbowed me in the stomach and pointed her out. She had just turned eighteen and was the most strikingly beautiful creature I had ever seen in my life. Far, far more beautiful than Voletta because Jade's beauty was real—it came from inside her.

So, on our afternoons out, the guys and I would always look for the "china doll" as they called her.

One day, she knew we were following her—making stupid comments under our breath and laughing like schoolboys. She sure did surprise us.

She turned right around and said, "You naughty men! You stop it, right now." She even stamped her little foot on the pavement. Well, I was gone.

Some of the other guys—can you imagine, grown, married, doctors acting like this—whooped and hollered and laughed. One little pout from Jade stopped all that.

She winked and then said, "You're all bad men, but I don't mind. I like you."

Suddenly, we all turned into big, stupid babies. She pointed at me; "I like you best of all."

She then turned and walked away. Of course, we followed her. She went to her parents' restaurant. So, that became our new weekly lunch spot.

I knew that her father didn't care for my flirting with Jade. I saw the upset looks he was giving me and I heard him reprimand Jade several times. But, it didn't stop us. I wish it had. Jade would still be alive, if it had.

One afternoon, the guys couldn't join me, so I went to the place by myself. After getting the evil eye from Hsin during the whole meal, I left. As I walked back to my car, I heard Jade come running out. "You forgot your doggy bag." She called.

I hadn't had a doggy bag. I didn't even have a dog. But, I figured, "What the hell?"

She handed the greasy sack to me and said softly, "I love you, Dr. Halifax."

I loved her, too.

The bag held more than moo shi pork. It had a note, telling me to meet her at 7:00 PM at the Bayou Vin Atténué. I told Voletta that I had a late shift and I met Jade as she had instructed. She stood waiting for me at the bayou dressed in a thin gown of pale green silk that fluttered in the breeze like waves on water. Her dark hair fell over her shoulders and set off her face like a portrait in oil. Framed by the gnarled oaks—their limbs dripping with Spanish moss, she looked something like a fairy welcoming me to some strange, beautiful, new land. She was perfection.

That night, Jade and I belonged to one another completely. I knew I was hers forever.

We met like that many, many times. She always worried that her mother and father were suspicious. I always worried about Voletta. Then, Voletta declared that she wanted a baby. She told me that if I wouldn't or couldn't give her one, she'd find a real man who could. I don't like to be challenged. The result was Shelby. So, I can't really say that I'm sorry I gave in to her. But, I didn't realize that once Voletta and I shared a child, I'd be tied to her in this hell forever.

I also didn't realize that I would soon be tied to Jade in the same way.

Unfortunately, Jade's mother and father found out that she was pregnant before I did. I thought that Hsin would kill Jade, he was so angry. Niu just shrieked a lot. I didn't want Voletta to find out. Hsin told me that he wouldn't tell my wife if I paid him the right amount. If I did that, he would take care of everything.

I don't know how I managed it without Voletta finding out. Her own pregnancy, I think, made her slightly more self-absorbed than usual—if possible—and keeping track of my bankbook took a back seat to complaining to her mother about how badly her ankles hurt.

However, I got my hands on the sum he requested and did as Hsin Ji wanted. I wish I hadn't. It wasn't the money—it was the price of losing Jade. I was forbidden to see Jade ever again. And I didn't. But, even that wasn't the dearest price. That was losing my other child.

I figured that when I got the news that Jade was finally moving out of her parents' place—after a decade and a half, we could be together again. This time, we would be more careful. We would meet in even more secrecy—we would avoid that Rittenhouse woman and her witchiness.

I could not believe that so much time had past when we finally met again at the bayou. She wore the same dress—the thin green fabric caressing her body as it rippled in the wind. That night, I gave her the pearl earrings. She opened the box greedily—as a child might. Again, she was perfection. Again, we were one.

Again, I lost her. This time for good.

That's what I think about when I steal a moment away from Voletta's drunken tirades. On those rare moments when I can sit on the patio and smoke a cigar, I look further up the hill at that gray reliquary and I think about Jade, our child, all the lost lives, all the lost opportunities. Shelby—all that she has missed.

And, yes, I still think Amelia Rittenhouse is a witch.

Amelia Rittenhouse

I heard the knock at the door. *They're still after you.* There had been several over the past few days. I ignored all of them. *You can't ignore them forever, Amelia.* Agathe would have answered the door. But, Agathe was gone—a vacant shell that once was my daughter.

Why had I never shown one bit of motherly affection toward her? *She didn't deserve it.*

She didn't deserve my affection. *No, she deserved better.*

No, she proved to be too much like her father. She had his eyes, his face, his hair. His anger.

Or was it my anger?

Some couples should not breed. We were such a pairing.

The very second I first saw her—bloody and pinched—her shrieks piercing my soul, I knew she was her father's. She even smelled of him. I toyed with the idea of keeping her. I had a heart then. But, no. She could not stay. There would be too many questions. Father helped. He did everything that was needed. In fact, I did not ever have to see her again if I hadn't wanted to. But, I had to have one last look. *Amelia, the baby martyr.* I had to give her something. I was generous. I gave her two things—a name and a piece of her history. My mother's name and her father's tune. Agathe—my father sighed as he bundled her up in a gray blanket. I knew it hurt him to lose two women of the same name. He gave her something, too. He gave her a chance.

A knock on the door. *Don't open it!*

Agathe was sent to the orphanage on Lake Pontchartrain. After a few years, when she proved to be un-adoptable, I arranged for her to leave the orphanage and to be sent anonymously to the home of a former colleague of father's in New Orleans—another member of the jewel trade.
How sweet. How motherly.

They were a very respectable family. Agathe would be raised with their own daughter. She was given a last name—Le Banni. How ironic. Sent to that new home, she finally had a new chance, a new life. But, much like her father, she sought me out and seduced me. And, much like I had with her father, I took her in. Again, I was defeated by force.

A knock on the door. No one may enter. *Leave us!*

My own father was as fine a man as could be. He took us away immediately after I had given birth to Agathe—the day after she was taken to the orphanage. Father tried to take my mind off of things. He loved his distractions. Took me away—me and Unwin. We went as far from Marionneaux as was possible. China. Father searched the mines. What about Unwin and me? Did we find what we searched for? Did it find us? Something always finds us. *Finds you and consumes you!*

A knock on the door—you can't find me. *It's him, old girl. Don't let him in. Don't let him find you!*

Agathe found me.

From China, Unwin came home with his love. I came home with my drink. Father did not come home.

Agathe wanted to come home.

A knock on the door. It isn't Agathe. She's not coming home. She never should have, never could have. There was no home to which to come. She should have stayed in New Orleans. I should never have let her return. But, someone needed to watch Unwin in my absence and keeping a girl was difficult.

After a time, they always ran off—too much pressure to be alone with Unwin. Someone needed to stay with him, someone I could trust to stay permanently. Who better than family—his niece? I thought she would have been loyal. I was wrong to expect a return on nothing. *Ugly, ugly, bitch! Of course you were wrong. You're always wrong.*

Had it been my fault that she was killed? I threw her as far from Marionneaux as possible. I threw her and I ran. I stumbled. Prostrate, I shall always run. *That's funny.*

And, then they would run to me.

A knock on the door. It isn't Agathe.

It isn't Unwin.

You know who it is! You know it's not Unwin.

Unwin—He wouldn't knock. He would come in. He would lift me up and carry me. Just as we did when we were children. *When was that, Amelia?* Hide and Seek. I would run, he would chase me—laughing, catching me and lifting me up, spinning me around. I wouldn't have to run anymore. I should never have run from him. Hide and Seek.

A knock on the door. It isn't Unwin.

He does not want to come home.

I would forever be prostrate.

If Unwin returned, would he speak to me? I hadn't heard his voice in forty years. Or has it been seventy. No, it's been forty. The day he escaped forty years ago—I heard his voice. He spoke. But, not to me. He spoke to Mingmei. To her grave…to her shell.

He wouldn't speak to me. *That's why you have us, Amelia.*

Agathe had called me in a panic. She hadn't been with Unwin long. She had no idea where he might have been. She couldn't find him. I rushed back from California and found him immediately. I was glad I rushed or I would not have heard him speak that one last time.

"I love you," he cried to her, "I love you. Why don't you speak to me?"

She didn't speak. And, afterwards neither did he.

His liquid eyes lost their shimmer. Thirty years of hope were dashed. Perhaps, perhaps, perhaps he hadn't really seen his love die. He had convinced himself it wasn't true. He had convinced himself that she had lived, had grown older while he was locked away in this house. He ran from one prison to another that day.

I brought him home again. And, I stayed with him. I thought that perhaps my presence along with Agathe's would be all that was needed to sustain him.

I spoke to him—to his shell. He didn't speak. And, neither will I. *Let the silence protect you, Amelia. We mean you no harm.*

A knock on the door. It isn't for me.

There's a beauty in this silence that I had not ever noticed before. *Of course.* Could this have been what Unwin has known since I brought him back and locked him away? Was it the awakening in Oz? This color is new to me. So much more than red. There's gold, there's blue, there's violet and green—all in this silence. All sparkling above me. And, the floor is so smooth beneath my back. Why would I want to move? It's a blessing. My reward. My mind may still run, but my body will not. I will not run.

A knock on the door. It doesn't matter.

Oh, no. I will not be defeated—not this time. I cannot be defeated now! I am impenetrable. Nothing can touch me. I will not be reached!

The door is opening. Unwin?

No, it isn't my brother.

It's him. Agathe's father.

He's speaking to me.

I will not answer.

He will not argue with me.

Don't let him tell! Don't let him tell! Amelia, don't let him tell!

He can't hurt me now!

He peers down at me.

My mind shouts, my mouth is still. "Daughter killer! Mothers and daughters!" He cannot deny it because he doesn't hear me. "You cannot kill me!" He cannot. How could he? I will not be defeated. He had killed me long ago. He had killed Unwin then, too. He could not defeat us again.

He kneels next to me.

I remember his voice, "Shall I tell them, Amelia?"

Don't let him tell!

I won't let him.

Does it matter, fool? Fool!

I had been a fool then, I had told him, "No." I let him defeat me. Twice! And, in the process I failed. I will not fail again.

He touches me. Not so beautiful now am I? Or was I ever? *Never.*

Will you slice me as you did the others? Come on, I'm ready. You can cut my body all you want. You cannot cut my mind. You never could! I'm stronger than my brother. You cannot cut my spirit. That, you had torn years ago. My spirit was never as strong as Unwin's.

He speaks, "I'm sorry."

You're not.

He's not! Throw him out! Bar the door!

"I'm sorry about Agathe."

You're not.

Be calm, don't let him hurt us…you.

"I would not let her tell them." He hisses.

I look at him. Once he was so handsome. He had courted me gently once—until he grew impatient. He seemed so much younger than I at the time. Now, he just seems older. Now, I am without age. I am part of the light now.

"I wanted you to know. I'm sorry."

No, you're not.

He's gone. He's left me to the sparkle of the crystals above me. He's left me to my heaven. He's left me to my silence. *He's gone. Rest, now.* The floor is so smooth on my back.

The chandeliers shimmer and spark.

So much color.

NO! *No!* A shadow. Don't take my light!

An angel?

Have they come for me?

Angels would not come for you, Amelia.

No, it's not an angel. I have no claim to a real heaven.

She's no angel.

It's Rosa Frobischer.

A shadow from my past. One of many.

Rosa.

I wasn't entirely comfortable leaving the girls at the bookstore alone. I worried that whomever had broken in would come back.

Eulabel and Yolanda had done an excellent job making sure the window was repaired. As I was leaving, I did a quick scan of the store—nothing too deliberate so as not to upset the girls. I couldn't see that anything was out of place. But, Marionneaux wasn't the sort of town that was prone to random acts of vandalism. Murder, apparently, yes, but not just windows broken for no reason. Someone had gotten into my bookstore because they wanted something. I wondered if they got whatever it was that they were seeking.

I made a hasty exit and got back into the limousine, asking the driver to bring me to the mansion at thc top of La Colline Cramoisie. He did so without question or hesitation. I couldn't help but think about the cab driver that brought me from New Orleans to Marionneaux when I first returned to Louisiana. What a ride that was. I had to laugh. There was no comparison.

On the way up D'Arbonne Street toward La Colline Cramoisie, I spotted Eulabel walking toward the café. I asked the driver to pull over.

"Eulabel!" I shouted out the window. She seemed startled at first. And, then recognizing me came over to the car.

"Look at you, Miss Hollywood Rich Lady!" She laughed with her drumbeat chortle. Something about her made me feel safe.

"Get in," I said.

She hesitated, but did as I requested. "I don't think I've ever been in one of these," She laughed. "Is there a bar?"

I nodded that there was and pointed in its direction.

"Well, don't I feel like Miss Rita Hayworth!" He voice was a tattoo and she mimicked a beauty queen wave. I saw the driver smile.

She looked squarely at me. "You know her?"

"Who?" I asked distractedly.

"Hayworth!" She sighed.

"Yes," I nodded, "I met her a few times."

"What was she like?"

"Beautiful." I shrugged.

"What else?"

"That was about it," I shrugged again.

She laughed—that staccato laugh.

I smiled.

"Thanks for making sure the window was fixed," I said.

She frowned. "Mrs. F. I didn't tell you the whole story."

I nodded. I had suspected as much.

"That night," She took a deep breath, "I think someone looked in some of the boxes in the back."

"That's odd," I said, "Nothing but books back there. You don't suppose it was some desperate, but oddly literate criminal?"

She laughed. "No Mrs. F. Not book boxes. Stuff boxes."

"Oh," I said sharply, remembering the boxes of Jade's things that I let Dove keep in the back room.

"I don't think they took nothin'," She said.

"Well, we'll see," I sighed, suddenly in a hurry to get back to Dove and Shelby. But, I had to finish the journey I had already started first.

"Don't worry about it, Eulabel," I continued.

She inhaled deeply. I couldn't tell if it was out of relief or out of a need for oxygenated courage.

"There's more," She began.

I raised my eyebrows and pressed my lips together. "Go on."

"When I went to look at the broken window, I saw…" She stopped.

"What?" I said patiently.

"The Loch Ness Monster," She said with a funny grin.

"Pardon me," I asked, pushing my head forward as if being somewhat closer, I could understand better.

"You know…the Onion." She said again—her cheeks plump with amusement.

I shook my head and was about to say that I did not, but suddenly, "Oh, Unwin Rittenhouse." I tried to sound calm. "You don't think…"

"No, I don't. I mean, da man is like seven hundred years old." She laughed.

"He's only about five years older than me," I said sarcastically—wondering how I knew that.

The smile left her face, "I guess, me too, come ta think of it."

We both laughed.

"I'll get to the bottom of it," I said as confidently as I could.

"How you figure?" She asked with wide eyes.

"I'm on my way up there now," I pointed up the hill.

"To the Rittenhouse place?" She asked loudly.

"Yes," I nodded.

"By yourself?"

"Yes." Odd to say, but I was going by myself. Who could have imagined?

"Oh, lordy, woman. I'm going wit' you." She said firmly.

"I don't know that Amelia Rittenhouse will speak very freely if you're there," I said honestly, adding, "Only because you're a stranger and she's so…"

"Screwed up?"

We both laughed again. I knew I shouldn't, but I couldn't help myself. Having Eulabel around was like going to a funeral with Jimmy Durante—which I have done—and which is a strange and impossible thing to get through without something of a giggle.

I shook my head, "That isn't what I was going to say."

"I'll wait in the car," She said, stroking the velvet bench. "But, Mrs. F., I sure would feel better if you didn't go alone."

I looked out the window, at my watch, at the driver and finally back to Eulabel. "All right." I nodded. "I don't think I could say 'no' to you if I wanted to."

"No, you could not," Eulabel grinned. "I have that way about me."

I laughed, "Between you and me, I'm glad not to go alone."

"Well, I coulda gone and guessed that!"

I smiled, "Driver." I pointed to the top of La Colline Cramoisie. He drove on, Eulabel and I looked out the windows. There were an unusual number of tourists on the hill that evening—strolling along, looking at the grand houses. Some of the faces were familiar, others were not. Was that Hsin Ji? No, it couldn't have been. It was just a man enjoying a summer evening. It was nice weather for a stroll.

As we drove toward the Rittenhouse estate, we passed the Halifax house and spotted rotund Marie L'Ebène chugging along on her scooter up the banquette to her daughter's house. She was being followed at a close distance by Augustin. They apparently thought it was a nice time for a stroll, too. I shivered. I hadn't really seen Augustin L'Ebène since the night of the one and only dance to which he escorted me. I had only seen him at a distance across the street the day after Jade had been killed. But, seeing his face made me feel as though I was sixteen again. It wasn't a good feeling.

The cold glint of his eyes shone even from several feet away. Thank God, Shelby hadn't inherited that glint, the way Voletta had. Even sunken and withered with age as he was, he still looked very much as he did the night of that dance. The event was a very fuzzy memory, but something about seeing Augustin's face again—even at a distance—brought back a flash of it.

I remembered being unhappy—standing in my pomegranate dress in the middle of the high school gymnasium. I was trying to dance, but Augustin kept pawing me—breathing heavily on me—making my neck feel damp. I felt a shiver of irritation in my arms as I remembered. I kept telling him to keep his hands to himself, but he wasn't. I remembered feeling trapped and suffocated.

I squeezed my eyes tightly shut—trying to ignore the crimson slash I saw behind the lids—I opened them again and looked first at Eulabel and then over my shoulder at the back of Marie and Augustin. I suddenly felt glad that Shelby hadn't gone right home. At least she could avoid a visit with her grandmother and grandfather.

"You got that funny look again," Eulabel said. She didn't smile.

"It's just Augustin L'Ebène," I pointed over my shoulder with my thumb.

"Oh him. He's a creep," She said flatly.

"Yes," I nodded. "He took me to a dance once. He was…aggressive."

She nodded, "The older boys always are."

The limousine stopped outside the gates of the Rittenhouse mansion.

"I won't be but a few minutes." I said as I waited for the driver to open the door.

"If you're not the hell outta there in ten, I'm comin' in after ya." Eulabel said. She wasn't kidding.

Little did either of us know, I would hardly need ten minutes.

I opened the creaky gate and walked up to the steps, pausing at the path to the side garden and remembering Agathe as I had seen her that first day.

She wears her hope like diamonds
All colors save but one
Diana's orb will free us
Reflected in the sun.

I suddenly felt as though I was going to vomit and began to chew my bottom lip.

I wouldn't have to fight with myself about whether or not to ring the bell that last time.

I walked up the front steps and noticed that one side of the double front doors was open. Light streamed out into the nascent nightfall. Someone had finally turned on those three massive chandeliers—the facets of their prisms shot color out the crack between the doors.

Why was the door open?

I pushed it further ajar and walked slowly inside.

I would get no answers that night.

Amelia Rittenhouse lay on the floor—stiffly—looking very much like some misplaced burial statue from Westminster Abbey—some stone effigy of a recumbent queen lying atop her sarcophagus.

I walked as quickly as I could to her side. The features of her face had slipped on one side, the corner of her mouth pulled down in an unsettling, permanent grimace. Her eyes were open. She blinked.

She was alive.

"Oh God! I'll call for help," I said.

She didn't answer.

I hurried back to the limo, feeling every bit of my eighty-six years in my legs.

"Oh, no, no, no," Eulabel was shouting at me through the open limousine door, "What's happened?"

"Amelia," I panted. "I think she's had a stroke."

We called the paramedics.

I felt very deeply sorry for Amelia as strange and awful as she had been to me. I remembered the young woman—drunk and rowdy—dancing her life away, dripping in sequins. The heiress to a jewel fortune in sequins—that image summed up Amelia Rittenhouse perfectly.

Seeing her like that on the floor made me realize that she wasn't as hardened as I had thought—as she thought, either.

She wasn't invincible.

And, the worst part was that she was alone. She had no daughter to care for her—and, no brother. She had nothing but her art collection and her silence.

I was awake. But, I didn't open my eyes. With them closed, I could make believe I was sleeping. I could make believe…

But, the light had become too bright and it cut through my eyelids, making all my thoughts glow red. I was thinking of Mingmei.

I did not want to open my eyes. I thought only of Mingmei.

She was beneath me…sleeping…always sleeping in her box. She was safe from the light.

How funny, I first saw her in the light—my Mingmei. Mingmei Sun. How funny. I saw her in a garden—holding her baby. They were both so beautiful.

She looked—oh, she looked like a doll, like a lovely puppet. She was so bright and smooth. So beautiful.

I fell in love with her immediately.

She smiled at me. She smiled at ME!

I talked to her. But, she did not speak English. She knew I loved her. She could tell—not by my words. She could tell by my eyes. She held the baby up for me to see. She said, "Niu." She let me hold the baby.

I wanted them both. They would be my family.

I ran to Father like a little boy. I told him about the girl and her baby. He laughed at me. Or maybe he was laughing out of a shared joy—laughing for me. I couldn't tell.

But, I went back anyway.

She explained to me with her hands and her eyes. Her husband was dead. She was alone except for Niu.

Niu was sleeping now, too. Right next to us in her own box.

I asked Mingmei if she wanted to come home with me and my father and Amelia. She may not have known the words, but she knew what I meant and she said yes.

Father said, "No." He acted as if I had asked to keep a stray kitty or puppy dog that I had found.

But, father died.

I took Mingmei home with us. She left China and came all the way back with us. She and the baby. It wasn't easy, but we got all the papers we needed. She was mine. We would be married.

She stayed with me and Amelia in the house. Oh, it was so beautiful then—beautiful because of her, because of Mingmei.

We were to be married. The night before…

No, no, no, no, no!

The night before…

She wanted to go swimming. She wanted to swim with me.

I had to make calls. Father was dead, so someone had to make calls. Amelia was too sad to make calls. She didn't care about the business then. I didn't either, but I had to. I was the man of the house. That's what father had said before he died. He told me to take care of everything…the business, Amelia, the house. I wanted to. I wanted to take care of Mingmei and Niu, too.

I would have.

She wanted to swim. A bayou is no place to swim. But, she liked it. She pointed over the terrace to the bayou.

"Fine, fine," I nodded. "I'll meet you there when I'm done."

I kissed her on the cheek.

It was so soft. And, she was so beautiful. She was perfect. She loved me so much. More than Amelia did. She even wore the necklace I gave her. Beautiful garnets—the best from our supply. All those red stones—all those diamonds—none of it was as beautiful as she was.

She was dead when I got there.

Lord, please, help me! She was dead when I got there! She was!

I didn't know what to do with the baby.

Amelia would know.

Amelia would take care of Niu. She promised.

But, Amelia fooled me. She locked me in my rooms. She told me that everyone would think I killed Mingmei. She told me she had to protect me.

She wouldn't let me tell her. She wouldn't let me explain. I couldn't tell her what had happened. I couldn't tell her that I had found Mingmei. She wouldn't let me. She wouldn't let me tell about Rosa. Poor Rosa.

Why didn't she let me talk? She always talks so much. I guess she talks for both of us. I don't have to anymore. Amelia talks too much.

That was all over. It was all finished and there I was on some bright morning—an old, old man—finally with Mingmei again. Only Mingmei was in her grave. It was easy to pretend that we were cuddled up together even though she was beneath the stone. If I imagined really hard—she was alive and we were both still young. We were snuggling with the baby next to us. She was, too…

The sun was getting hot. Too hot for a sick old man in a cemetery. Too hot to be cuddling on a grave. Too hot to pretend I wasn't.

I opened my eyes.

Mingmei was gone again. And, so was Niu.

But, there was Niu's husband. He's not a nice man. He has greedy eyes.

He was watching me.

I wonder how long he had been there.

I tried to shut my eyes again.

My arm! My arm! He grabbed my arm so hard and twisted it. He pulled me to the ground.

“Hello Monster,” He said. Mean, mean man.

He made me cry.

“You’re hurting me!” I spoke! After forty years I spoke! Pity it had to be in pain. Pity it had to be to him.

He made me go with him.

And, he shut me away. Just like Amelia.

She never really wanted to protect me

Eulabel Watkins

That night when Mrs. F. come runnin' out of that old house, I thought my heart was gonna stop. Who knew if that old witch had said somethin' mean? Mrs. F. isn't as tough as she'd like ya to think. And, then I thought that maybe the Rittenhouse woman attacked my old Hollywood lady friend.

I had to hold myself up in the seat I was shakin' so hard.

But, then Mrs. F. says that Amelia Rittenhouse had a stroke or something. So, the driver man calls the police and the ambulance people.

She and I and the driver go into the house. And, there's that old Rittenhouse just lyin' on the floor like she's dead or somethin'. I can tell you, I thought I was just gonna scream. Or laugh.

Mrs. F. tries to talk to her, but old Amelia ain't answerin'. She ain't even movin.'

Her face is all pulled down and she looks like half of her is melting. She don't really even look like a person. She looks like one of them empty shells you find on the beach.

I guess it was a stroke after all. I have no idea how long she been lyin' there. By the looks of it and the smells of it, it could have been several days.

That's what happens when you're all alone—no one to remember you—when you're alive or when you're dead.

Hsin Ji

Did Monster think I not remember? Did he think I would not know him? The monster. The downfall of all of our family. If he had left Mingmei in China seventy years ago, everything would be different.

It can still be different.

I can still fix things. I can get that Douglas to pay again. I can make sure no one finds out.

I should never have hit Dove. Her mother's sins—not her fault. Dove should have a chance.

I will start by putting everything where it belongs.

I can make it different for Dove.

Yes, I will start with Douglas Halifax.

"Your father's name is Douglas?" I asked, still kneeling on the floor among the scatters of Jade's few remaining belongings.

Shelby nodded. Her face was a blank.

We were silent for a moment. Shelby kneeled next to me—the knees of her pants had gotten dirty on the floor of the storeroom. She didn't even try to brush them off when she stood. I wanted to do it for her, but she didn't seem to care.

"Lots of men are named Douglas," I said.

"Lots of men in Marionneaux?" She asked me in a scary kind of emotionless way.

"I'm sure there's more than one Douglas." I nodded. "The letters didn't have a last name."

Shelby turned away from me.

"Besides, the letters were written recently, I would guess. Your father has been married to your mother for how long?"

"Eighteen years next month," She answered—still strangely emotionless.

"So, Jade's boyfriend couldn't have been your father." I tried to answer with authority.

"Married men don't have girlfriends?" She asked with a little sadness and sorrow in her voice. I was glad, at least, to hear some feeling from her no matter what it was.

I sighed. She had me there. "Yes, they do sometimes. But, not nice men like your father."

"You've met my mother," Shelby moaned. She was more like herself. "Nice men who are married to nice women don't cheat. Nice men married to women like my mother, well…"

"How old is your father?" I asked.

"I dunno," Shelby said distractedly, "I think he's about forty. Why?"

"Well, Jade was thirty three when she died." I began, "Your father is almost ten years older. I'm sure her boyfriend was a man her own age."

"Yea, it would be just plain weird for a married man to have an affair with a younger woman," Shelby hissed.

"Now, you're being mean," I said, sinking back down to the floor. "You're acting like…" I stopped myself.

"Like my mother!" Shelby shouted.

I didn't answer.

She began to cry and sat back down on the floor next to me.

"I'm sorry," She said finally. "I'm just scared."

"Me too." I said.

"You too...what?" She asked.

"Sorry and scared," I said softly.

We both giggled.

As Shelby wiped her eyes, I noticed how tired she looked. The bandage wrapped around her skull didn't help.

"You know," I said cheerfully, "Your dad is a really nice guy."

Shelby nodded, "Yeah, most of the time. Sometimes Mommy makes him so crazy that he shouts at me or, worse, ignores me. But, all in all, he's a nice guy."

We sat in silence again.

I didn't like the feeling. I looked at the ring that Rosa had given me—the citrine sparkled in the light of the bare bulb over our heads. Tiny bursts of white and yellow glinted off the facets in the stone and danced against the surface of the jade that surrounded it.

"I wonder who took Jade's letters," Shelby said after a minute.

"Whoever killed her, I guess." I sighed.

"I guess," Shelby agreed, looking worried for a moment and holding the diamond heart pendant in between her thumb and the edge of her hand.

"Rosa's birthday gift to you is very pretty," I said, trying to change the subject.

"Yes," Shelby smiled.

"Is your party still tomorrow?" I asked.

"I think so," Shelby answered, "That's what Mommy said last time we talked. You're coming right?"

"Of course!" I laughed.

"Good. I need you there." Shelby said nervously.

"I wouldn't miss it," I patted her shoulder.

She helped me clean up the mess I had made. We carefully packed Jade's things up again.

Shelby chuckled.

"What?" I asked—smiling in anticipation of whatever she might say.

"It's funny. You wished your dad was more like mine."

I nodded.

"I wish my mom was…" Shelby stopped.

I was afraid for a moment that she was going to say she wished her mother were more like mine—mute or dead.

"Was more like Mrs. Frobischer." She said finally. And then corrected herself, "Rosa."

“Me too,” I nodded.

We went into the bookstore and sat at the table by the magazine racks. We didn’t look at anything. We just waited for Rosa.

Eulabel, the driver and I waited until the paramedics took Amelia Rittenhouse away. I was tempted to go to the hospital with them. But, what right did I have to do so? I was sad for her. But, also for Agathe, Jade, Dove, Niu and even Shelby.

We would never get the answers we needed from her.

We dropped Eulabel at her house and the driver took me slowly back to D'Arbonne Street.

I couldn't help but think about Augustin L'Ebène. I could almost feel his sticky breath on the back of my neck. How different he was than George. George was gentle and loving—even in his moments of rage. Those moments were all directed inwardly. He never took his frustration out on me.

George and I had only quarreled once. Our maid had dropped and dented one of his awards. It wasn't even a major award—some small honor from this guild or that. I didn't bother mentioning it to him at the time. He was engrossed in writing a new picture. I didn't want to interrupt him—or upset him. And, knowing how much he valued all of his trophies, I thought I would spare him the disturbance until the script was finished. It must have slipped my mind or perhaps I made it slip my mind. But, months after he had finished the script—months after the picture had both begun and finished shooting—he found out.

We had hosted a small cocktail party the evening of the film's premiere. It was a quiet pre-show gathering of talent from the picture. Afterwards, we would all file into our respective vehicles for our grand entrance.

George was showing off his multiple trophies—myself included. We had all gone into his study and he was explaining the significance of this statuette versus that loving cup versus that avant-garde representation of the three muses. When he picked up the trophy that had been dented, my heart jumped.

He turned to Marlon Brando and began his acceptance speech over again. Brando, in typical fashion belched out, "Yeah, Georgie, that's a pretty one, but what's with the big crater in its ass?"

George's face turned to granite. And, then melted in embarrassment.

It was the only time he ever really shouted at me. And, unfortunately, it was in a room full of people. He made me promise never to keep anything from him again.

I swore that day I'd never keep another secret.

I had since broken that promise. I needed to tell Dove that I knew someone had gotten into Jade's things. And, I needed to do it before she noticed for herself.

Dove and I sat together and waited for Rosa. I felt like I did right before I went on stage the time I was in the school's beauty pageant. At least Dove seemed comfortable. I tried not to let my nervousness show.

I wondered if my father was the Douglas that had signed those letters to Dove's sister. I convinced myself that Dove was right. I convinced myself that it couldn't have been.

Averill Cage once told me that he thought his dad had a mistress in New Orleans. He said that it's very common for rich men to keep another woman on the side. Averill seems to think it's like some sort of badge of success for a man to have lots of affairs. I guess maybe Averill was right. But, I just couldn't see my father doing something like that.

All that talk about how nice my father was…and when Dove wished that her father were more like mine, it broke my heart. I felt bad that her father had hit her and run off. I knew my father would never do that. I felt guilty for having a decent father. But, I supposed my mother more than made up for it. More than anything, I felt most guilty about keeping a secret from Dove.

I should have told her that her father had called while we were in New Orleans. I had no right to keep that from her.

I was angry with myself—no matter how much I tried to convince myself that it was all right to do it. Keeping secrets wasn't the sort of thing I did—not really. Maybe I kept secrets from Mommy now and again, but I only did that to make sure she didn't get mad at me. But, I wouldn't have normally kept something hidden from Dove. She wouldn't have had any reason to hurt me. There was no reason that I should have kept a secret from her—well other than I didn't want to see her get even more upset. I know that I did it to keep *her* from getting hurt. Still, I wasn't usually a secret keeper. The whole thing just made me so confused.

Averill says that when…ummmm…he says…oh, who can remember?

Maybe I was wrong to keep what I knew from Dove.

I knew I had many less than nice qualities, but keeping secrets wasn't among them. That was the sort of thing that Grandmother L'Ebène and mother did—not me.

Perhaps my father was good at keeping secrets, too.

Just as I was about to tell her, Rosa walked in.

"How'd it go with Miss Rittenhouse?" Dove asked.

Rosa looked shocked, "How'd you know that's where I went?"

"Considering everything that we learned from that tan-headed woman in the jewelry store, that seemed to be the most logical place for you to go." Dove answered.

Rosa grinned. "You're too smart."

"Nah," Dove blushed, "You just can't hide anything from us."

I blushed, too.

Mrs. Frobischer looked worried for a second, and then she said, very seriously, "Girls, I have something to tell you. When I told you that someone broke a window here, I wasn't…" She paused. "I didn't tell you everything."

"Oh?" Dove said. "Does this have something to do with the fact that Jade's stuff has been gone through?"

"Then you know?" Mrs. Frobischer nodded. "I was afraid of that."

"Yes," Dove said without any anger or sadness. "Her letters from her boyfriend are missing."

"Ahhhh," Mrs. Frobischer said. "I wasn't sure what was in the boxes. I didn't look in them. Are you sure that's all that's missing?"

Dove nodded.

"Love letters," Rosa muttered.

"Yeah, from some guy named Douglas." Dove scrunched up her nose.

Rosa looked at me. I knew what she was thinking.

Luckily, it didn't come up, "Mrs.," Dove began, "I mean, Rosa. Why didn't you tell us? About Jade's stuff, I mean."

"I didn't know for sure until earlier this evening. You see, Eulabel called me while we were in New Orleans and told me someone broke into the store. She said nothing had been stolen. See, she was trying to protect us, too. But I suspected differently. I should have mentioned it to you, but we were all so upset. I didn't want to make it worse," Rosa answered, "Especially for you." She pointed at Dove.

"Sometimes, it's worse to keep something a secret," Dove said sweetly, "It always hurts more later."

"I know," Rosa took Dove's hand. "I'm sorry."

I felt even guiltier then.

I didn't know how to feel when Augustin handed the box to me. Should I have felt guilty? Probably, but I didn't. I felt excited—an excitement I hadn't felt in decades. I was so warm, I thought I might perspire and ruin my eye shadow.

"It certainly is beautiful," I cooed.

"Yes."

Shit. I was disappointed. He should have said, "Not as beautiful as you." It would have been a lie, though. And we both knew it. Besides, he never said things like that to me. He had used all such compliments up long before we married.

"Do I dare wear it?" I asked.

He nodded. Never a chatty man, my Augustin. He took the box from my hand and snapped it shut.

"I'll give it to you again before the party," He smiled and his eyes danced like jewels. "It'll go nicely with the gift I gave to Shelby."

"Augustin," I begged, "Do tell me what it is! What did you get Shelby?"

His pride got the better of him. He broke down and told me. I hooted with glee! How clever of him! How clever of Voletta—she'd proven to be more like her father than I could have hoped.

I couldn't wait.

VI
Sandcastles

Rosa Frobischer

I woke up with a painfully stiff neck on the loveseat in the living room. Dove, curled up in the yellow and blue striped wing chair by the fireplace, gurgled softly with each deep breath of her heavy slumber. The morning was still dark. I saw no point in going back to sleep.

As I watched Dove sleep, I wondered if I shouldn't wake her and send her upstairs to slumber in her bed where she might be more comfortable. However, she was sleeping so soundly, I was hesitant to bother her. In any case, she wouldn't wake with the discomfort that I had. The young are more flexible when it comes to sleeping in odd places. So, I opted not to disturb her.

She and I had spent the night watching films on TV and eating whatever we could find—alternating between sweet and salty until our bodies were so overloaded, we couldn't take in another calorie. Empty pretzel bags and ice cream cartons lay spent on the floor and coffee table as a mute testimony to our emotionally charged gluttony. I knew that as a responsible guardian, I should encourage Dove away from such foods—especially given the fact that she's so unhappy with her weight. But, there'd be time enough for healthy eating and we both found such comfort in our nutritionally empty snacks; I saw no harm in indulging for one night.

One of George's films had been on television, and as we watched it, I told Dove about all the behind the scenes turmoil that I could recall. She seemed thrilled to have a glimpse into those days of old Hollywood. It was a good distraction for her. George would have been pleased.

I hadn't wanted to go upstairs to my own bed—still tormented by my dreams of faceted, suffocating red. I thought perhaps that if I stayed on the couch and did chance to fall asleep, my raw psyche would be fooled by the change in location and not see fit to replay the dream. I had been mistaken, and the red reel started up on time.

Dove, ever loyal, wanted to stay downstairs with me—insisting that staying up all night would be fun. I wondered what sort of dreams she herself was avoiding. I wished, whatever they were, I could take them away.

We both felt Shelby's absence keenly—having grown used to our trio during our time in New Orleans. While we didn't say it, we were both worried about her. Shelby had gone home to her mother and father, pleading silently for me to find a way to keep her with me for one more night. She cried in the limousine before it dropped her off at the rambling yellow clapboard Queen Anne house on La Colline Cramoisie. She dreaded seeing her mother. I certainly couldn't blame her for that. The few times that I had seen Voletta Halifax, I was more than unimpressed with her maternal instincts.

Shelby, thank God, demonstrated more with each passing day that she was growing to be very much unlike her mother. Yet, as she developed, I found that she became increasingly more withdrawn. Gone was the exuberant and blithe girl whose only thoughts were of clothes and parties. In a way, I mourned the loss for her and wished she could regain some of her selfish innocence. It all seemed a cruel price for maturity.

As the darkness outside began to filter lavender and orange through the heavy clouds that hung in the morning sky, I cleaned up our mess as silently as I could. In all actuality, Dove slept so soundly, I could have belted out a number from *Oklahoma* and she wouldn't have been awakened. To confirm my suspicions, a distant clap of thunder made a rolling appearance. Dove didn't stir. We were in for a storm. At least, the girl could rest beforehand.

I went in the kitchen and put a kettle on to boil. Some nice, warm tea would help purge my body of the night's red.

I thought about George and how when we were first married, he would bring a tray to me in bed each morning—tea, toasted brioche with lovely little jams, poached eggs and fresh fruit—all on the best china and served next to a cut white rose in a crystal bud vase. George was very sweet.

Those were the moments that I missed the most intensely. Why hadn't I enjoyed them more? Why hadn't I done the same for him? I had provided many services for George, but breakfast in bed wasn't one of them. If he had wanted me to do the same for him, he would have told me. He always told me everything that he wanted. But, perhaps he had been waiting—just patiently waiting—for his breakfast in bed. Perhaps that was my one failure as a wife.

That, naturally, would add to my total failures as a human being. Oh, but that was before. I'm sure of it. If only George had lived to join me in the after. I'd have given him breakfast in bed every blessed morning.

I would do it for Dove. In this case, breakfast in chair. And while, I couldn't imagine that she'd be hungry after our wicked, fat-saturated retreat into caloric debauchery, I hoped that the message behind the act of providing her such a luxury would be noted and appreciated.

It was, and Dove ate eagerly. I was glad to see it.

As the rain began to fall steadily—shrouding all of Marionneaux in a close, misty veil, Dove and I ate our breakfast and rested as much as we could despite the rapping of the rain on the windows.

We both needed our strength for the day that was to come…for the party that evening. We needed to be strong for Shelby.

The limousine dropped me off outside my house. I'm surprised I didn't enjoy it more. I usually always enjoyed a limo ride. I had often begged Daddy to keep a driver on staff and to buy a limo for us, but he said it was too showy and that he didn't want his family to be "one of those kinds of families." The Cages had a limo and a driver. Were they, "one of those kinds of families?" Well, yes, actually, I think they were and are. But, I still I remember how much I wanted a limo of our own.

Mommy had said that she'd make him change his mind—not for my sake, but because she wanted it, too. But, they never mentioned the prospect of a limo or a driver ever again. I guess they both got too busy with other things to worry about it. Who cares anyway? I don't really care about limos and drivers and stuff like that so much anymore. None of it seems important. If it had been, I'd have enjoyed that ride back from New Orleans more. Maybe it was because I was going home that I didn't enjoy the ride. How funny it sounds to say that. I felt more at home with Rosa than I ever did with Mommy.

Rosa and Dove offered to come in with me. I told them that they didn't have to. I think they knew I wanted them to, but they didn't press once I said "no."

I just didn't want them to see what it was like at 324 Rue de La Colline Cramoisie. Was I ashamed? Yes, that was part of it. But, I also didn't want them to have to deal with it. I didn't want Dove to have to face my mother. I didn't want Rosa to have to endure the smell of bourbon coming from the morning room or see my father's sad eyes. If I could spare them that much, it would be one of the nicest things I could do for them. And, for me, too. I didn't want to have to deal with my friends' pity.

I walked in the front door and put my suitcase down in the crook of the staircase. I didn't have to go any further than that to know where my mother was—the rancid smell of spilled alcohol and throw up came creeping out of the cracked morning room door. She drank herself sick again.

I knew I should have peeked in the morning room door to say hello and to see if she was all right. But, I just didn't feel like it. I was already in something of a bad mood and I didn't really want to make it worse. I couldn't shake feeling bad over not telling Dove about her father's phone call. I was also worried about Jade's letters. Surely they had to be from some other man named Douglas who wasn't my daddy. I tried to think of anyone else in town named Douglas. I couldn't. What was that other doctor friend of Daddy's named? No, no, he was Daniel. What about…no, his name was Donald. But, surely there was another Douglas somewhere in Marionneaux.

However, what weighed most heavily on me at that moment was that I was sad to see our trip over. Even though parts of it were difficult, I enjoyed my time in New Orleans with Dove and Rosa more than I had ever enjoyed anything else. I pulled at the diamond heart that Rosa had given me and ran it along the bottom of the thin chain from which it hung.
I decided to leave my suitcase where it was. Therese could get it in the morning. Or, if not she, than I could. It didn't matter. We were both equally able.

I walked up the stairs. My head was throbbing, but not nearly as bad as it had a few days before. I paused at the landing and looked over the rail at the morning room door.

I was sure Mommy would want me to take the bandage off before my party tomorrow night. I just hoped the wound had stopped oozing and crusting. Stupid party! Funny how it had been all I could think about two weeks before. It suddenly didn't seem important and I wasn't looking forward to it. Sweet Sixteen—right.

"Shelby!" I was startled by a woman's voice behind me at the foot of the stairs. I thought it would be Mommy. But, it wasn't. How weird that they had begun to sound so much alike. Mommy's voice had been made gravelly by her constant drinking and Grandmother L'Ebène's just naturally husky from age and smoking…and meanness.

I turned around, "Grandmother."

"Girl, it's very late." Grandmother L'Ebène scolded.

"It's 8:30." I said calmly.

"We expected you back hours ago." She answered sharply, leaning on the railing. It was strange to see Grandmother out of her motorized scooter thing that she used to slowly prowl around town. She really was huge…just three big circles—like a snowman or something.

"Your mother was worried sick," Grandmother L'Ebène scolded me.

"I don't…" I began to say that I didn't think it was worry that had made Mommy sick, but I decided that I wouldn't. Instead I said, "I don't know why she would be. I called and left a message saying I'd be back around now."

Grandmother L'Ebène ignored me; "You need to get straight to bed. You need your rest. You have to look perfect tomorrow."

"I will," I sighed, "Don't worry."

"It's a very big night and we're all counting on you."

"Counting on me for what?" I said before I had a chance to censor myself, "It's only a birthday party—not a meeting of the Joint Chiefs of Staff."

"Don't take that tone with me, missy!"

"I'm sorry." I answered quietly.

"Well, just go to bed."

I turned to go up the stairs and then feeling brave, I said nastily, "Why are you here anyway? Do you live here now or something?"

"You little bitch," Grandmother growled. "If you must know, I had to come and keep your mother company in her time of distress."

"Next time," I said, "Check the phone messages before you declare me dead. Sometimes you can actually learn something more from answering machine messages than when the delivery man from the liquor store is coming."

I then turned my back and walked as quickly and calmly as I could up the rest of the stairs while Grandmother stuttered in rage below me. I couldn't help but smile.

I walked down the hall to my room and was surprised to hear talking from Daddy's study. I paused outside the door to listen. He was talking on the phone. Actually, a better way of putting it would be to say that he was shouting on the phone.

"I won't do it!" Daddy was shouting. "I'm not going to give in to you. Not this time."

There was silence for a few seconds. And, then he said, "Go ahead and do it. I'm not frightened anymore. There's nothing left to lose. You can't hurt me."

And then he slammed down the receiver with so much force that it sounded as if it had cracked the base unit clear in half.

The noise startled me, and I squeaked.

"Who's out there?" Daddy shouted. Before I knew it, I heard his heavy footsteps on the bare wooden floor. I knew if I ran to my room, I'd look guilty. So, I just stayed put.

The study door swung open and Daddy stood in its frame—breathing heavily. He wore beige shorts and a light pink T-shirt and his hair was all mussed. I couldn't help but think how young he looked—much younger than Mommy did even though they were close to the same age.

"Were you listening outside my door?" He demanded.

"No," I shook my head. "I just got in and I wanted to say good night."

He ran the back of his hand across his forehead and the hardness of anger softened in his face. “Oh, well, hi. Welcome home.”

I nodded.

“You seen your mother?” he asked.

“No,” I sighed, “I smelled her.”

Daddy smiled.

“But, I did see Grandmother L'Ebène,” I said.

“Oh,” He frowned. “She’s here?”

“Yeah,” I nodded again.

“Any idea why?”

“Grandmother said it was because Mommy was stricken with worry when I wasn’t home yet.” I explained quickly.

“Uh huh,” Daddy grunted. “Your mother…” He sort of stopped talking for a second, saying instead. “Well, I’m just so glad you’re home, my princess.

I smiled

“Are you ready for your big party tomorrow?” He asked, scratching his left shoulder through the thin T-shirt material.

“I guess,” I shrugged.

"Hey, what's this?" Daddy smiled. "I thought you were so excited. What's happened?"

"Oh, nothing." I lied, "I'm just tired."

"Well, then off to bed with you," Daddy answered, looking over his shoulder back into his study as if he expected something to leap out from behind the desk.

"Okay."

"Shelby!" Daddy said as I began to walk to my room.

I turned around. He met me in the hall and bent down a bit, sweeping me into an enormous hug. He smelled faintly of sweat, cologne, cigar smoke and hospital. I buried my face into his big shoulder.

"You missed me, then?" He said.

I nodded—my face still pressed against him. He gently stroked the back of my head—being careful not to touch my wound.

Finally, he let go of me.

"Daddy," I said as I looked up at him. "Do you still love Mommy?"

He squinted and leaned against the wall.

"No," He said. "I won't lie to you."

"Did you ever?"

"Yes, once…a long time ago," He shook his head. "I thought so anyway."

"Why do you stay here?" I asked.

"For you, of course." He said softly.

"Oh," I sighed.

He nodded.

"Good night," I said and then I walked to my room.

I went into my room without turning on the light and shut the door. I undressed in the dark and squinted to look out the lace curtains at the thickening clouds and mist outside the window. The poor moon—it seemed to be struggling to shine brighter.

I put on my nightgown and walked to my dressing table. Hanging next to it was a garment bag. I could see through its clear plastic, the dress that Mommy had picked out for me. It looked strange in the weak, sickly light. Its green was washed out in the dimness of the room and looked almost silvery.

I took off the necklace that Rosa had given me and laid it gently on the crystal tray that I kept atop the dresser. I then opened the top drawer to get out some moisturizer and instead paused as if my eyes had been caught in the invisible pull of a magnet. There lay the wrapped box that Grandfather L'Ebène had given me—right where I left it in the drawer next to the pile of broken bits of the china doll that he had crushed the afternoon he crept into my room.

I covered the doll head shards with a handkerchief that I pulled from the back of the drawer. I then took the wrapped box out and put it on top of the dresser for a second—ultimately deciding that I preferred it to stay in the drawer. Grandfather L'Ebène had told me not to open it until the evening of my party. I could wait. In fact, I didn't care if I ever opened it.

I climbed into bed and pulled the covers up to my chin.

I dreamt of the china doll.

And Dove…

I kind of panicked when I woke up in a chair in the living room. I had just been dreaming about Mama and Jade. They were alive, in the kitchen as I remembered, making noodles. Mama was singing. That part, I don't remember ever happening. But I wished it so often that it seemed real.

The shadowed river listens,
Waiting for the rain,
Lies lost in such sharp silence
Her beauty will wane:

That's when a clap of thunder shocked me awake. I kept my eyes shut. I wasn't ready to face another day yet—not even a day with Rosa. I just needed a little more time behind my eyelids to get ready. I drew pictures on the back of my eyelids. I drew Jade and Mama and sweet, wonderful Rosa. They all looked frightened.

I kept my eyes shut until a second loud boom from the sky scared me so much that I couldn't sit still any longer.

I must have screamed because Rosa came rushing out of the kitchen. She was wiping her hands on her apron. I remembered Papa wiping blood on his apron. It was from the freshly slaughtered chickens. I suddenly felt sick to my stomach.

Rosa instructed me to stay put and she rushed back into the kitchen. I watched the rain hit the windowpanes. A few moments later, Rosa came back with a tray of food and proudly presented it to me as if I was some kind of princess.

I wasn't hungry, but I didn't want to hurt her feelings. I could tell she went to a lot of trouble to make a special meal for me.

One of the books that I always liked was about a little boy who had tuberculosis. No, not the cheeriest of books. But, it was sweet and it made me feel things. So, this boy was really very sick, and his mama would bring him trays of food in bed. I thought that was really cool. I didn't think anyone would ever bring me a tray of food—ever. Anywhere.

So, I ate it quickly. I hoped that if I choked it down, it might stay down.

We both ate and talked about Shelby's party. The store was always closed on Mondays so we were in no hurry to get anywhere. With knots in my stomach, I helped Rosa clear the dishes and then we sat still and watched the rain. As I sat, I ran my index finger across the top of one of the cotton pillows on the couch. I guess I was drawing invisible scenes.

Every time I blinked, I thought about those poor slaughtered chickens…and Papa.

Bastard! He think he can ignore me? Doesn't he know that I have the power now? Douglas Halifax has no idea what I can do. I show him.

I hung up payphone and made sure that no one saw me. I rushed back to the bridge where we sleep. It's dark. There was the Monster in his box.

Such a big man. You think he'd be able to break free of the tape I use to tie him up. He sleeps in his refrigerator box. Maybe he don't sleep. But, he keep his eyes shut. He's so old…he got no fight left in him.

"Hungry, Monster?" I laugh.

He opens his eyes, but says nothing.

I laugh again.

"There's no food for you!" I say.

He look sad. I don't know why, but I feel bad for him.

"Hey," I say, "You gonna be free soon."

"I will?" He asks.

Good, I think. He's not gonna die. Monster is old monster.

"Listen," I say, "I tell you a story." It's nice having Monster to talk to. I've been lonely under the bridge.

"You remember Mingmei?" I joke. I know it's cruel, but I do it anyway.

"Mingmei," he says, too.

"Yes." I nod, "I marry her daughter."

"Niu," Monster says.

"Yes. When I was a young man, I live near Lake Pontchartrain. I used to bring linens back and forth to the orphanage," I say. He's listening. I kind of wish I had food for the Monster.

"Anyway," I say, "There's a girl there—right?"

Monster nods. He's lying on his side in the box with his hands and feet all taped to each other. He looks like a baby—big old baby.

"She's very pretty and nice and quiet—makes a good wife. And, since she been there a long time, I ask the orphanage lady if I can have her to be my wife."

Monster sighs.

"So, shc says, 'yes in a year.' I'm happy then and I make plans. I will take the orphan girl and we will start a life. I will even take her to church, I think. So, I wait a year and then I get to make the orphan girl my wife. She come out to meet me—all dressed in rags. She looks horrible! But, her face is pretty. Orphanage lady gives me a box with her few little things in it. But, in the box there's this black bag. I ask what it is. The orphanage lady shows me. You know what it is?"

"No," Monster says all quiet and serious like.

I laugh, "Not to worry, Monster. I tell you. It's a necklace all red and sparkly. It's like a million dollars or something. I want to sell it. But, Niu, she says 'no.' She says we have to keep it cuz it's all she has to remember her mama."

"My necklace," Monster cries.

"You know about that?" I laugh. I knew he know. "You Monster. When we move to Marionneaux, we hear all about the legend of the murdered oriental girl. We figure out that was Niu's mama. They have the same name. We learned all about you and how you brought Mingmei and Niu here. And, we have the necklace."

"You have it," Monster says—he still is crying and I feel bad.

"Well, okay. I used to have it. We hid it in the floor, but Dove found it."

"Dove?"

"Yes, my…" I don't want to talk about Dove. "Anyway, we have the necklace, but it's gone again. Dove was trying it on and I told her not to because it's a whore's necklace and Dove is not a whore."

"Mingmei wasn't a whore." Monster yells. I don't like yelling. So, I hit him. He cried more.

"So, it's true—eh?" I say, "You kill Mingmei?" I should not tease him, I guess, but I like it.

"No," Monster is crying hard.

"Anyway, it doesn't matter now," I say, "Let me finish. Niu gives me a baby. We name her Jade. Niu is good mother to Jade. She sings to her. Sings her a little song she learned from some older girl she knew for a time in the orphanage. Some Aga..agata…agah…tey girl somethin'."

"My niece, Agathe." Monster cries.

"Oh, you just know about everyone and everything, do you Monster?" I kick him—hard. It makes me laugh and feel sad at the same time. "I know all about that, too! I'm smart!" I feel bad again.

"See," I say as I sit down next to him again, "My baby, Jade—she grow up to be a whore like her grandma and she has an affair with this white man who married and all. And, she has a baby, too. We try to cover everything up, but then she goes to work for your sister and she and that man start again. So, she really was a stupid girl. I'm not going to let Dove be like that. So, I need money."

"I have no money," Monster screams. I get up like I'm going to kick him again and he quiets down.

"I know. I don't want your money. I want money from Douglas Halifax. But, he don't wanna give it to me. So, that's why I need you. See, you gonna scare him for me a little. And, then he give me the money so I will make you stop being scary."

"How?" Asks the Monster.

"You just leave that to me," I say.

"That makes very little sense," Monster says.

"Oh! Now you have like whole sentences!" I kick him harder than ever, over and over; "No one cares what you say. You stupid…"

I stop kicking. He's so tired he cannot even cry no more.

"Now, we sleep," I say and lie down on my dirty blanket. Monster says nothing more that night, but I hear him make little noises. I don't know if he sleep.

I sleep then and wake up wet—it's raining.

I wish I still had that necklace. I'd sell it for money and then I wouldn't need Douglas Halifax or Monster Rittenhouse.

But, wait, I think—there's no one in the big mansion. Old lady Rittenhouse is near as dead. Nobody there. I don't have to be wet.

I poke at the Monster.

"Time to go home," I say.

What's to become of my home? *Your home?* All of father's things? What if they take it all away? *It has already been taken.* I will never return there again. *No. You lost! You let them eat you.* Will they find the will? *Which one, Amelia? Whose will?* Does it matter? *No, old girl. Not anymore. They took it all and they took you, too.*

Rosa Frobischer took me away from it. I was happy there on the floor. It was smooth and cool. Now, I'm in this blasted bed and these women poke at me and prick my skin. They're taking my blood. *We always warned you about the parasites, Amelia. Did you listen? Did you? Now, they'll drink your blood.* I think of Jade's blood, Mingmei's blood. Agathe's.

I have tubes in me. I won't let them suck out my life. They can't. *Too late, you dirty old thing! Too late!* Is it? They can take my blood, but not my life.

Rosa Frobischer called the ambulance. *Can't you see why she did, old girl?* I was happy on the floor. Now, all the sparkle is gone…nothing here but beige. And no color. *Please…*

I hate it.

I miss the red walls and the sparkle. The sparkle and the red. Just like the necklace. Mingmei's necklace.

I wonder if Unwin will go home. *What home, Amelia?* Who will take care of him? Poor Unwin. Even if I were home, he'd cry. He'd want me to speak. He loved it when I spoke to him. *You fool, you fool! If he loved it, why didn't he talk to you for forty years?* My silence plus his silence. *You might just as well have killed him, Amelia.*

But, he could have sat with me on the floor and looked up at the sparkle—the sparkle on the red.

Mingmei's necklace.

When I went for Unwin that night so very long ago, and found him struggling over Mingmei's body, I hid. *Don't think of it.* I waited. *Don't remember. Let her, if she wants to! Let her remember!*

I must remember. When the men from the city took her body away, the necklace fell off. I took it. I put it in my pocket. It would be for her little girl—that Niu. *That was nice, Amelia. Nice of you to throw her away with a souvenir.*

I wish Unwin could have seen that I sent it with her to the orphanage—her inheritance. So, when she grew up she could sell it. That was more than we sent with Agathe. That was more than Agathe would have deserved, but that poor Chinese baby deserved better. It was the nicest thing I ever did. The only nice thing I ever did. I was kind to that baby. She would not grow up with my brother's love. She would not grow up to share his life, but she could at least benefit from his gift of wealth. That was the nicest thing ever.

Nice for whom?

I did it for her—and for Unwin. Maybe the only thing I ever really did for Unwin.

I wish I could give Unwin his life back. *But, you took...* Yes, yes I took it from him. I was afraid—always afraid. But, not anymore. Nothing can touch me now. Not these tubes or needles, not these nurses…not the sucking sound of the machines. I'm stronger than all of it. *Not stronger than me, Amelia! Not stronger than us!*

I miss my brother.

Unwin Rittenhouse

He hurt me, that man. Bound my hands and kicked me. He would give me no food. Agathe was nicer even though she was sometimes like her father. At first she tried to talk to me. She was young then, we both were younger. She would feed me. Sometimes she would sing a song to me about the river and the moonlight on the water. It reminded me of Mingmei in her necklace. Sometimes, I would cry. But, sometimes it was nice to be sung to. Agathe always gave me food. It was good food, too. After awhile, she stopped singing. But, I could still hear her below me through the window sometimes when she walked in the garden. She stopped trying to talk to me, too. At least talking nice to me.

Many times Agathe brought me food and would sit with me while I ate it. At those times, I loved her and I would not want to cry. I would think that maybe she wasn't so bad. But, the next time, maybe she would bring me food and slam the tray down—the noise scared me. She would say mean things and tell me she didn't care if I ever ate. Her eyes were so cold at those times. Her eyes shone like silver. I hated her at those times and would think how much she was like her father.

Poor Agathe. I don't think it was her fault. No one ever loved her. She was trapped just like me. It's no wonder she became more bitter each day. She never knew who she was. And, she was so lonely. I don't think I was good company. She should have stayed with people who would have made her laugh—people who would have talked to her. I would not talk then. I wished I could see her again. I would talk to her.

She always had so many questions. I could tell by her face. For forty years I looked at the questions on her face. Then one day I thought I would answer the question. I thought she would soften to me and sing again. Even though it made me cry, it was better than silence.

Yes, that day, she brought me my food and slammed it down. She called me names, "ugly" and other things. But, I smiled at her. I knew why. She laughed when I smiled and she said, "Hey La Bas! Are you so stupid that you don't know when a person hates ya?"

I just smiled.

She narrowed her eyes at me, "What's wrong with you Uncle Ugly?"

Then I took out the piece of paper and handed it to her. It had a name written on it.

She looked at the paper and read the name. "What's this?" She asked me in an angry way.

I just smiled.

"What in the hell does this mean?" She yelled.

I smiled.

She sat down across from me in the little wooden chair. It creaked under her weight.

She read the paper again. "Is this?"

I smiled.

"Is this my father's name?" She asked—her tone was softer. Maybe she'd sing to me.

I smiled and sat back ready to be sung to.

"It is, isn't it? This is my father! Oh Jesus!" She sounded happy and angry all at the same time. "Oh, you just wait!" She called out.

I stopped smiling. I was afraid Amelia would hear.

"Do you know what I'm gonna do?" She screamed at me. I wanted to cry, but I was too scared.

"Oh, I'm gonna get what's mine!" She yelled.

I was very scared then. I did cry. That isn't what I wanted. I wanted a song.

She got behind me and pulled my hair. I cried harder. I did wrong! I did wrong! I shouldn't have told!

"And, I'll be free of you and your ugly, ugly face, you stinkin' freak." She said in a mean whisper.

I got down on the floor and lay on my stomach—I mashed my face in the floor and tried not to hear her.

I waited until she was gone before I got back up. I didn't eat; all I could do was cry. No one would ever sing to me again.

Agathe hated me still and Amelia would hate me even more when she found out what I had done. That's why I ran away when the poor girl died and Agathe ran off to tell Amelia.

I didn't look at Jade before I left. I already knew what had happened to her. And, I didn't want to be sad. I never got to see Jade up close, but I used to watch her. She looked so much like Mingmei. I would sneak around upstairs and watch her when she worked. I was falling in love with her—Jade.

But, she had to die. Just like Mingmei. Why? Why? Why?

That's why I had to run when I had the chance.

But, I couldn't run away from Hsin. He had bound me. That mean man, Hsin, he brought me up the alleyway in the rain in his car. It smelled of copper and garlic and he made me stay on the floor. He hit me to make me get in the car. I hated him. But, I felt sorry for him, too.

I screamed when I saw that he had taken me home. The back of the house looked like a skull. It scared me. But, he hit me again. He made me get out of the car.

He broke the window in the back door and forced it open.

Amelia would be so mad! Oh, she'll be mad at him. She'll be mad at me, too. I didn't want her to yell at me. But, I thought that maybe she'd be happy to see me. Maybe she'd be so happy that I'd come home that she would let me stay out in the big rooms alone and not hide. And, we could talk! I could talk to her! We could talk and maybe even sing!

But, when he dragged me into the front hall, I knew Amelia wasn't there. I couldn't smell her. I couldn't hear her.

"Where's Amelia?"

"She no come back!" He laughed. "She no come back ever!"

I thought maybe Amelia was dead, too. I wanted to cry, but I knew he'd hit me.

"Where you stay?" He asked me.

I pointed up the stairs to the hallway on the left. He dragged me up there and found my old rooms. He threw me inside and left—locking the door behind me.

My old prison. Again. This time I want to talk, but everyone's gone.

Where was Amelia? Was she in the cemetery, too? Was she with Agathe? Was she with Mingmei? And, the girl, Jade?

"I'm all alone again."

I was free to cry, but I didn't want to. I was too tired.

All I wanted to do was sleep. But, I was too scared to sleep, too.

"Who will take care of me?"

All the women were gone. Oh, no, wait…what about the girl in the cemetery who talked to graves? The chubby one?

"Maybe she could take care of me."

Maybe, then I could sleep.

What was her name?

He had said it. Oh, yes…Dove.

Rosa and I barely moved that whole day. We sat and watched television. Rosa seemed too tired to do much else. I was tired, too. I wanted to get up and get my pastels and paper, but I guess I didn't want it enough.

We called Shelby. But, Therese told us that she was too busy to come to the phone. Rosa had promised that we would try to go to the party a little early to help her get ready. I told Rosa how I always helped Jade with her hair when I was a little girl. Rosa told me that she used to help her husband George tie his bow ties when they went out. I think we were both really looking forward to helping Shelby get ready for her big party.

We promised we'd help each other, too. I still didn't know what I was going to wear. Before I could ask Rosa about it, we had a visitor.

Eulabel Watkins came over with armloads of shopping bags and brought them into the kitchen. She brought us a lovely lunch of cheese, fruit and meat pies made by her sister, Beatrice, in Natchitoches. Eulabel stayed for awhile to keep us company. Watching TV with Eulabel was a new kind of experience. She always ended up shouting at the screen as if the pictures were just small people in a box. She was a welcome addition to our afternoon.

The rain continued steadily for most of the day until it was time for Eulabel to leave for her sister Yolanda's house. I had mixed feelings about the rain. On one hand, it served to break the heat and humidity of a summer day in Marionneaux and I knew that the plants desperately needed it. I had always enjoyed rainy days at my parents' house. Maybe it wasn't so much the rain that I enjoyed. Maybe it was more that I liked being with Jade.

When I was a small child, Jade would wrap me in my slicker and we'd go to the bayou and watch the raindrops hit the water—rings swelling out of the center of each drop. We would sit under the shelter of one of the mossy trees and watch those circles spread out until they disappeared.

She would hum to me softly as we sat there in our damp sanctuary—

The shadowed river listens,

Waiting for the rain

—teasing me that we were like the chickens huddled in their coop.

Once did I wish I was a chicken? Did I wonder what being a chicken felt like?

I wondered who was feeding the chickens since…since everything changed. Or had Papa left them to die, too?

But, the rain—on that particular day, I found it annoying as well. First, because Rosa seemed to hate it so. And, second because I knew Shelby's party was to be indoor-outdoor with candles and dancing set on the veranda by the pool in the back of that beautiful yellow house.

Luckily, the rain stopped just in time for us to get ready for the party. We looked out the diamond-shaped panes onto the newly washed streets and lawns. Rosa sighed, "Maybe it's a new beginning."

Maybe it was.

As Eulabel was about to leave, she looked at Rosa who nodded with a sly grin.

"Well, I'd best be goin'," Eulabel said, fumbling with her raincoat and making a show of unfurling her umbrella.

"Thanks for lunch," I said.

"Anytime, anytime Miss Dove, anytime." She grinned.

"Tell your sister the meat pies were wonderful!" Rosa beamed.

"She does do a gooooood job, dudn't she?" Eulabel laughed. "She moved to Natchitoches when she got married and took up with a fine lady who runs a little bed and breakfast. She makes them meat pies for all the guests. She brings 'em to me sometimes. Or if she don't feel like the drive, she sends 'em frozen."

"Well, if you ever have any extra, I wouldn't mind if you brought them here." Rosa smiled her sly smile again.

"Well, looky," Eulabel chuckled, reaching behind her. "Looks like I got me 'nother shoppin' bag right here."

"Is it meat pies?" Rosa giggled.

I had a feeling it wasn't meat pies.

"No," Eulabel said, dramatically putting her head into the large pink bag. "Don't look like no meat pies to me."

I squinted and suddenly felt as excited as if I were four years old on Christmas morning. I actually didn't really know how that felt, but I had read about it in enough books that I was pretty sure the way I was feeling was close.

I looked at Rosa. She winked at me.

"Well, what could it be?" Rosa teased.

"Ohhhhhhhhhhhh," I squealed, "What is it?"

Eulabel pulled out a light pink cardboard box and placed it on the ottoman. "Looks like it's some kinda clothes," she laughed.

I looked back and forth between Rosa and Eulabel.

"Go on," Rosa motioned to the box. "It's for you."

I rushed over to the box and pulled the top off—sending crème colored tissue paper flying into the air.

I gasped when I saw what was inside. A dress—a beautiful golden satin dress with beads around the collar and the bottom of the skirt. The beads looked like sparkling drops of rich honey. The sleeves were of a sheer bronze-colored material and ruffled gently down into points on either side—they looked like angel wings. The skirt of the dress had a floral design all in beads the color of amber. It was truly lovely.

"Oh!" was all I could say.

"Mrs. F. picked it out before ya'll went to N'awluns. I picked it up for you this mornin'." Eulabel explained.

"Oh, Rosa! Thank you!" I rushed at her with a hug, being careful not to knock her over.

"And, thank you Eulabel," I said, looking over my shoulder.

"I was wonderin' where the thanks was for ol' Eulabel." She laughed in her great big way.

I hugged Eulabel, too.

"I didn't know what I was going to wear tonight!" I exclaimed.

Rosa just nodded.

I hugged the dress to me while Rosa walked Eulabel to the door. I had my very own party dress—and not just any party dress. It was a real honest-to-goodness designer dress!

"I feel like a…"

"Princess?" Rosa asked.

"Yes!" I laughed. I thought maybe I shouldn't be so happy considering all the things I had to be sad about. But, I figured it was okay for a little while. I went from chicken to princess. I imagined walking into the party just like a princess would.

I would wear the jade ring with the golden yellow stone that Rosa gave me in New Orleans. It would be perfect.

Then, I remembered the garnet necklace and how Papa hit me when he caught me trying it on. I shuddered and hugged the dress closer to me. I wouldn't think of it. I wouldn't let myself. Not that night!

"Don't wrinkle it, now," Rosa joked, "I'm not so good with an iron."

"I hope it fits," I exclaimed as I flicked the dress out in front of me and let it catch the air like a sail caught in sunshine.

"It'll fit." Rosa assured me.

"You're," I started and felt tears well up in my eyes. "You're the…I just, I never had such a beautiful thing and you're so good to me. You're just the best…" I didn't know what Rosa was the best of. She wasn't my grandmother or my mother.

"Friend," Rosa suggested.

I nodded.

"It takes one to know one," Rosa joked as she tapped me on the shoulder.

"Now, go try it on. Then I'll give you the shoes."

"Shoes!" I squealed again.

Rosa laughed, "Yes, shoes, too."

I couldn't wait to get dressed.

I avoided it all day—the chaos downstairs. It was supposed to be all for me. But, I just didn't care. It didn't feel like any of it was for me. And, even if it had been, I wouldn't have wanted it.

I stayed up in my room the whole day and, for awhile, watched the rain fall and splash against the slope of the black slate roof outside my bedroom window. Earlier in the day, I found a book downstairs and secretly carried it up to my room. I knew Mommy would be furious with me if she found out I was wasting my time reading when I was meant to be getting beautiful for my party.

Luckily, she was nowhere to be found when I crept into the library, so smuggling the navy-blue bound volume back into the safety of my bedroom was a far more simple and danger-free adventure than I had originally thought it might be. With my stolen *Jane Eyre,* tucked into my window seat, I found what I had been looking for. I found a little escape. I felt a certain kinship to Jane and I found it difficult to stop reading. After that day, I read whenever and whatever I could.

The phone rang a few times, but no one came to tell me the call was for me. I was surprised that Rosa and Dove hadn't called. Maybe they had and no one bothered to tell me.

As the time for me to get ready drew closer, I sat at my dressing table and eyed the garment bag that hung next to its buttery ruffles. It made me feel a little dizzy. Or maybe it was the dull ache from my now bandage-less head.

In a way, I was glad Mommy had insinuated her taste upon me. At least I didn't have to pick out my own dress. I wasn't much in the mood for fashion. And, I was in no hurry to get dressed.

Averill says that sometimes he gets fed up with everyone, too. That's when he says he has the most fun. I don't know what he means by that. He won't tell me. Maybe someday he will. He's such a silly boy, that Averill Cage. I hoped he'd show up at the party. I think Mommy had invited him. He was on my list.

Mommy knocked on my door and entered without waiting for me to tell her to come in.

"You're not ready yet?" She hissed. Yet, she was oddly sober. I could tell by her walk. She didn't smell of bourbon and her voice was softer than usual—less gravelly, less like Grandmother L'Ebène's, and more like Grandfather's.

"The party isn't for two hours," I sighed. "There's time."

"We could at least do your hair," Mommy said with a disturbing charm to her voice. I wondered if that was how she had attracted Daddy when they were young.

"Okay," I shrugged.

"Aw, what's wrong? Is my big sixteen year old not feeling well?" She ran her fingers through my hair.

I shuddered. "Ow! Careful of my stitches,"

"Yes, that's right," Mommy's voice was sweet, but her eyes flashed—silver like Grandfather L'Ebène's.

"I know what we'll do," She said, opening my dresser drawer to get out my curling iron. As she did, she noticed the handkerchief covering the bits of broken china that had once been the head of the laughing Asian girl doll. She pulled away the handkerchief.

Upon recognizing what they were, she laughed shrilly—breathing in sharply in a rhythm that made it sound like what I guessed was the noise a dying pig makes.

I made a face and got up from my dressing table.

"Sit down!" She shouted, adding "Darling…" in a bizarre purr. Maybe she wasn't as sober as I had originally thought.

"I think we'll just curl the ends so that your lovely black hair flows over your shoulders." Mommy said with an unusual quickness, as I sat back down. She stood behind me and spoke to my reflection in the round mirror in front of us. "That way, we won't have a complicated hair-do that will pull your…stitches." Something had distracted her.

Something else in my top drawer.

"Is that your grandfather's birthday present?" She asked, plugging in the curling iron.

"Yes."

"You haven't opened it yet?" She asked in a screechy, mean kind of way. Mrs. Frobischer, I mean, Rosa would have called it "strident."

"No, he told me not to until I got dressed for the party." I explained, fearing she would find fault with that somehow.

"Good," She grinned—there, again, was the steely glint in her eye.

She put the curling iron in my hand and said, "I'll leave you to your toilette." And then, she left in a cloud of perfume. I coughed.

I sat and stared at my reflection in the mirror for a good ten minutes before I started to curl my hair as I had been instructed. I looked more like Mommy than I had realized. Maybe if I smiled more…

Once my hair was curled and I had applied the little make-up I was allowed to wear, I reached for the green dress and freed it from its plastic bag.

It was a pretty dress. Not as stiff and a little more free flowing than I would have liked. It was a nicer color than I remembered—it kind of reminded me of a dusty version of the color of Dove's ring.

I put it on and looked at myself quickly in the mirror as I zipped up the back. Eh—it didn't matter. In its loose, somewhat gauzy silk, I felt something like a fairytale character. Not a princess, but like an elf or a—oh, no one cared. Like I said, it didn't matter.

Another knock on my door and another uninvited visit from Mommy. This time she didn't come in, she simply stuck her head in the door.

"Oh good!" She mooed—filling the room with her boozy stink. She had either started or continued her daily binge.

"Now for your grandfather's present."

"Okay," I said, taking the box and unwrapping it. Mommy began to leave.

"Don't you want to see it?" I called after her.

"No," She laughed. "I've already seen it."

She began to shut the door and before it closed she said huskily, "Don't forget to show your father before you see anyone else!"

"Okay," I shook my head and stuck my tongue out at my own reflection in the mirror.

I unwrapped the box and opened it.

Earrings. What was the big deal?

Marie L'Ebène

Voletta did the right thing to tell us when she discovered that Douglas was screwing that oriental girl again.

Our daughters—mine and Augustin's—know that we'll always do anything we can to take care of our precious babies.

We had such high hopes when we suggested she pursue Douglas Halifax. His family was one of the wealthiest in the parish—a long line of pharmaceutical geniuses and doctors that Augustin had become acquainted with through his medical practice. Halifax was big and handsome, that was for certain, and had a promising future ahead of himself as a surgeon. But, even if that failed, there would always have been that Halifax money to fall back on.

The first time Douglas strayed, we instructed Voletta to stick with it. Divorce wasn't an option. We wouldn't settle for half...she would have to hang on and hold out for the whole thing—the rich widow act.

In fact, when she tried to give us the details of his infidelity; we wanted to hear none of it. The less we knew about the particulars the better—especially given Augustin's temper.

But, the second time, she was right to tell us everything—our dear, wronged baby.

She reminds me so much of myself sometimes—but only sometimes. I'd have castrated Augustin if he…no, that would depend on who the woman was. Never mind. As I was saying, I rose above my family and married well—but, not nearly as well as Voletta had.

The L'Ebène family was well off, but nowhere near Halifax money. Nevertheless, I got Augustin with much less effort than poor Voletta had to use to snare Douglas. All I had to do was be at the right place at the right time. And, I certainly had been.

Funny how it's all coming back now.

I had to laugh as I got dressed that evening. I put on my favorite champagne crepe gown—I didn't want anything to compete with the beautiful gift Augustin had given me. Yes, it was foolish to wear it. But, so few would recognize it—it would be my own little joke on all of them. My own symbol of my triumph over all of them! I couldn't wait to see the look on Rosa Frobischer's face—that ridiculous hag. She would have no idea what had hit her and that was the beauty of it. I would win. I always win.

And, my dear Voletta would win, too.

I wished I were with Shelby when she modeled her outfit for her father.

Voletta Halifax

Goddamn it! Where are those hairpins? Oh, here. Oh, oh, oh….I should stop laughing!

Where's my…oh…mmmmmmmmm…my favorite brand. Mmmmmmm…ah, cold. Goddamn! Too much ice! Oh, stupid Therese! Oh…

My roots need touching up. Why am I laughing?

Lipstick on my teeth.

Therese! Therese, bring me another—less ice this time!

Right about now, my dear, dear…Shhhhhh…Shelby will be showing off her birthday outfit to her dear daddy.

How lovely she must look! Right, Douglas? Too bad I can't watch.

Mmmmmm…Therese! I said bring me another!

Ahhhhhhhh, Douglas…Too bad I can't SPY on you like I did when you went to meet your little Asian slut!

"Oh, my darling, you're lovelier than ever…" Kiss, kiss, kiss, Douglas. Oh, oh…oh.

So, how does your daughter look? How does she look in a copy of your whore's dress! How does she look in your slut's earrings? The very ones that came off her mutilated body!

Tell me, Douglas, tell me!

And, Shelby, did you get all of Daddy's love this time? Did you? Did you ever?

Silly little pearl earrings—the other day, Grandfather acted like they were the crown jewels. I guess they were nice. As nice as anything else he would have picked out for me.

I put on Rosa's diamond heart. Mommy hadn't sanctioned it, but I doubted she would notice and it was the one item that I had that I was proud to wear.

I paused for a moment to look out the window. Behind the slate roof I saw that the clouds were beginning to clear and the rain had stopped completely. Rented waiters were lighting votive candles around the veranda. Their sharp lights sparkled in the gently moving water of the pool.

At least I could stay outside away from my grandparents and Mommy. I thought perhaps Rosa, Dove and I could sit by the pool and have our own private party. None of Mommy's friends would want to be outside on such a thick and muggy evening.

Yes, we would sit by the pool. But, Rosa wouldn't like that. Perhaps we could sit in the garden, then—if we kept our backs to the view of the Rittenhouse place looming above us at the top of La Colline Cramoisie. I guessed there would be time enough to decide.

I looked at the clock on my dressing table. Rosa and Dove were late. I figured I'd better hurry to see Daddy.

I checked myself in the mirror. The dress fluttered as I moved. It was a little too—eh—what does it matter?

I turned to look at the time again. I had about half an hour before the guests would arrive and I knew Rosa and Dove would be coming a little early to chat with me before the party. Finally, I smiled.

Mommy said that I should show my outfit to Daddy before anyone else saw it. I didn't know quite why. I figured that Daddy would be even less interested in it than I. But, if anything, it would be a good chance to show him Rosa's diamond heart.

I thought about taking one more quick look in the mirror, but I decided it wouldn't do any good. So, I went out in the hallway and walked to Daddy's study door and listened. I heard him moving around in there.

Why not have a little fun? When I was six or seven, I would play little games with Daddy. I'd knock on his study door and hide. He always knew it was me, but would pretend that he had no idea. He'd then come looking for me and when he'd find me he'd laugh, "It's you!" And, then he'd tickle me and we'd laugh and laugh.

Daddy didn't laugh much anymore. Maybe if I played the game—even though I was grown up—he'd think it was sweet and at least smile for remembering. I thought it might even cheer me up a bit, too.

I knocked on the door—suppressing a giggle.

When I heard him move his desk chair, I tiptoed further down the hall and ducked behind the corner that led to the other bedrooms.

"Who is it?" He said as he opened the door.

I thought maybe he chuckled—or sniffed.

"Shelby?" He asked. I heard him come down the hall. I decided I'd surprise him, so I stepped out in front of him and spun around to show him my dress. I heard no laughter.

"It's you!"

At first I didn't even know what had happened. I didn't feel the sting until a few seconds afterward. I was certain that the back of his hand had left its impression on my face. All I knew was that I ran. I ran as fast as I could in that dress. Even behind my bedroom door, I could hear him screaming.

Rosa Frobischer

Finally, the rain stopped and I could relax a just a little bit. Of course, rain or no rain, the afternoon still would have been sheer delight. Dove loved her dress—and the shoes! I could hear her in the room next to mine happily talking to herself as she got ready.

I soon realized that time was running out for my own preparations. We had, after all, promised Shelby that we would arrive early. I had dressed for so many parties throughout my sixty eight years of marriage that I had the routine down pat. I wouldn't need long to put myself together. Granted, it look longer as I got older, but I was still the fastest dresser I knew—well, at least the fastest in Hollywood.

I went to my wardrobe—black, black, gray, black, charcoal, gray, black. I couldn't help but sigh. One of George's greatest pleasures, he admitted once, was seeing me dressed to the nines. He always told me that I wore a gown better than anyone, even in a room filled with Deitrichs, Crawfords, Bergmans, Sotherns and Leighs.

Eve Arden had overheard this comment and asked me to give her a little of whatever it was that I slipped into George's morning coffee to keep his interest. But, George, ever the clever one, replied, "It's what she slips in her slip that keeps my interest."

I blushed, but Eve and George slapped each other on the back like a couple of fraternity brothers in the locker room.

Standing there in front of my wardrobe, I wondered if George would have approved of the past six months I'd spent in the drab of mourning. I suspected he could still see me from wherever he was. He probably rolled his eyes every time I donned another bland outfit.

And, frankly, I was getting a little bored with all black myself. George knew I missed him. God, how I missed him. I sometimes felt as if I was losing him a little bit more every day. I sat down on the edge of the bed and looked at my left hand, moving my ring finger from side to side so that the diamonds on my wedding ring and the seven-carat stone on my engagement ring would catch the light. That shower of color—that burst of light—that's how I felt every time George looked at me.

I lay back on the bed—I'd have to fix my hair again anyway. A trickle of moisture leaked out of the corner of my eye and rolled toward the duvet cover. I wiped my temple. How I hated water…

The day that George proposed to me, he took me to the beach in Santa Monica for a picnic. I wasn't too thrilled with the idea at first, but knowing how much I detested being wet; we sat far enough away from the ocean to satisfy me.

I remember watching George run back and forth between me and the tide with buckets of water. We were building a sandcastle. And, George, of course ever the screenwriter, was telling me a story as we built it. Over the course of two hours, we had begun to build one of epic proportions. I was so engrossed in my love for George that I had no concept of time. He entertained me with his story.

It was a story about a "showbiz" frog that found a beautiful princess in Louisiana while doing some research for a picture. The girl and the frog ran away together. I asked if the princess kissed the frog and he turned into a handsome prince. He said no, the frog stayed a frog, but the princess didn't care because she loved him so much.

"You're no frog," I laughed.

"Hey," George laughed, "What makes you think this story is about us?"

George continued. He told me how the frog and the princess had been in love from the very first moment they saw one another, but the frog was a kind and decent frog—an old fashioned frog.

I told him he didn't make any sense.

He told me to be quiet. We both laughed. All the while we built our sandcastle higher and higher—oblivious to the day around us and the clouds that had begun to fill the sky.

"As I was saying," George continued in a rather vaudevillian way, "The frog was an old fashioned frog and the princess was a good girl. So, naturally, the next step would be for the frog and the princess to marry so they could live in the same damn house."

I laughed. "All the frog would have to do is ask."

"Shhhhhh! You're ruining it," George put his fingers to his lips in a schtick worthy of the Marx brothers.

"Fine. Continue," I said—affecting an air of seriousness.

"So, the frog took the princess to the beach. And, they built a sandcastle. The castle was big and beautiful like the life they would build together."

I nodded.

"And, the frog asked the princess to reach into her beach bag and take out the white box." George winked.

I did as he suggested.

"When did you put that in there?" I asked—beginning to become emotional in anticipation.

"Shhhh!" George became Groucho again. "Open it."

And, there was that ring—even in the dim light of the clouds, it shone like a star.

I don't remember exactly what I said—something silly about it not being as beautiful as George, but I do remember saying yes and I do remember George's arms around me. I also remember the first time I ever really felt safe.

We sat there for quite awhile before the rain fell—my hand on top of his (so I could look at my ring). But, suddenly, almost on cue, the heavens opened.

"Don't worry, it's not an omen," George joked.

"Oh! Our sandcastle!" Our creation had begun to crater in the rain—its beige walls dimpling under each drop.

"Water ruins everything!" I moaned as I gathered up my bag.

George swept me into his arms and kissed me. "Not everything," he whispered afterwards as he held me. We lingered one moment more before running to the car.

I sat up—seventy years later—catching a glimpse of myself in the wardrobe mirror. I had faded. The diamond had not. And, neither had my love for George.

Oh, Dove and I were running late. George hated for anyone to be tardy.

I stood up and opened the other side of the wardrobe—pulling out a never-worn pomegranate red dress with a Greek key design in scarlet silk embroidery.

That night, I would make George proud.

VII
The Party

Douglas Halifax

I hadn't meant to hurt her. I didn't even know what I was doing until after I hit her.

"Shelby!" I hollered after her. But, she had already gone running down the hallway to her bedroom. I followed her.

"Shelby!" I repeated pounding on her door. She would not answer.

I quickly realized that screaming and door beating were hardly the way to get an audience with my daughter. My daughter—the only person left that truly loved me—the girl I just slapped on the evening of her "sweet sixteen" party.

I was already agitated when I heard the knock on my door. Hsin Ji had called again—making demands and threats—promising if I didn't give him more money he would scare it out of me. And, then I opened the door and saw her.

She rattled me. That dress—pale green silk just like Jade's. In the dim light with her dark hair cascading over that dress, I thought for a second that I was seeing some wraith of my lost love. And, then I saw the earrings. And, I thought that Shelby was playing a cruel joke on me. But, how could she? In order to do that, she would have had to know about my affair with Jade. Unless Voletta had told her, there was no way she could have known. And, Voletta was far too cunning to do that—she wouldn't risk her inheritance. Of course, she could have let it slip in one of her inebriated fevers.

As I stood outside of Shelby's door, I began to realize that my child had been used as a pawn in someone else's sick game.

I took a deep breath, this time saying, "Shelby," as gently as I could. "I'm sorry, please let me in so we can talk about this."

Silence.

"Please, Shelby. I'm so sorry."

I heard the door unlock, but it remained closed.

I opened it to see Shelby walk back to the farthest corner of her darkened room. I turned the light on. Shelby squinted—her eyes rimmed pink from tears—a large red hand-shaped welt was rising on her left cheek.

"Shelby," I said walking toward her. She cringed. So, I stayed back and stared at her.

Those earrings—identical to the ones I had given Jade.

"I'm so, so sorry, Princess." I said softly.

"Why?" She shouted angrily. "Why did you do that?" She began to sob, "I was playing the game we used to play when I was little. I was trying to…"

"Oh, sweet heart," I began.

"Shut up!" She shouted. "I hate you!"

That stung.

“You—you are supposed to be the good father. You’re the father that Dove always wishes she had.”

I winced.

“But, you’re just as bad as hers!” Shelby continued.

“I…” I began. But, I wasn’t ready to tell her yet.

“You hit me! You son of bitch!” Shelby threw a hairbrush at me.

“I deserve that,” I said, sitting on the corner of her bed. I decided not to scold her for her language.

“Why, Daddy? Why did you hit me?” She wept, throwing herself into the chair by her dressing table.

“I was confused.” I said in my shame, “I thought you were someone else.”

“Who?” She asked. I couldn’t tell her.

“Where did you get those earrings?” I asked instead.

“Who did you think I was, Daddy?” She growled at me in a tone that reminded me too much of her mother. I had hoped that my love would guide her away from a resemblance to the L'Ebène side of her. I feared I had just pushed her in the opposite direction.

I took a deep breath, “Where did you get those earrings?”

“Damn you!” She shouted, “I got them from Grandfather L'Ebène!”

And, it all made sense, then. Voletta had told her parents. It all made sense.

“And, the dress?” I asked.

“Mommy made me wear it,” Shelby answered, again speaking softly. “I hate it.”

“It confused me,” I admitted again.

“Why?” Shelby asked once more, this time more calmly.

I didn’t answer.

“Who did it remind you of?” She repeated—still with an unnerving calm.

I still didn’t answer.

“You owe me that much!” She shouted, and then her voice fell into a childlike desperation. “Jade Ji? Was it Jade Ji?”

My eyes widened in shock. “Why do you ask me that?”

“Jade’s letters. From Douglas. Are you Jade’s Douglas?” She nearly whispered.

“How?” I felt a rage well up inside me again, I knew it wasn’t with Shelby, but I was still furious and it needed to be released, "Did you go into my study and read my personal papers?”

She shook her head and laughed coldly. “No, Dove told me about letters that Jade had from a man named Douglas. But, you answered my question.”

My body went numb.

She continued, still laughing, “They were stolen from Mrs. Frobischer’s…Rosa’s, I mean. Dove had stored some things of Jade’s there.”

“I have them now,” I said, trying to control myself.

“Obviously,” Shelby laughed eerily. “So, it’s true.”

“Yes.”

We sat in awkward quiet. Below us, a swell of voices signaled the arrival of the guests.

“I loved her,” I said finally.

“How nice,” Shelby spat. “Did you kill her?”

“No!” I shouted—furious that she would think so. But, I quickly realized that her whole concept of me had been dashed. She didn’t know what to think.

“Do you know who did?”

“I think I do…now,” I nodded.

“Don’t you owe it to Dove to do something about it?” Shelby asked me, her voice regaining strength.

I looked at her.

“Don’t you owe it to your daughter?” Shelby said.

“My daughter? How did you…” I stuttered.

Shelby's eyes widened. "Me. I meant me!" She began to raise her voice again. "Oh God! Dove is your daughter!"

"N..." Why lie to her? "Yes, yes, she is." I nodded.

"And, Jade—is her mother?"

I nodded again.

"Dove is your daughter." She coughed the words. "You threw away your own daughter! Wouldn't it have been kinder if you'd killed her before she was born?"

I stared at Shelby like some stunned, mute idiot.

"Wouldn't it have been kinder than letting that sad little girl grow up fat and lonely in a crappy, dirty house with those horrible people? Wouldn't being dead have been better than thinking that the woman who gave birth to her was her sister?" Shelby screamed. "She lived her whole life thinking no one ever loved her!"

"Who?" a voice at the door asked boldly. "Who did?"

I turned. There stood Rosa Frobischer and Dove. It was Dove who had spoken. She looked frightened and angry.

Rosa stammered nervously, "Therese let us in. Sorry we're late, but...I see that you're in the middle of something. We'll come back later."

"NO!" Dove said.

"Dove," Rosa shook her head. "This doesn't concern us."

"I'm sorry, Rosa," Dove said fiercely, "But I have to know. Who are you talking about?"

"Dove," Shelby growled, "You deserve to know." She looked at me with acid eyes, "Tell her!"

"Tell me what?" Dove was shaking—the beads on her golden dress shimmered like raindrops…or tears.

I wouldn't answer. Rosa Frobischer blushed and looked awkwardly into the middle of the room.

Shelby grinned viciously. "Dove, you know how you wished your dad was more like mine. Well, guess what?"

"No, no, no!" Dove put her hands to her ears. "I don't hear you!"

"What's wrong Dove?" Shelby said—her eyes wild, "This is what you wanted, isn't it?"

"No!" She lowered her hands. "Hsin Ji is my father." Dove whispered.

"He isn't," Shelby said—suddenly becoming sweet as she was overcome with affection for her sister. "Jade is your mother and *my* father," Shelby looked hatefully at me and scowled, "Is also yours."

"I don't understand!" Dove's shaking became worse.

"The 'Douglas' from the letters," Shelby explained. "Is Douglas Jacob Halifax."

Rosa came up behind Dove and put her arms around the girl. "Not now. This isn't right. It's too much for her."

"Rosa, she should know," Shelby answered forcefully, but with the same affection she had shown Dove. Her voice had somehow changed. Would Shelby ever speak to me the same way again?

"No! No, he is not. Hsin Ji is my father," Dove repeated, shaking her head frantically and looking at me.

"He isn't," I said to the daughter I had denied. "Hsin Ji is not your father."

"He isn't?" I asked, still staring at Douglas Halifax. I didn't understand. Nothing made sense. Nothing! "What do you mean, Mr. Halifax? Shelby, what does he mean?"

"Dove, honey," She was trying to be gentle. "I told you."

"Tell me again!" I screamed. I didn't understand. "Who? Tell me who my father is. Tell me! I'm too stupid to understand! Tell me who my father is!"

"I am," Douglas stepped toward me..

"Don't come near me!" I yelled. He stood still. Rosa held me tighter. I wanted to die. I had no idea what was happening. Who was I? Who? I didn't know. I didn't want to know. I felt as if I had just been punched. I felt as I had the day Papa—Hsin—whoever the hell he was, hit me.

That's when I noticed the handprint on Shelby's face. My heart stopped.

"Who did that to you?" I asked.

"Our father," Shelby replied bitterly.

"Our father," I repeated. "So, another father that hits." I laughed. "Lucky friggin' me!" I had never spoken like that. I didn't care, though! I just didn't' care. I laughed again. I had to—otherwise I was afraid I'd simply die.

Douglas looked nervous.

“You hit her?” Rosa asked. I could feel her muscles tighten.

“I didn’t mean to,” Douglas stammered.

“Didn’t MEAN to?” Rosa was very angry!

“Didn’t mean to. He didn’t mean to!” I laughed again. “Tell me, did you mean to get my sister,” I stopped, feeling my face turn hot. I shouted, “My mother—did you mean to make her pregnant and then leave the baby—ME—did you mean to leave me to be raised by elderly, careless…old…who never…Oh GOD! Did you mean to do that? Did you?”

“I was young,” Douglas stuttered.

“Was it because I was Asian? Were you…were you....ashamed?”

“It had nothing to do with you being Asian.”

“Are you sure? Maybe we’re good enough to…but...” I began to sob again. I didn’t understand!

Shelby rushed to my side, taking my hand and linking her arm through Rosa’s—they had enveloped me. Rosa and…my sister…Shelby was my sister!

“Think of it this way,” Shelby said, trying to calm me, “Daddy is actually all right. At least he isn’t scary like your—like Hsin. He doesn’t make creepy phone calls. And, he won’t run out on you.”

“Right!” I shouted, “He’s already run out on me once! Why shouldn’t he again?”

Shelby began to cry.

I squeezed her hand, "I'm sorry. This is hard for you, too. I'm not upset with you." And, suddenly I thought about what she had just said. "What did you mean about creepy phone calls?"

"Yes, what did you mean?" Douglas looked frightened.

"Let's all try to calm down," Rosa said, running her left hand through my hair.

"I should have told you," Shelby turned pink, "But, Hsin called while we were in New Orleans."

"Why didn't you tell me?" I demanded of my sister.

"I didn't want to upset you!" Shelby was shaking.

"That wasn't your choice to make!" I yelled. "You're liars! All of you are liars!" I tried to free myself from Rosa's arms. She wasn't a liar; she was the only one I could trust. I hoped I didn't hurt her feelings.

"Let me go!" I squirmed. She released me.

I just had to get out of that room.

"Dove!" I heard Rosa shout after me.

I ignored her

I ran down the hallway and heard a shrill laugh behind a partially open door. I recognized Voletta Halifax's laugh, so I turned abruptly at one of the many sharp corners in the hallway. I had to get away from all of them!

I ended up sneaking down the back stairs—just like a servant. Hiding!

Avoiding the sound of the partygoers, I darted out a back door, catching my dress on the door handle. I heard a rip and the sound of amber beads bouncing on the tile.

Only once I was on the veranda could I breathe. At least I felt free for a moment…until I saw him—the man I just discovered was my grandfather.

"Come on, Monster," I say. Monster isn't moving very fast. Someone will see us. If I kick him, he'll cry and give us away.

"Hurry up," I pinch him. He did not cry, so pinching is good.

"I hate you," Monster says.

I laugh—quiet like.

"I don't care." I say

We finally get into the yard. Douglas Halifax's yard.

"You stay in bushes," I tell Monster.

Monster does as he is told.

Sometimes he is a good monster.

I quick-like take a look around. There is no one in the garden. All kind of fancy candles are lit up around the pool. Rich people light candles, but they don't need to. They have lights! Stupid candles. They look sparkly in the water. They make me think of the necklace.

I should not have hit Dove. She did not know. She would expect more from a papa. Too bad I'm not her papa. But, she should expect more from her grandpapa, too. It's not Dove's fault that my daughter was a whore.

I should not have hit Dove and I should not have left Niu alone. She was no bad wife. She just scream sometimes, but she always so afraid. Afraid of loneliness. I guess that happens when baby grows up with no mama or papa. At least, Dove had that.

I feel bad that Niu is gone. We were man and wife a long time. And, sometimes it was happy. Like when Jade was a baby. Niu would sing. I had such hopes for Jade. She was going to be the one that did things right. She would have more than noodles and frying pans and chickens.

But, Jade ruined everything. No, Douglas Halifax ruined everything when he took my baby's love and made her cheap. Dove came from them. So, it's hard to say if Dove would grow up cheap like her mother—a cheap whore. My baby was a whore. It makes me feel so…hurt.

Maybe that's why I never love Dove as much as she need me to. I did not want to be hurt again. And, 'sides, I was afraid she would become a whore, too.

Fear is funny with power.

That's why Monster is here. He is fear. He makes me have power.

Maybe I can come back and save Dove when I get money. Maybe…or maybe she want to love Douglas, too. Maybe Dove won't forgive me.

I try with Jade. I try to forgive. Money helps. But, I cannot forgive even with money. Even when he give us money to raise the baby, I want my little girl back, too. I want everything. But she not come back and I just get mad. I try to make her love me. I buy her pin with red stones. But not even Douglas' money make her love me more than him. Sure, she say she love me, but I know Jade only could love that Douglas. Even when I have his money, she love him more. Even when she not see him anymore, she love him more.

So, all I had was the devil's money and no love. All his money did is make me into a whore, too. Who wants a whore's love anyway?

If I can't have love, I'll have money. Other money is long time gone. I want more. Douglas can give that to me. He owe me! He owe Dove!

Someone comes.

Dove! I hide, but she sees me.

I come out from the bushes into shadow.

"How could you?" She screams.

"Shhhhhhhhh." I say. "Shhhhhh." I don't want people inside to hear and see me with Monster. Surprise would be ruined.

I am happy when she lowers her voice.

She looks terrible—dressed like a cheap slut all in sparkles.

"You are like your mother in that dress—like a hooker!" I say angry, but quiet.

"Which mother?" She makes a noise like a snake at me.

I want to hit her again, but I don't. Maybe she can't help it.

"My real mother? Jade—my sister?" She sounds like sick animal.

"Yes," I say. "So, you know."

"Yes, I know." She says.

"How could you lie to me?" She asks.

"Seemed to be right to save you and give you chance. Besides, there is family honor. If people knew that Jade is pregnant without husband—family honor is ruined."

She laughs at me and walks back and forth, back and forth.

"What about MY honor?" She asks all mean.

"Who cares about little girl's honor?" I say.

She laughs again. She looks sick.

"What about Mama…Grandmother…Niu! What about Niu?"

"What about Niu?" I ask.

"Did she earn the right to honor?"

"What?" I ask.

"Or did you take that away from HER, too?" She makes noise in her neck like she's going to throw up.

“I did nothing,” I say waving my hands to quiet her down.

“Did you kill her?”

I say nothing.

“Did you kill her? Answer me! What are you afraid of?” She is screaming now.

“No. I did not kill Niu.” I answer loud, too. Someone will hear us, but I am not afraid. “I am afraid of nothing!” I shout.

Afraid. Oh no! Monster! I run to bushes, but he is gone.

My old voice cracked as I screamed after her, "Dove." She was quicker than I was. I gathered my crimson skirt up above my ankles and went as quickly as I could after her. I wasn't sure what direction she had taken.

Shelby and her father were still arguing when I ran after Dove. I didn't want to leave Shelby alone, but she hadn't followed me and I didn't want Dove to get too far.

I went to the end of the hallway past Voletta Halifax's bedroom door. She was standing in the frame watching me in slushy, Dickensian triumph.

"Having fun?" She belched.

I couldn't think of anything to say to her. I suspected she was somehow behind all of this coming to a head at once. I was filled with such a prickling need to verbally accost her; I didn't know where to start.

"Harridan!" I growled, "Where did Dove go?"

She swigged her rather substantial drink and pointed to the sweep of the maple staircase a few feet ahead of me. Those stairs led straight to the foyer where most of the guests had gathered. Perhaps Dove had been slowed in the crowd.

Without saying another word to Voletta, I went down the stairs as quickly as I could without tripping over my dress.

As I descended, I scanned the gathering swarm of bodies below me for Dove. However, I saw no sign of her. I did, on the other hand, see Marie L'Ebène propped up against the newel post like a side of ham in beige pleats. My wish was to walk right past her, but as I turned the last step, she grabbed my wrist in her knobby claw. She pinned my hand to the banister.

"Dear Rosa. Who knew you were here?" She mewed—how odd to see her standing—her great hulk straining against her gown.

She regarded me with contempt—looking through her false lashes at me, the black, caked hairs of which did little to mask the wickedness in her eyes.

I tried to shake free of her grip, but she was strong from grasping the handlebars of that contraption she employed to terrorize Marionneaux.

Her mouth was wet with saliva, and she took her other claw and rubbed it against her cheek—dragging it down her chin to her throat.

And, then I froze in terror until I felt my whole body spasm in a flood of memory.

Around her neck, she wore a necklace of garnets set between trios of round diamonds. I knew that necklace. It was the one from my nightmares—the one around the dead girl's throat.

The room grew fuzzy and the flicker of the candles and brass chandeliers was replaced by the tremor of red—rising up first like fire and then spreading like blood in water.

My knees buckled under me and my hand—trapped beneath Marie's—gripped the banister tighter so that I would not fall.

I felt as though there were two of me—one in the present and the other—Rosa, but not Rosa Frobischer—another Rosa, younger, also in a red dress surrounded by the stench of floor polish and sweat—both of us trapped.

And suddenly, there was but one Rosa. Young Rosa. I was at a dance in the school gymnasium and I felt arms close around me—not the comfort of George's arms, but a malodorous vice.

"You're so beautiful." He smelled of dirt. "Come on, little Rosebud," That horrible voice said, "I'll be so gentle."

"No," I heard myself speak. I shivered. Someone was touching me—my breasts—his hands making wet stains on my dress.

"No," I repeated.

I felt a knee run up my thigh. "No," I squirmed.

Trapped. Hot breath making me sweat.

"Come on!" The voice was sharper. A hand slipped into the back of my dress—a wet hand.

Red, red, red…I struggled to see through it.

"Let's get out of here and I'll make a woman of you," The voice said—it was raspy and dripping with honey and vinegar. He whispered his song in my ear, “The shadowed river listens…” His hands were slick.

A hand closed around my arm. I was being pulled!

“NO!” I shouted and as I did, the red began to clear in slashes like sunlight through Venetian blinds.

“I hate you,” I screamed. “I won’t go with you.” I let my voice fly from my throat. “I hate you Augustin! Let go of me!”

And, there was his face! Framed between red slashes. Augustin L'Ebène seething with anger and frustration.

But, I wasn’t young. It was seventy years later and I wasn’t at a dance in the high school gym. I was standing on the staircase at the Halifax’s house and Augustin L'Ebène was standing in front of me still. I had left that far away gymnasium behind, but Augustin L'Ebène still remained! In the present, he also held my by my thin arm.

“You hush,” He cooed as the crowd began to look at me. “Marie, let’s take her outside for some air.” He tugged at me.

“I won’t go with you,” I screamed, yes, it was me—old Rosa.

Marie continued to press my hand firmly to the rail and turned to look at me as if she would slap me with her free hand—the folds of her neck scraped against the necklace and again, I felt the wash of red. I smelled copper—the metallic smell of blood! I could taste its sharpness.

My body shook. Someone in the room gasped.

I went back again…

Augustin! Yes—he's standing over a dead girl's body at the bayou. A dead Asian girl! She's naked except for the necklace—Marie's necklace, but it isn't Marie's.

Augustin is cutting the girl's body with a thin, silver knife. Oh God! At the bayou, I'm screaming!

In the foyer, I am screaming, too. "Oh God!" It's Shelby's party. I'm shouting "Oh God!" Augustin killed that girl—he killed Mingmei. He cut her to shreds.

Augustin killed Mingmei and I can see it! I saw it! I can…did…

In the present, Augustin tightens his grip on my arm. Marie presses harder. People are running around. Someone else screams! Where am I?

I'm drowning! God help me! I'm drowning in red!

"Let her go!" A voice bellows.

I try to see through the red. Where am I? I'm standing somehow on my own—No, no I'm not—someone's holding me up!

I pinch my eyes shut so I can see who it is.

Unwin! Unwin Rittenhouse. I recognize his long fingers before I even see his face. He's got me!

I open my eyes. Unwin has me still!

Augustin and Marie have released me. Unwin has me before and he has me after.

I grunt and struggle—gasping. The smell of blood—like new copper pennies.

I'm free now and I can't control my arms.

My hand catches on something.

Unwin rushes to grab my right arm, but my left still is thrashing.

People are yelling and suddenly I feel as though I'm being thrust forward.

I feel warm liquid on my left hand and then I hear a splash!

George!

Help me!

Marie L'Ebène

I should never have worn that necklace. I knew it was too dangerous, but I never would have thought that the Frobischer bitch would have remembered.

I remembered everything. I always remembered everything. I had to. It was my power.

I felt sick as I watched them at the high school dance. Rosa was the luckiest girl in school to have the attentions of a college man like Augustin L'Ebène. He was handsome and came from a good family.

He never would have noticed me—not with the "beauty" there.

He wanted her so much. Watching them dance—the way he pressed his body against hers and whispered in her ear, the way his hands wandered over her body—it made me sick. What made me sickest was the way she teased him in that red dress and then rebuffed him. Didn't she realize what she had literally right there in her grasp? It never pays to be such a prude. I knew I would never have resisted him, I would have let him do whatever he wanted to me. It never came to that.

He was absolutely right to storm out of that dance the way he did. She deserved to be alone.

Augustin didn't. He needed company. I could tell. That's why I followed him—oh, no, not close enough for him to see me. I made sure I didn't lose sight of him. I would have followed him anywhere, but luckily he only went as far as the Bayou Vin Atténué.

Of course, by the time I got there, he had already found another slut. This one—a naked savage. But, a savage in diamonds and garnets. I looked at that necklace around her yellow neck. I wanted it, and I wanted him. Ultimately, I got both.

Stupid loose Chink, she was another tease…that yellow beast, she struck him when he kissed her and wouldn't give into his needs.

He was a rough man, Augustin L'Ebène, just the way I liked them. He was strikingly attractive with his chiseled body and his wavy black mane. His hair was thick with sweat and it fell into his silver eyes that night as he perspired in the moonlight of the bayou trying to satisfy himself with the china girl. I gasped as he peeled off his jacket and shirt—his smooth shoulder rippling as he struggled to hold onto her. He was glorious and I wished I were the savage girl!

As he went to undo his belt and finally find what he sought, the savage kicked him and tried to run. That's when he growled like an animal. He was beautiful.

I could finally believe the things I had heard—the whispers amongst the servants at the club about how he had fathered a child with one of the rich girls from the hill. He was all man.

He ran after the savage and she screamed and threw such a tantrum and fit. I had to bite my cheeks to keep from laughing. That's when he took his pocketknife out and flipped it open. It glinted in the moonlight.

He reared back and raised his leg like a stallion—kicking the girl squarely between her tits. She landed with a squeal into the bayou mud. With one hand he held her throat and with the other he began to cut.

Blood spattered his chest and sparkled like the garnets in the china girl's necklace.

I wanted him.

But, then I heard footsteps in the fallen leaves behind me and I ducked further into the bushes.

It was that Rosa.

"Augustin!" She called, "I'm sorry. It's just, I'm not ready…"

Then she froze when she saw him arched over the savage body—the blood both spurting and oozing out of her yellow skin.

Rosa screamed.

And Augustin growled.

The savage was dead—time for one more!

He sprang off the dead girl's body and grabbed at Rosa, who, of course, struggled.

Oh, the names he called her. I loved it!

He grabbed her by the neck and with all his animal strength, he threw her into the bayou. The water was thick with oriental blood so that you could hardly see Rosa in her red dress.

He spun around and his eyes glinted silver in my direction.

I would give him what he wanted.

But, before I could show myself, that gawky giant from the biggest house on La Colline Cramoisie lumbered out of the brush—howling. Unwin saw the Asian girl and shrieked like a ghoul before plunging his hands into the water and pulling Rosa out. "The Beauty" sputtered and gasped.

I had to. I laughed.

And Augustin saw me—his eyes registering hate. I knew I would have him forever.

Unwin Rittenhouse drug Rosa off and left her in the brush. She must have gotten up on her own steam after awhile because as Unwin and Augustin grappled with one another, I saw her pale face watch the men for a moment and then noted a flash of red out of the corner of my eye. She was gone before Augustin and I fled.

Unwin may have been taller, but Augustin had the muscle. He quickly felled the miserable freak and he ran toward me. I had gathered up his knife, shirt and jacket while they struggled.

He rushed to me and grabbed me by the arm as he had done with the other two.

"You're not going to tell anyone about this?" He purred in my ear.

Another interruption! That tramp, Amelia Rittenhouse, comes screeching after her idiot brother. "Unwin!"

Amelia stares at Augustin and me with her yellow, lunatic eyes and notices the blood dripping down Augustin's bare torso. She shrieks and runs to her brother who stood sobbing over the savage's body.

"Do you want me to tell them?" Augustin says after slowly going up behind her.

She shakes her head.

"Shall I tell them, Amelia?" He asks. "Shall I tell about our child?"

Oh! I was thrilled. I then knew everything! I had all the control.

She shook her head.

"Good," He said. "Then keep quiet." He added, looking with derision at Unwin who was blubbering, "Keep him quiet, too. Whatever you have to do." He inhaled deeply, "And, if I get wind that there's been talk about this, I'll say that your idiot brother did it. Who will they believe? Me or the town tart?"

Amelia didn't answer him, but we all knew that she understood. She tried to convince her brother to come with her.

We ignored them.

Augustin again grabbed my arm and growled, "Now what will it cost me to keep your mouth shut?"

He spun me around and kissed me like a wild beast.

I broke away and whispered in his ear, “Just you.”

We went off together and called the police saying that we heard noises at the bayou.

From that moment on, he was mine.

Augustin L'Ebène

I was no stranger to a woman's bed. That's true. I'll have you know, however, since I married, I never took a woman other than Marie.

Yes, yes, before her, there were many. Before Marie, I took what was owed to me.

They owed us—women. We L'Ebène men have been wronged for too long. It was up to me to make them pay. I'd make them all pay for what she did to my grandpappy. Yes, they'd all pay for her…the "Elegant Ogress." For her and for the others…

I had to prove that I was more than a....no; it's a sin to dwell.

I will not be an entryway to sin! I was only a little boy, then. Pappy meant me no harm. I won't pay for family sin. I've done my penance. I'm not the one that must repent! I'm not the sinner. I did no wrong. It wasn't my fault.

Let's just say that I learned early what to expect from a woman and how to always be the one with the power. The only woman who ever bested me was Marie.

We belonged to one another. I traded myself for her silence. We made a good team.

We had a family—of reasonably attractive girls. The first two were lost causes and we married them off as quickly as possible. But, Voletta—she was my female self.

Nothing but the best would do for her.

I thought Douglas Halifax was the best.

I was wrong.

Everything had gone so smoothly after that night at the bayou. Marie was good to her word. Rosa said nothing and within months of that night, she met some Hollywood dandy who took her away with him after only a few days. I knew she was a tramp at heart. She would have had more fun with me—a real man.

Amelia Rittenhouse went away, too, after she got rid of that ugly damn brother of hers. Just the threat of someone knowing that she had my baby was enough to keep her quiet. I didn't know what she had done with the kid, but I heard she was a girl. It wasn't until years later that I met her.

So, for the time being, I was safe. The law is a tricky thing. I knew I was right in what I did. It was justice and Miss Oriental Queen got what was coming to her. So, God did as God does and let the just be free.

Marie turned out to be a good wife. And, as I said, she gave me three girls.

I loved Voletta. I loved watching her, the smell of her…the feel of her. She was my pride. She erased all the sins of those around me and made me believe that purity of heart such as my own could be matched. She was my equal, my spirit—my clone. The other two girls Marie gave me were more like their mother. They didn't have my power. But, the moment I first saw Voletta's eyes, I knew she would grow up to be just like me. I knew she would be a conqueror! She would fight and win! She would finish the fight for me! She would make the world pure! All she needed was a benefactor.

In that spirit, I gave her to that Douglas Halifax. She snared him, bedded him and then tried to train him. He seemed weak-ish and I figured by the time she was fifty, Voletta would be a rich widow.

Douglas, sad to say, wasn't as weak as I had counted on. Voletta told Marie that he cheated. Fortunately, that had ended—for a spell. Only the second time, she told both of us all the details.

Imagine—a Chinese girl, and what's worse—the granddaughter of the oriental whore that had teased me on the bayou. Well, we couldn't have that. So, I took care of it. I took care of it the way I had taken care of her grandmother. This…Jade! She deserved it even more than the first one. And, it was so easy.

In fact, I found that I got the same rush that I had the first time. I felt like a young man again—completely. My favorite part was ripping the earrings out of her ears—the way the flesh popped. You just don't get to do things like that as a doctor! I thought I'd keep them as a little souvenir. Thinking about it, I later decided they'd be a better gift for my little Shelby. Douglas should have given them to her in the first place.

Of course, I had heard that Rosa Frobischer had returned, but she seemed to have no memory whatsoever of that night at the bayou. I didn't feel she was a threat. Then, she started keeping company with my granddaughter and Douglas' bastard Asian child.

I saw the three of them the day after I got rid of Jade. They were carrying brown boxes into her little bookstore. I figured that those boxes would be worth looking through. I didn't want anything left around to link my daughter's husband to that china girl.

I swore I'd get in there and I did—luckily, I found those letters in time. It made quite a nice little surprise for Douglas when I put them in his study. I felt like I could do anything. The blood of that girl made me feel alive again. I prayed that Douglas really suffered because of it.

Before I could worry about finishing off that fool Douglas, I had a few other things to take care of.

I had recently received two letters from an Agathe Le Banni. In the first, she claimed she was my daughter. I had no doubt that she was telling the truth. At first, I saw her as no threat either.

Too bad for her that she went on to say some other things that made me think differently. She said that she had learned from Amelia's journals what had happened that night when Mingmei received her final judgment. She told me what she intended to do with the information. That by itself was enough of a reason to dispose of her.

The second letter also hinted that she had seen what had happened to Jade. I don't know if she really did nor not. I couldn't risk it. Agathe sealed her fate when she licked that envelope.

Agathe meant nothing to me. It was easy to get rid of her. In fact, it was only fair that I should be the one to spill her blood. It was my blood after all. And, in a few short minutes, a lifelong problem was erased. Amelia Rittenhouse had no power over me anymore.

In fact, last I saw Amelia, it was very clear to me that she didn't have any sort of power left at all—not even enough to peel herself off the floor. I didn't have to worry about her any longer.

Rosa on the other hand—that woman was always around! Still a little tease after seventy years. She had aged better than Marie, but she had been more attractive to start with. Why is it that the pretty ones are always the prudes?

She was getting too close to the yellow savages. God knows what sort of misinformation was flying around their filthy hut. So, I thought I'd go right to the source and have a look around that nasty little shack of theirs—that Ji family. It would be easy to get rid of anything that connected them to my daughter's family. But, I found so much more.

The moment I walked in that door, I felt called by some force I couldn't explain. And, then I realized what it was! God led me to it. Right there in a dingy little room was the necklace! On the floor no less! The gaudy garnet number that Rittenhouse had given his Chinese harlot. Marie had always wanted it as sort of a trophy. So, I picked it up for her. And, that's when I saw that freak—Mingmei's daughter. She just stared at me and wouldn't answer me like she was some kind of dummy.

I don't have to take that from one of them! She was just what I always dreamed of—one that wouldn't fight back! She didn't even talk.

So, I teased her with the necklace. "Look, look how pretty you are!" She still wouldn't say anything.

I didn't have time to cut her. So, I just cut off her air with those rocks. There was beauty in the way the skin of her neck pushed through the spaces between the stones as I choked her with that necklace. It was short and quick—and frankly, I did her a favor by doing it.

Done! Took care of a lot of problems.

Everything was fine. Voletta had a nice little plan to make sure Douglas knew that he was at her mercy—those little earrings came in handy after all. And, I had planned to spend the rest of my life in peace and quiet.

But, I guess I got a little cocky. I asked Marie to wear the necklace to Shelby's party.

Then, the Frobischer cow remembers.

And who knew old, ugly Rittenhouse was still around? I didn't see that coming.

And, now, I can see nothing.

Unwin Rittenhouse

Poor Rosa—I could have guessed what that bad, bad man did to her. Why did she go after him again so very long ago? Why would she have gone to find him at the bayou? Some people will apologize to the person that hurt them. Some people will forgive anyone for anything.

I understood her.

Poor, poor Rosa—again at Augustin L'Ebène's mercy. I had to do something. I think I scared the people when I walked in. I was scared, too—so many people, more than I had seen in decades. But, I had to help Rosa Frobischer. I had to keep her from Augustin.

I should have killed him all those years ago. I should have killed him when he—when he—killed Mingmei, when he threw Rosa in the water. I pulled her out—she was coated in Mingmei's blood. At least she could live.

I should have killed him. But, I couldn't. I couldn't hurt someone.

I still remember that night—Amelia tried to convince me to leave. She said she understood what had happened, but she wouldn't go to the police. She wouldn't tell them the truth. She begged. She begged me to leave with her. But, I wasn't going to leave Mingmei there—not all alone. I stood over my love and wished she would breathe. She did not. And, then I wished she could at least be at peace in her slumber. I prayed that I, too, would slumber.

But, then the police came. They yelled at me. I got scared. I ran. I should not have left Mingmei, but I was frightened. I hid behind the trees and I waited until they were gone. Amelia hid, too. She was so good at hiding.

Later, I listened to Amelia. I didn't know what to do. I should not have gone back with my sister. I should have killed Augustin when I had the chance. He had hurt too many people.

I wasn't going to let him hurt Rosa again.

All the people at the party in their fancy clothes looked at me like they were seeing a ghost. Poor Rosa, she was trapped by Augustin and that awful Marie—she smells like raisins. They had Rosa cornered on the stairs.

"Let her go!" I yelled in a voice that I never knew I had.

He did. And I held Rosa up.

She was struggling still—not against me, but her arms…they had a power of their own.

Perhaps she had the strength to do what I could not.

She broke free of me—her hand flailing at him. The first blow cut him from his brow to his chin, his eye—cleft and growing wet with red—that stone, that big diamond on her left hand slicing through his skin.

Her arms spun—blow after blow—the diamond cutting his face, time after time.

The growing crowd around the stairs pushed towards us and we were moved by their force—their clothes spattered with Augustin's blood as he struggled against Rosa's spinning arms.

We were forced through the open doors and onto the patio. Augustin screamed as he fell into the pool. The water was soon red.

I was so tired, but I took Rosa in my arms again and led her to sit down.

Thank goodness that the pretty, chubby girl was there. She would take care of Rosa. And I could rest finally. I wished I could rest.

I watched for a moment as the chubby girl comforted poor Rosa. She really was quite beautiful, that girl. So much like my Mingmei—not only in the way she looked, but also in the way she moved and the way her eyes shone as clear as water. Maybe Mingmei wasn't as gone as I thought.

Hsin, my grandfather, cursed me—telling me I was lost to him—that my blood was all Jade and Douglas Halifax. I had been too strong, he said. He looked around the bushes for a moment and then was gone. I never saw him again.

I read a book once where…no, I had never read a book like that. I didn't care to remember any more books. I had my own life to deal with.

I stood alone on the veranda—staring first at the flickering candles and then at the shimmer in the ripples of the pool water as the glowing moon began to reveal itself from behind its gauzy shift of clouds—making a white ring in the haze that surrounded it. The moon seemed to swell as it liberated itself from the murky fog as if at any moment it would burst forth in a shower of sparks like fireflies…or diamonds…or snow.

I felt like none of it was true. Yet, I knew it was true because I felt the moisture on my own skin. But, still, I wasn't sure. My mind was muddy from welcoming my adulthood.

Lost in my own world—in my own loss and in my strange new self, I had not heard the commotion beyond the French doors at first.

Suddenly, I was snapped back into reality as a great swell of people burst out of the doors—led by Shelby's grandfather, struggling to walk backwards—his face and hands bloodied. He was immediately followed by Rosa—her hands coated in blood, her arms twirling at him like a machine. Next to her was Unwin Rittenhouse looking stronger than I had remembered seeing him at my—at Niu Ji's, my grandmother's, funeral. He looked as he must have looked when he loved Mingmei Sun.

As if in slow motion, Augustin L'Ebène, fell backwards into the pool, his blood spreading out into the water in vermillion ribbons. I vowed to paint that image one day.

Unwin Rittenhouse cradled Rosa and lowered her to a stone bench by the pool. He looked at me and I immediately came to Rosa's aid. When I looked up again, he was gone.

As the sirens blared up the street—I'm still unsure who called the police—I held Rosa as we watched Augustin L'Ebène claw his way through the ruddy water to the side of the pool and try to pull himself out.

I didn't need to know what had happened.

No one needed to tell me that he had killed three generations of the women of my family and later, I would discover that he had killed his own daughter as well.

My best friend's—no, my sister's grandfather had destroyed my family.

The only thing that hurt me more was finding out what he had done to Rosa…and perhaps knowing that he had also taken Shelby from me.

Rosa went after Dove. At first, I shouted at my father—I was angry. Angry about the lies and the secrets, yes. But, also angry that he had been so unhappy with mother that he had to seek love from another person in the first place.

My yelling gave way to tears. I don't know how, but I ended up in Daddy's arms. We both cried.

And, then mother walked in.

In a drunken rage, she chastised him and called him weak. She called him countless other names that I dare not say. She berated me and told me I was an idiot to love him. And, then she gloated because she had been successful in her plan. She dressed me as Jade Ji and got to torture both of us—him for not loving her, and me for loving him.

The sound of her tirade grew faint as we all noticed the shouting downstairs. And then suddenly as if a volcano had erupted, a horrible noise rose from the veranda.

Mother screamed as she watched her father. He was covered in blood and plunged into the pool. Rosa had somehow injured him. Later, I found out that she had used her engagement ring as her weapon.

Grandfather had survived. He was, however, blinded. The paramedics came shortly after the police. He went from the hospital to the Marionneaux city jail where he waited to find what was next.

Grandmother, as well, found herself in the women's city facility for her involvement. And, mother was also questioned and later released.

That night, Daddy and I moved out of the yellow house halfway up La Colline Cramoisie and rented rooms in a local bed and breakfast on Fontenette Street—waking the angry owner and begging her forgiveness—until we could find a permanent place to live.

I hadn't had a chance to speak to Rosa during all of the chaos that followed grandfather's exit—she seemed stunned; focussed on something beyond my understanding.

I called the cottage for two hours after Daddy and I settled into the bed and breakfast. I knew it was horribly late, but I had to talk to my friends. I hoped they would want to talk to me. Rosa answered the phone when I called at 2:00 the next morning. She said she was fine. She said she loved me still. She told me where they went.

Dove had asked Rosa to take her to the cemetery to visit Mingmei, Jade and Niu. Rosa told me that she wanted very much to see me the following afternoon. She told me again that she loved me.

When I asked to speak to my sister, Rosa was silent for a moment. Then she answered. Dove did not care to speak to me. *Can you blame her, Shelby?*

Afterwards, I heard them trying to talk to me. I finally understood Niu Ji's aphasia—and Amelia Rittenhouse's. I answered their questions as best I could. I heard the words, "Self Defense."

Afterwards…

I stood there by that pool looking at the red water.

And soon, the moon grew brighter than I had ever seen it, as if it was trying to compensate for being so late in shining—its reflection on the water's surface glared with such a white brilliance that the red was erased.

It really was quite beautiful.

The moon and the water.

The white.

VIII
The White

I rarely—if ever—closed my eyes. I feared that if I did, they would try to take me—the doctors with their needles. Something changed…something beyond me.

That night, I lay there in that stiff bed—wishing for the cool smoothness of the floor, wishing for the deluge of color that I had once known. The darkness of the hospital room seemed to breathe with me—its thick lungs masking the absent walls.

Suddenly, the gnawing energy of my arms flushed away as if it were being rinsed out of my veins. My fingers and hands went limp and I didn't wish anymore.

For once, the silence did not bother me. The quiet did not taunt me and my insecurities didn't mock me. I was, for the first time in decades, not fighting.

And as the vinegar tingle of fear seeped away from my heart, my thoughts rose with scenes of times before Augustin forced his way into my being. I saw my father, strong and tall. I saw my mother—her face clear and perfect like the living marble of a Florentine St. Theresa. They stood on either side of us—me and Unwin. Our hands were linked. All of our lives steeped together through our hands—like a family.

We walked along the river—the Mississippi stretching beside us like a napping dog in dream pursuit of a rabbit. The light glanced off the azure ripples and shone on our faces. Our bodies, in a glimmer, were transformed with a radiance that expunged the shadows of our eyes. And with those dark relics gone, so was my betrayal—my desertion of Unwin, my banishment of Agathe.

I soon realized that Agathe walked behind us, we turned and motioned for her to join. She stood between me and Unwin and we all linked hands and walked through the strobe of brilliance along the river.

I tried to speak, but found I could not. I didn't need to. It was no great loss.

The phantasms faded away and I was again alone in the hospital bed—strangely not stiff anymore—it felt slick and alive beneath me.

The bare walls of the room reappeared and undulated with a blush that melted in the pure streams of moonlight through the narrow window.

I could live without the prisms.

I would let the whiteness enfold me.

Rosa Frobischer

The streets smelled clean. The air was alive with a fragrant marriage of roses and gardenia and I could detect no hint of the languid odor of swamp. The rain and the moon had blotted away its olfactory blemish.

This was after. This was now. I was Rosa.

This old hunk of rock could finally sparkle. "'Atta Girl, Rosie."

I knew myself. I was so glad to have met me.

I was the woman that George had known for seventy years. Funny how he had never introduced us before. Lovely, beautiful, brilliant, selfish bastard—he kept me all to himself. I loved him for it.

I loved Dove, too. She took my hand as we walked and asked me to go with her to see those that she had lost. I saw no reason why we shouldn't fulfill that wish—despite the hour.

She seemed tall—her stride was purposeful and yet, given a grace that I had never known her to have before. I let Dove guide me. And, while I didn't voice my yearning for Shelby to be with us, Dove was aware and silently told me that it was impossible.

I knew we would see him there.

Unwin Rittenhouse lay atop Mingmei Sun's vault on his stomach, his head to one side, his long fingers stroking the sides of the crypt.

He smiled when he saw us.

"She loved me," he whispered.

I did not know if he meant Mingmei or his sister, Amelia. It was not my place to know.

Dove and I sat on the concrete ridge of the planter below him. I took his long, wide hand in mine and held it to my shoulder and neck. He sighed.

"I'm tired." The words were barely audible.

"Then you must rest." I whispered.

Dove stood and looked into Unwin's eyes. I remained on the ground with his hand in mine. She stroked the gray tangle of his hair and sang softly. Her voice was clear and strong.

The shadowed river listens,
Waiting for the rain,
Lies lost in such sharp silence
Her beauty will wane:
She wears her hope like diamonds
All colors save but one
Diana's orb will free us
Reflected in the sun.

Unwin smiled, his breath slipping through his lips before he slept. His quest had ended.

Blanketed in the white gauze of the moon, Unwin Rittenhouse found peace.

The Loch Ness Monster was no more.

We stayed with his shell for awhile. I sat in silence and engaged in a communion with those spirits that I sorely missed while Dove said goodbye to her great grandmother, her grandmother and her mother.

When she had finished, she stood before me and smiled, extending her hand; she helped me to my feet.

Upon releasing me from her gentle grasp, Dove looked at her own hand and removed the jade ring I had given her. I nodded at her as she slipped it onto Unwin's left ring finger—the coolness of the stone gliding easily over the long digit.

Then, she took my hand in hers again and guided me home.

Once there, we made a call to have Unwin's remains moved. I asked that they set Dove's ring aside for her. I'd retrieve it in the morning. I knew one day, she'd want it back. One day she'd need it more than Unwin. He would be with Mingmei forever. They needed no rings.

When that had been finished, I spoke to Shelby. Dove would not. Instead, she went to sleep. And, so did I soon after.

I slept for hours—uninterrupted. When I shut my eyes, I saw a white softness. And, when I awoke the world was sharp again.

I immediately cleaned and polished my engagement ring—as quickly and as completely as possible. I did not want it off my finger any longer than necessary. I could not bear the thought of being without it. Nor could I imagine being without Dove or Shelby.

In the months that followed, Dove was a wonderful friend to me and regarded me as a mother would a child. As time passed, we stopped expecting Hsin Ji to return. We never saw him again. Dove and I tried to make a home for ourselves—just the two of us.

But, Marionneaux was no longer a comfortable home for Dove and she soon convinced me to send her away to a boarding school. At first, I resisted the idea and gently urged her to make her peace with Shelby and Douglas. She refused. She said she could not do it yet.

So, after careful consideration we selected a Catholic school on Lake Pontchartrain. I should say that Dove selected it based on their academic reputation. She seemed confident in their curriculum, but I had my misgivings. George had much to say on the subject of the Catholic Church.

Before we met, while he was earning the right to call himself a writer, my George had spent some years working for a publisher of Catholic teachings. During the course of his time there he had become so embittered about the hypocrisy of priests and nuns that he couldn't pass a church without spitting some invective. He often said that in or out of a habit, there was nothing more purely cruel than a nun was because they masked their lonely venom behind a papier-mache mask of faith.

I hoped Dove would not come to the same conclusion that George had reached and during the weekdays, I kept careful remote watch to make sure that she did not suffer at the hands of the clerics.

My weekend visits to the school were partly to see Dove and partly to make sure the staff knew I was keeping an eye on them. On those weekends, Yolanda and Shelby watched the store. Shelby never gave me a message for Dove, but always told me to make sure her half-sister was safe and happy.

Although the nuns regarded me with controlled disdain, I was sure that my regular presence there each weekend was enough to keep them from taking their own private theological turmoil out on my young ward. Thankfully, I knew Dove would be looked after during the week. Eulabel's sister from Natchitoches, Beatrice, often visited Dove in the evenings and brought her little pastries and meat pies.

Dove seemed content, if not a little overworked. She made me proud every day—excelling in her studies, particularly as a fine young painter. In two years, she had moved on to Brasseaux University where she learned to control her talent—later settling into a job as a conservator at the prestigious Musée D'Orleans.

Each time I returned from a visit, received a call or a letter, I made sure to give Shelby all the news about Dove's new life. Shelby hungrily took in the details and nodded in approval.

Prior to Dove's departure to Lake Pontchartrain, my visits with Shelby were always in the bookstore, for a few hours each day. During those hours, Dove avoided D'Arbonne

Street completely. She had ceased working for me at the store and had taken a part-time job at the City Hall with Eulabel Watkins in the Marionneaux Cultural and Historical Center.

There, she worked as an intern—researching the lives of our late local artisans and aiding in cataloging the treasures of the Rittenhouse estate which had been left, according the Amelia Rittenhouse's will, in trust to the state.

The gray house at the apex of La Colline Cramoisie became a museum and was a major boon to Marionneaux tourism. What would Amelia have said if she had ever seen all those people come and go from her home? Dove and I often wondered.

After a point, Shelby stopped asking aloud if she could talk to Dove and while the question was always present in her face, we never spoke of answers. Dove had told me once that each time she looked at her half-sister, she could not help but see the face of Shelby's grandfather, Augustin L'Ebène—the man that had taken everything. That sorrow overpowered their sisterhood. I was sure Shelby understood without my saying anything. Instead we tried to enjoy our time together before we parted.

Shelby was determined to stay in Marionneaux. However, Dove did not return before I reunited with George. Our visits were always away from her former home—away from Shelby.

Shelby grew into a quiet, reserved young woman. Her growing fascination with literature pleased me. She began to read insatiably as if each page of every book held the key to lessening the burden she carried upon her young frame. Upon her graduation from high school, she worked for me in the bookstore full time—writing in the evenings or whenever she had a break. She'd write with such a feverish concentration that I often wondered from where the words were coming. At the end of the day, she'd rub her hands together and stare out into the distance for a while before springing back to life…and to me.

She and Douglas had found a mutual calm, but she avoided Voletta who had become a slouching shadow in the grip of years of alcoholism. When she turned 18, Shelby moved in with me—occupying Dove's old rooms. She began a bland, but serious courtship with a pale, strange young man named Averill Cage and I knew that one day they would marry.

We were content, Shelby and I, as far as our friendship was concerned. Ours was a comfortable life and we enjoyed our time together. Every few weeks, she and I would go to the Marionneaux Cemetery. We would visit the graves of Mingmei, Niu, Jade, Agathe, Unwin and Amelia Rittenhouse to make sure that their cement temples were kept clean and the meager plantings were well tended.

Sometimes, afterwards, Shelby and I would walk to the Bayou Vin Atténué and walk amongst the oaks. Gone were my rushes of crimson—replaced by the solid, cool images of wholeness. My mind projected faces—Mingmei's in peace with Unwin for eternity; Amelia's alone yet finally unafraid; Jade's with her eyes looking toward the freedom of a gentle future; Niu's forever bathed in light; and of course, George's handsome visage—waiting for me. As the breeze grew chilly and the sun faint, my phantom companions would join and fade leaving nothing behind but Shelby's soft, uncertain smile which spread beneath the clouds of her thoughts and her longing.

For, Shelby's young face always bore the lines of the haunted and the sparkle of her eyes had dimmed. She carried a familiar burden—the only remaining connection between herself and Dove—she, too, had lost a sister.